3B

# CHAT

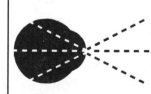

This Large Print Book carries the
Seal of Approval of N.A.V.H.

# CHAT

# ARCHER MAYOR

**WHEELER PUBLISHING**
*A part of Gale, Cengage Learning*

GALE
CENGAGE Learning

Detroit • New York • San Francisco • New Haven, Conn • Waterville, Maine • London

**LIBRARY OF CONGRESS CATALOGING-IN-PUBLICATION DATA**

Mayor, Archer.
    Chat / by Archer Mayor.
      p. cm.
    "A Joe Gunther mystery"—T.p. verso.
    Summary: "When a wintertime car accident leaves his mother and brother seriously injured, Joe Gunther takes a leave of absence to attend to them and investigate the cause of the crash" — Provided by publisher.
    ISBN-13: 978-1-59722-706-3 (hardcover : alk. paper)
    ISBN-10: 1-59722-706-4 (hardcover : alk. paper)
    1. Gunther, Joe (Fictitious character) — Fiction. 2. Police — Vermont — Fiction. 3. Traffic accident investigation — Fiction. 4. Computer crimes — Investigation — Fiction. 5. Large type books. I. Title.
PS3563.A965C47 2008
813'.54—dc22                                                    2007050356

Published in 2008 by arrangement with Grand Central Publishing, a division of Hachette Book group USA, Inc.

# ACKNOWLEDGMENTS

As always, I found myself happily dependent on the knowledge and expertise of others in the preparation, writing, and editing of this book. Also, as always, I'd like to thank them while taking full responsibility for any stumbles that I may have committed in applying their wisdom to the following tale.

My gratitude, therefore, to the following:

John Martin
Erik Johnson
Kathryn Tolbert
Michael Mayor
Elaine Sopchak
Andrea Moriarty
The Weathervane Music Hall
Eric Buel
Julie Lavorgna
Scott Passino
Jesse Bristol

JB Auto
Rick Bates
Jennifer Morrison
Scout Mayor
Brattleboro Police Dept.
Castle Freeman Jr.
And, of course, Kate and Melanie

# CHAPTER 1

*"Made it, Ma. Top o' the world,"* Leo quoted theatrically, his words shrouding his head in the cold night air. "What would you think if I went out like that?"

His mother twisted around in her wheelchair to look at him balefully. "I don't understand why such a wonderful dancer would do a movie like that."

Leo smiled down at her as he pushed her gently along a shoveled path, across the broad courtyard before Dartmouth's Hopkins Center for the Arts, universally nicknamed The Hop. "I warned you, Ma. I told you it wasn't *Yankee Doodle Dandy.*"

"You said it was a gangster movie," she persisted, "not an ode to a psychopath."

Leo burst out laughing. "Wow. You make it sound pretty deep. I just liked it when he shot the car trunk full of holes to let the guy inside breathe, or when he went nutso in the prison dining hall after finding out his mother died."

She faced forward again as they neared the curb. "How did I end up with such a disturbed child?" she asked meditatively.

"Hey," he told her. "You got one son who's a cop. Stands to reason the other should go to the dark side. It's nature's balance."

He went to pass by her on his way to unlock the car, when she grabbed his wrist in a quick-moving, wiry hand.

This time, her expression was soft and appreciative. "I've been doubly blessed, Leo," she told him. "Both my boys are just right."

He leaned over and kissed her wrinkled cheek, warm in the evening's chill. "I love you, too, Ma. I hear they're playing Polanski's *Repulsion* next week."

She tapped the side of his head playfully as he moved away. "Oh, now, *that* sounds like a comedy."

"You have no idea," he admitted.

She watched him bustling about, unlocking doors, starting the engine to get the heater going. It wasn't all that cold, even though it had been dark for several hours. Dartmouth's trademark Green was coated with a new layer of snow, which shimmered under the glow of dozens of traditionally designed streetlamps. These, along with the formal brick buildings looming darkly beyond them, and the enormous library's beautifully lighted clock tower at the far end, lent the entire scene a timelessness, as if she might have been waiting for her son to hook up a horse and sleigh instead of a Subaru.

"All set," he said, stepping behind her once more and easing her chair off the sidewalk to where it nestled beside the car's open door.

She reached out and took hold of the two handles Leo had attached just inside the opening, one high and one low, and nimbly used them to assist herself inside. Her legs were too weak to support her, but they did move, which was a godsend in situations like this. She was already attaching her seat belt by the time Leo opened the car's rear door to slip in the folded wheelchair.

He joined her moments later, making the car rock as he virtually fell into his seat. An enthusiast by nature, he never did anything by half measures, including the most mundane of actions.

"You want to stop somewhere for ice cream or cocoa or something?" he asked.

Now she was looking at the facade of The Hop, from which they'd just come on their weekly Friday night outing. Designed by

9

the same architect who later did Lincoln Center in New York, it looked like the kind of place that would offer a broad sampling of the arts — modern by one light, slightly worn by another. She and Leo came here frequently, local beneficiaries of the college's mission to be a generous cultural neighbor.

"No," she answered him. "Not tonight. Drive me around the Green, though, will you? I love the buildings."

Leo backed out of their parking space and slipped into the thin traffic, taking his first left to engage the long eastern reach of the Green.

"Feeling touristy?" he asked.

She was watching the buildings go by, but also the students, huddled in their winter clothing, marching determinedly in small groups or singly, intent on their mysterious goals, which could as easily have been the next beer or a rendezvous as some scholarly pursuit. Although she'd been a local her entire life, even if from Vermont, just across the river, she'd never had the envious, resentful view of the college so many other "townies" harbored, nor had she delighted in the supposed depiction made of the place in the movie *Animal House.* She worshipped education, and while her sons had become a police officer and a butcher and hadn't benefited from Dartmouth's offerings, she had made sure they developed an appreciation of music and literature and art, and she'd trained them to be analytical, appreciative, mindful, and kind.

She knew that college students could be self-indulgent, narcissistic, and careless with the gift they'd been offered. Those were the clichés. But as Leo slowly circled the Green, quietly allowing for her meditation, she relished the fantasy she'd held forever, of places like this being the incubators of the mind, where kids learned to think, sometimes despite their best resistance.

"You should've gone here, Ma," Leo finally said.

She turned away from the buildings to look at him. "I came close enough," she said after a thoughtful pause. "I got access to that library and passed along what you and Joe could bear. It would have been fun to actually sit in class, but I can't complain — I've read what a lot of their professors wrote."

Leo laughed again. "And you got to fall asleep in class. We were always taking books off your lap after you dozed off."

She whacked his shoulder. "Once in a blue moon, after spending all day chasing you two around."

"You did good, Ma," he said after a pause.

It was a gentle taunt. He delighted in mangling English around her, since she worked so hard not to do so herself. But this time, instead of correcting him, she chuckled and admitted, "I think I done good, too."

He smiled and hit his right turn indicator at the stoplight, preparing to go down North Wheelock and across the bridge into Vermont, at the bottom of the hill. Of course, much of what they'd just been talking about dated back a few years. His mother had slowed down recently, reading less and watching more television. And since landing in the wheelchair, she'd retired the use of that library card.

Their years together were numbered, clearly.

In the darkness of the car, his smile faded away. As silly as it sometimes sounded when he admitted it out loud, he'd lived with his mother all his life so far, and he was fair and square beyond middle age. His older brother, Joe, had been the restless one, leaving home early to join the service, seeing combat halfway around the world, going to college for a few years in California. Even now he lived in Brattleboro, near the Mas-

12

sachusetts border, sixty miles to the south.

But Leo had never seen the attraction. He and their mom lived in the farmhouse he'd been born in, and his room overlooked the fields his father had once tilled. When the old man died so many years ago, leaving behind two boys and a young widow, the three survivors had looked to one another for their grounding. Joe had used that as a springboard to go forth into the world; Leo had seen it as all he really needed. He began working at the market in Thetford Center, just down the hill from the farm, and settled into a life of dating girls lacking in serious intentions, working in the barn on old cars from the sixties, becoming the most highly prized butcher for twenty miles around, and establishing an easy and permanent friendship with his mother.

Which he knew was closing in on a natural end.

"You're awfully quiet all of a sudden," she said softly.

They had just reached the bridge spanning the Connecticut River, a newly rebuilt structure, which its designers had accessorized with a series of gigantic, evenly spaced concrete balls — a source of some humor in a school renowned for its testosterone.

"Just thinking about the movie."

She let it go. Whatever its virtues, *White Heat* didn't merit an excess of reflection. Leo had something private on his mind, and she had a pretty good idea what it was, or what she feared it might be. While grateful for a lifetime of Leo's company, she was not unaware of the peculiarity of a middle-aged son still living with his mother. The thought that she — or her circumstances, first as a widow and then as an invalid — had encouraged this situation only made her feel guilty. That said, she was also a pretty good observer of people, and her take on her younger son was that he was not only happy with the status quo, but increasingly worried about what to do after she died.

She could sympathize. She'd been in much the same boat when their father died. A good and decent man, much older than she, he'd had his greatest influence on them all only after his death, when they discovered the huge void he'd so quietly filled.

She suspected that Leo, more than Joe, would find the world an oddly empty place, at least for a while, once she followed her late husband's example.

She stole a glance at him as he turned right onto Route 5 on the Vermont side of the bridge and began heading north, parallel to the interstate, which he knew she didn't enjoy as much.

"Thank you, Leo," she said.

He looked at her quickly, both his hands on the wheel, a good and practiced driver. "What for? I thought you hated the movie."

"For taking me anyhow, for not choosing the interstate, for being a good son. I'm not sure I tell you enough how grateful I am for everything. You've given up a lot for me."

He laughed, though a little cautiously. His mother wasn't prone to such comments. "Totally selfish, Ma. Do you know how many times I've used you as an excuse to shake off some female with big plans? Unbelievable. There are women up and down this valley who think you're the worst thing since Cruella de Vil. You should be calling a libel lawyer instead of patting me on the back for being such a wonderful son."

She smiled and shook her head. She should have known better. Leo was her showman, quick to grab a joke when faced with a serious moment.

She decided to allow him his choice. "Really?" she reacted in kind. "No wonder I've been getting those strange looks. Good Lord. I always thought it was my breath, or maybe something horrible coming out of my nostril."

They were surrounded by darkness now, moving quickly and alone along the smooth, twisting road, paradoxically comforted by the dark, semifrozen expanse of the large river to their right. New Englanders often felt at home while isolated in the cold. It was that aspect of their environment that most outsiders compared to their demeanor, but which they themselves saw as simply encouraging strong character.

Leo was surprised. "Are you kidding about that?" he asked. "Have you really noticed . . . ?"

He suddenly stopped speaking, his hands tightening on the wheel. "Damn . . ."

Alarmed, she looked first at him and then out the window, expecting a deer to be standing in the middle of the road — an almost common experience. Instead, the road was beginning to shift away as they slid out of control on a slight curve.

"Shit," Leo said through clenched teeth. "Hang on . . ."

She was ahead of him there, clutching both the dashboard and the uppermost handle beside her. "Leo," she said, almost a whisper.

Ahead of them the landscape changed from the comfort of the black macadam to a blizzard of white snow as they plowed through an embankment that exploded across their windshield. They could hear beneath them the tearing of metal against the remnants of a hidden guardrail, along with their own seemingly disconnected shouting. They were first jarred by several abrupt encounters with buried stumps or boulders, and then became weightless as the car began to barrel roll, causing their heads to be surrounded by flying maps, CDs, loose change, and an assortment of now lethal tools that Leo normally kept in the back.

In the sudden darkness following the loss of both headlights, Leo's mother focused solely on the muffled sounds around her, coming from all sides as they continued farther and farther downhill. She began thinking about the cold water that might be waiting at the bottom — if that was the way they were headed.

And then it was over. In one explosive flash, she felt a shocking blow to the side of her head, the sense of some metallic object, perhaps a lug wrench, passing before her face, and then nothing.

Leo opened his eyes briefly before shutting them again with a wince, brought up short by a burst of pain in his left eye. He paused

17

a moment, trying to sort through the throbbing at his temples, to remember what had happened.

"Mom?" he asked suddenly, attempting to see again, ignoring the pain. He shifted in his seat, looking in her direction. The car was black and utterly silent. Carefully, he reached out and touched her, the tips of his cold fingers slipping on something wet on the side of her head.

"Oh, Jesus," he murmured. He made to turn toward her and shouted in agony, the entire left side of his chest suddenly spiking as if electrified. He sat back, panting, and coughed, feeling as if his lungs were full of phlegm. He gingerly pushed through his overcoat at his ribs with his good hand and winced.

"God damn it," he said, mostly to hear his own voice. "Mom?" he repeated then, reaching out a second time, but lower, groping for her shoulder, which appeared to be fine — maybe merely because it was there at all.

But she wasn't moving.

It was cold, and the other thing his fingers had felt was snow. Somewhere there was a broken window. He had no idea how long they'd been here, had no clue if they were visible from the road. He didn't even know if they were both alive.

He followed her shoulder up to her neck and burrowed his index finger between her collar and the scarf she was wearing, probing for a pulse. He was a butcher, he thought ruefully. At least he knew his way around a body.

His fingers were too cold. If her heart was beating, he couldn't feel it, but he doubted he could have anyway. At least that was the comfort he gave himself.

"Okay, okay," he said softly. "Probably just as well. No pain, no struggling. She's got her coat on. Could be worse."

Still using his right hand, he touched the window next to him. Intact. He didn't feel as though they were on their side, and he couldn't hear running water, which meant they hadn't reached the river. So far, so good.

He felt down to the door latch and pulled it. Nothing. Probably jammed. With even fewer expectations, he tried the electric window toggle. He was rewarded with a gentle whirring sound and a cool waft of air against his cheek.

"No shit," he muttered, noticing how hard it was to breathe, to actually move his lungs. The window had lowered all the way. He considered shouting, but with the cold air had also come a wider silence, as from a chasm without bottom. He knew this road — it either had traffic or was empty. There were no pedestrians and few homes.

He had to get out.

He moved his feet and found his lower body uninjured. That was good. But even at 100 percent, struggling out the side window of a small car wasn't easy. And, he knew by now, he was far from 100 percent, just as he knew that wasn't phlegm in his lungs.

"Ma?" he said, barely whispering by now. "Can you hear me? I got to try to get help."

Nothing.

He sighed, gritted his teeth, took hold of the steering wheel with his good hand, and pushed up with his feet, hoping to launch himself at least partway out the window.

The pain was beyond imagination. It felt like lava, filling him with heat and blinding red light, exploding inside his head and making him gasp for air. Beyond that, he could feel something fundamental shift within him, as if the cellar of a house had suddenly vanished into the earth, leaving everything above it precariously poised above a void. For a split second, he could almost see himself hovering in the air, somewhere between heaven and oblivion.

And then he, too, collapsed into the blackness and the utter, all-encompassing quiet of a winter night.

**Brett:** so wut u doing
**gIRl:** chatting with u
**Brett:** cool
**Brett:** u in school
**gIRl:** nope
**Brett:** why
**gIRl:** home - school get out at 220
**Brett:** oh cool
**Brett:** so u ain't got no bf to be hanging with
**gIRl:** nope broke
**Brett:** that sucks
**gIRl:** i guess

# CHAPTER 2

It was postcard serene — trees coated in white snow, hanging low over a tumbling brook whose boulders were collared with sugar halos of ice, sparkling in the sun. The painfully blue sky overhead daubed the darkly rushing water with the hint of a bruise as it emerged, cascading, from a large, cavernlike culvert projecting from under a quaint backcountry dirt road.

Joe Gunther studied that road a moment. It emerged from the woods like a fairy-tale prop, entered the sunshine, its snowy shoulders dazzling in the light, leaped the culvert, and vanished as magically into the darkness of the trees on the far side. There were no railings hemming it in as it spanned the water, not even a curb. In fact, if viewed from a low enough angle, the road appeared to cross the brook as if by the stroke of a paintbrush.

"What do you think?"

Joe glanced over at Sammie Martens, his only female squad member and as close as he had to a lieutenant.

"I think it's dangerous as hell," he said. "Bet more than one driver's gotten white knuckles crossing this thing."

"Not to mention the odd pedestrian," she added ruefully.

Joe nodded and grunted his agreement, approaching the edge overlooking the water. Sam joined him to stare down at the swirl and tumble of the stream gushing out below them. There was a pile of boulders right at the mouth of the culvert, then a widening where one of the banks tabled out slightly to form a small beach before the trees downstream crowded in once more and narrowed the channel to create a miniature whitewater chute that raced off around a bend.

At the edge of the snow-clad beach, the water slowed and flattened enough to create a pool — no doubt a popular swimming hole during the summer. Not that Joe had been hard-pressed to conjure up such an image, since floating facedown in the middle of the pool was the body of a fully clothed man.

"You think that's what he was?" he asked her.

Instead of answering, Sammie merely shrugged.

By the water's edge, a diver for the Vermont State Police was adjusting the last piece of equipment on his cold-water suit. Before lowering his face mask, he called up to Joe. "You ready for me to go in?"

Joe gave him a thumbs-up.

Another state police officer, this one looking cold despite his zipped and snapped bulky ski parka, approached from the other side of the short bridge. Joe and he had just been introduced minutes earlier. He was Jeff Dupree, originally from Virginia, and he was still getting used to the cold weather, even after five years up here.

"You find anything up that way, Jeff?" Joe asked as he drew near.

The young man shook his head before reporting in a soft Southern accent. "A couple of houses about a third of a mile up. One's empty; the other had no idea — older couple that keep to themselves. They told me the road dead-ends about a mile up, at least in the winter. The town doesn't plow it. I didn't see any tracks by the side of the road along the way that told me anything."

Joe nodded. "Thanks. You got their names and information?"

Dupree tapped his chest with a heavily

25

gloved hand. "Sure do."

Joe smiled at the sight. His own jacket was unzipped and he was without gloves, considering this an unusually warm day. He returned to watching the diver below.

He and Sam were the only representatives from the Vermont Bureau of Investigation, the state's independent major-crimes unit. The others, and there were five of them by now, were all from the state police. It hadn't always been so. In the not so distant past, the troopers would have owned this scene and been led by detectives from their own BCI division. But, recently, by a governor's signature, the VBI had been put in charge of all major cases, the only concession being that, generally speaking, the unit should be invited in by the initial responders rather than simply take charge.

It had been an awkward arrangement at first, and not just with the state police but the large municipal forces as well, with considerable grumbling from all sides. But since VBI was composed of the best from all departments, and since Gunther, as field force commander and number two in the bureau, had bent over backward to be accommodating, supportive, and self-effacing, relations were improving all the time.

It also didn't hurt that a majority of the

new VBI was made up of old BCI members who loved the increased autonomy and lack of heavy-handed structure.

Below them, the diver slowly waded into the dark water, eddies collecting around his calves as he picked his way between unseen obstacles. The body floated spread-eagled, as if snorkeling, about ten feet out.

"Any theories yet?" Joe asked more generally. Sam had been here an hour already, ever since a 911 cell phone call from an out-of-town jogger enjoying the sylvan isolation had gotten everyone moving.

She shook her head. "The road's been plowed, the snowbanks don't show anything, there's nothing lying around like a wallet or a bag, there's no car parked nearby, and Jeff just told us what he found — or didn't — up the road. I don't know what the hell happened. If this guy's a drunk who missed his footing, what's he doing way out here? We're fifteen miles from Brattleboro. If he drove here, where's his car? If he was driven here by someone else, what's the story with that?" She glanced over at him, clearly frustrated. "I sure as hell hope he has some ID, 'cause this could be anything. Maybe he fell from a plane."

"You got a canvass going?" Joe asked.

"VSP did that right off the bat. There

aren't a lot of houses around here, but they're spread out, so it'll take a while to hear back from everybody. I'm not holding my breath. There's something about this one that makes me think it won't be a slam dunk."

"Foul play, as they say?" he asked.

"Just a hunch."

That counted for something. Sam Martens had been working for Joe a long time by now, dating back to when she was one of his detectives on the Brattleboro PD. Wiry and energetic — and as privately self-doubting as she could be forceful with others — Sam was a dogged, intuitive, natural digger. Joe had been delighted when she opted for the VBI, joining his own three-person, Brattleboro-based squad. This small group, while responsible for cases in Vermont's southeastern corner, had also virtually become a flying squad, often called on to support other VBI teams across the state because of Joe's status within the organization. He wasn't big on pecking orders or playing favorites, but his trust in Sam played a role in making this arrangement possible.

The diver had slipped fully into the freezing water by now, barely disturbing its surface except for the bubbles escaping from his regulator. It had once seemed like overkill to Joe, all this scuba gear for a job that might have been achieved with a pair of waders, but Vermont's waters proved deadly for people who didn't treat them with respect, and by now he'd become easier with a little more caution holding sway over a mishap, especially for a dead body. Besides, as he'd been told more than once, these calls were good practice for when a life did hang in the balance.

The diver, clearly milking the moment, circled the body, examining it from all sides. They even saw the reflected flash of his waterproof camera as he took a picture.

Eventually, though, he reached out and began shepherding the source of his interest toward shore, where a tall, skinny man waited quietly. This was the death investigator from the medical examiner's office, who, along with the state's attorney and the police, formed the judicial three-legged stool on which rested the fate of the unexpectedly dead in Vermont.

Joe nodded, half to himself. "Well, guess we'd better introduce ourselves to the mystery guest," he said, and moved toward the embankment, where a rope had been rigged to help with the snow's slippery surface.

The ME's rep was Alan Miller, a twenty-year EMT whose primary job was as a carpenter. Joe, who'd worked with him a number of times, had always found him to be a quiet man of peaceful demeanor, and sometimes wished that he'd found a happier part-time occupation. Death investigation seemed a dour way to complement the more optimistic pursuit of emergency medicine.

But Miller clearly didn't see it that way. His face lit up when he saw Joe — or better Sammie, Joe reasonably suspected.

"I didn't see you two hiding out," Miller said, shaking hands. "Find anything interesting?"

"Nothing," Sam responded gloomily, ignoring him in favor of the corpse now being hauled onto the small beach area.

Miller followed her gaze just as the body was rolled over onto its back. "Well," he said, "maybe we'll get luckier here, or at least up in Burlington."

Joe didn't say anything, hoping he was right. Burlington meant the ME's office and Dr. Beverly Hillstrom, a prime example of how a state like Vermont could still sometimes attract the very best professionals. More than once, she'd pulled a miracle out of thin air when Joe thought he had run dry of possibilities.

Miller pulled on a pair of latex gloves as he approached the deceased. "Not a very remarkable-looking guy, is he?"

That was hard to argue. The body was waxy-pale and tinged with the blue typical of cold-weather deaths, but he was relatively fresh, possibly dead for under ten hours, and the rushing water had kindly washed away the seepage that a dry corpse produces in short order.

"Looks like a clerk out of an old movie," Sam agreed.

The man appeared to be in his mid-thirties to early forties, bald with a fringe of hair above his ears and around the back. He was neither fat nor thin, tall nor short, handsome nor hideous. Joe had to agree with Sam — this was a portrait of utter blandness. The Invisible Man in three dimensions, dressed for winter.

Miller was now standing astride him, as if getting ready to squat down and sit on his chest. In fact, he merely hovered so his hands could roam freely just above the man's surface, carefully unbuttoning and unzipping and peeling back layers of clothing, searching through pockets as they were revealed. He didn't actually take anything off, but by the time he was finished, most aspects of the man's anatomy were available for inspection.

But in terms of revelations, despite the treasure hunting aspect of the process, the conclusion matched the introduction — and Sam's opening appraisal.

As Miller reiterated when he finally stepped free and peeled the gloves from his almost numb hands, "Nothing. No bends, folds, or mutilations."

Joe pursed his lips without comment. He didn't like cases like this. It wasn't the extra work they represented — the lack of identification, the absence of a clear and reasonable story. Rather, it was the lingering scent of menace he disliked — the palpable suggestion that they'd ended up dead without ready explanation because somebody else had engineered it that way.

It was possible that this man had fallen off the bridge in a drunken stupor, or suffered a heart attack while taking an evening stroll, but Joe doubted it. This body had been stripped of the conventional identifiers we all carry, and Joe's instincts told him that Hillstrom and her associates would end up telling a tale of homicide. Looking down at this innocuous mystery, he could almost feel the malevolence that had brought it about.

Sam glanced up at her boss, one eyebrow

raised. "What do you think?" she asked.

I think there's a nemesis out there, ready to be engaged, he thought, but he actually said to her, "I think we use a fine-toothed comb."

A shout reached them from the road above. "Special Agent Gunther?"

They all looked up at Jeff Dupree, his hand in the air as if waving farewell to a train.

"What's up?" Joe asked, raising his voice above the tumble of the water.

"I've got dispatch on the cell phone. Something about a car crash."

**Lonely:** any hot girl wanna chat ??
**Hottie:** yea
**Shez:** add me
**Dislove:** dude
**Gangsta:** ron how tall r u??
**Shez:** n u can hav a look
**Hottie:** what is it
**Lonely:** any hot girl wanna chat ??
**Hottie:** kk
**Dislove:** bored
**Hottie:** so u gonna talk me something about
  yourself
**Boss:** hey all Im Back Whats good?
**Hottie:** yourself
**Dislove:** any guys? . . .
**Gangsta:** ron r u there??
**Hottie:** shez u there
**Shez:** em wot u wna no
**Ron:** back yes I am
**Lonely:** boss
**Lonely:** can we chat ??

**Hottie:** I don't know that is for u 2 tell me

**Ron:** im 6'1″

**Doo:** uhhhhhhhhhhhhhh

**Doo:** hi

**Shez:** well iv got an 11inch touge n breath frew ma ears

**Hottie:** oh I c

# CHAPTER 3

Joe positioned his chair in the corner, by the window, where he had a clear view of both the bed and the door and where he could stretch out his legs if need be. It was a strategic decision, based on the chance that he'd be spending a lot of time here, which, sadly, was what he was anticipating. Unless things deteriorated even more.

He looked across at his mother, lying peacefully in bed. At least he had that to hold on to. There were no tubes stuck down her throat at the moment, and only a single IV dangling from a metal pole beside her. She just looked asleep, aside from the ugly bruise extending from her left temple. Soon, he'd been told, if she stayed this way beyond some short-term deadline, a feeding tube and oxygen would be introduced. Maybe more. But, right now, her vitals were stable, her breathing deep and regular, her heart-beat strong, and her brain waves energetic.

He had been led to believe that among the overall patient population at the Dartmouth-Hitchcock Medical Center, his mother was actually in pretty good shape. She just wasn't waking up.

Leo, typically, wasn't quite as enigmatic. Like the man himself, his injuries were prominent, visible, and easily diagnosed, if not so simply set right. Leo had been Joe's first stop in the hospital, once both patients' conditions had been made clear on the phone. For all Leo's much publicized joviality, he was a worrier, always nervously hovering over the target of his attention. It was one of the reasons he was so popular as a butcher, fussing over every customer. Joe knew from the moment he'd heard of his brother's broken ribs, collapsed lung, fractured shoulder, and concussion, that Leo's biggest problem was going to be his inability to get to their mother's bedside. To Joe's mind, regardless of who was in worse shape physically, Leo was going to be needing the most care.

And that wasn't even factoring in the man's guilt.

Fortunately for Joe, his brother was so beaten up that he couldn't give much voice to his concerns. When Joe visited him in ICU, in fact, picking his way through all the

37

monitoring equipment circling the bed, all Leo managed was a halfhearted smile.

Joe wasn't even sure he could talk. "You okay, Leo?"

Leo winced, as if at some joke Joe couldn't fathom. "Top of the world," his brother whispered, adding, "How's Ma?"

Joe slipped his hand into Leo's and gave it a squeeze. He made his voice sound upbeat. "Haven't seen her yet, but you're in much worse shape. They told me she's fast asleep — breathing fine, though, and everything else looks okay. No breaks, no messed-up major organs. The doc on the phone told me not to be overly concerned — that sometimes the body just needs to rest awhile. Sounds pretty good."

Leo closed his eyes, and Joe realized he was fighting back tears.

"Leo," he told him, "it was an accident."

Leo took a ragged breath, reopened his eyes, and murmured, "It was the car, not the road."

He coughed once then, not forcefully, but the effect was telling. His face contorted, and one of the monitors began chirping. A nurse gently moved Joe out of the way in order to adjust something.

"I'll look into it, Leo, and I'll take care of Mom. Just get better, okay? I'll be back in a bit and give you an update."

Now, in the stillness of his mother's room, Joe thought of the deeper meaning behind Leo's parting words. In Leo's world, there were really only four areas to which he paid any attention — Mom, the butcher shop, his short-term girlfriends, and cars. The barn their father had once filled with farming equipment, livestock, and hay now housed a mismatched, dust-covered, much tinkered-with collection of automotive relics. Leo never worked on the Subaru he used to chauffeur their mother — she'd made it very clear that she wanted a professional doing that — but Joe trusted his brother's mechanical instincts and knowledge. If Leo thought the car had somehow been the root cause of this accident, Joe was ready to believe him.

He pulled out his cell phone and dialed.

"VBI Dispatch."

He recognized the woman's voice. It was that kind of state, where people joked about there being only a few dozen residents, grand total. It was more like six hundred thousand really, but that still made it the second least populous state in the country. The number inside the law enforcement community was even more minute by comparison.

"Hey, Gloria. It's Joe."

Her voice instantly slipped into maternal mode. "Oh, my God. I just heard about your family. I am *so* sorry. How're they doing?"

He wasn't surprised. Vermont was a small town in some ways, spread thinly across a hilly map. It didn't take long for everyone to know your business. Fortunately, that was one of the aspects of living here that he cherished. He had no wife, no children, not even a significant other at the moment. The fact that virtual strangers — even a disembodied voice on the phone — knew his life's latest news actually came as a comfort.

"They're hanging in there, thanks. I'm at the hospital now. Actually, I was wondering if you could do me a big favor in connection with that."

"Anything at all."

"Could you find out who was working the car crash that banged them up? I'd love to talk to him or her."

Gloria couldn't keep the keenness from her voice. "You suspect something?"

Joe made an effort to laugh easily. "Whoa. You need to cut back on the cop shows, Gloria. I just want to find out who's on the job."

She laughed in return, but he could

almost hear her cataloging his request for future in-house gossiping. "It's the company I keep, Joe. You guys have made me paranoid. I don't even *watch* cop shows anymore. Give me about five minutes and I'll call you back."

Joe made sure the phone was set to vibrate, and returned it to his belt. He went back to gazing at his mother's pale profile, propped on a white pillow, uncomfortably reminiscent of a carved tomb lid in a medieval church.

She was certainly deserving of a monument of some sort, he thought, though a much more upbeat one. In all his experience, he'd never known a person with more considerate sanity. Just as he'd always looked to his quieter, utterly dependable father for his own reliability, so he blessed his mother for whatever sagacity he could claim. She'd always been thoughtful, patient, and encouraging, though never shy to speak her mind. She had taught her boys to do as little harm as possible, to be considerate of the less fortunate, to be slow to judge, and to maintain a sense of humor. She'd been the only girl in a family of a dozen kids, where the mother had finally died in childbirth, so she'd had good practice. Still, Joe had sometimes wondered how she

41

would have fared with two daughters.

In any case, he'd lucked out, and he knew that his brother felt the same way. It was going to be a huge threshold to cross when they lost this woman.

The cell phone began vibrating at his belt, and he yanked it free to answer.

"Gunther."

"Joe, it's Gloria. The Windsor County sheriff's got your case. A Deputy Rob Barrows is investigating. If you have a pen, I've got his cell number."

Joe pulled out a black notepad and scribbled down the number she gave him, thankful that he was where cell coverage was better than most places. As with many things technological, Vermont tended to lag toward the back of the innovation herd.

"Thanks, Gloria. You're a peach."

"You just take care of that family," she said, hanging up.

Joe dialed the number she'd given him.

"Barrows." The voice sounded young but confident.

"Deputy, my name is Joe Gunther. We've never met, but —"

"I've heard about you, Agent Gunther. This is a real pleasure. Sorry about the circumstances, though. How's your brother and mom?"

Joe was happy not to have to break the ice, go into a whole song and dance about who and what he was, or, worse, ingratiate himself with someone who had a beef against the VBI.

"They're in good hands," he answered vaguely, becoming aware of how often he was going to have to respond to that inquiry. "I was wondering if you'd figured out what happened yet."

Perhaps instinctively, Barrows came back with "What did your brother say?"

Joe was pleased by the reaction. It made him feel he might be talking with someone who truly understood his job.

"Not much, given the shape he's in, but he said it was the car, not the road, and I'll give the man his due — he does know cars."

Barrows didn't argue. "The road looked good to me. They weren't on much of a curve, and I didn't find any signs of ice or snow on the surface — road crew had done a good job. Course, I was there after the fact. What did he say about the car?"

"Just that, nothing more."

Joe could almost hear the other man thinking. Generally in an accident like this, with no death resulting and no involvement by anyone else, the physical aspects of the vehicle examination were pretty much limited to the condition of the tire treads. It didn't make sense to go looking beyond driver error, and it cost a lot more money.

"Could you do me a favor?" Joe therefore asked, to help the man reach a less hasty conclusion.

"What's that?"

"Could you keep the car where no one can mess with it until I get someone to check it out?"

Barrows hesitated before asking in turn, "I don't want to step on anyone's toes here, sir, but are you not telling me something?"

"Absolutely not," Joe reassured him. "I have no reason to think this wasn't just what it looks like. But given what you and I do for a living, wouldn't you be curious?"

"I see your point," Barrows conceded. "I'll give it a closer look myself — I know cars, too. And I'll make sure it's kept under lock and key."

"Thanks, Deputy. I owe you one. I'll see you a little later."

"That would be my pleasure."

Joe snapped the phone shut and was putting it away when it vibrated in his hand.

"Hello?"

Gail Zigman's voice was tight with concern. "Joe, I just heard. How are they?"

Joe was startled by his reaction. After

something like twenty years, he and Gail were no longer a couple, and hadn't been for over a year by now. But whether it was his own present vulnerability or simply the preexisting pattern that any couple establishes after so much time together, he was caught between feeling genuine relief and a sense that this was one conversation he just didn't have the stamina to maintain. One reminder at a time of the price of loss seemed ample.

"Hi," he muttered stupidly.

"Are they all right?" she repeated.

"They're alive," he finally managed. "Leo looks the worse for wear, but he's conscious. Mom is just asleep."

"Asleep?"

"That's what I call it. They're not saying 'coma' yet, but that's probably just for me. Maybe it's a kind of twilight until things become clear."

There was a long pause, followed by "My God, Joe. I am so sorry."

"Me, too."

"Do you know what happened?"

"Not yet. All Leo told me was that it was the car, so maybe the brakes went out, or something in the steering. I'll look into that later."

He could almost hear her thinking, examining the angles. Gail was a lawyer, a legislator, someone with ambition who knew how to organize things. After ending her relationship with Joe, she'd moved altogether from Brattleboro to Montpelier, the state capital, so she could fully concentrate on her new political career. If Joe were to bet on it, she had the governorship in her sights.

"What are your plans?" she asked.

"I'm on leave until I get a handle on this."

"Would you like some company?"

He had a split second to respond correctly, and almost inevitably chose poorly. "It would mean a lot to them."

Her comeback drove home his error. "I know that's not true for you, too, but I won't get in your way. I promise. I would just like it if you said it was okay," she said. "I feel so awful about this."

He scratched his forehead, thinking a rap with his knuckles might have been more appropriate. "Gail, you'd never be in the way. They both love you, and I could do with the help. I'd really appreciate whatever time you can spare."

"You're sure?"

"Absolutely. I'll clear it with the hospital, too, in case they have rules or something about visitors."

Her voice was soft, almost tearful, in

response. "Thank you, Joe. I'll be down as soon as I clear a couple of things up here. Give them my love."

Despite his fumbled comeback to her offer, it remained true that Gail's presence would be helpful, even if painful. He hadn't been the one to end what they'd shared, but it had certainly been his profession, in large part, that had precipitated her decision. He'd been a cop for enough decades to have made a few enemies, and survived enough bullets, knives, and explosions to understand anyone's desire to gain a little distance from him. But he did miss her, and having her nearby again was going to be tough.

He rose and stood before the window, looking down on the snow-dusted trees that circled the hospital.

It would allow him to be practical, though, and perhaps a little self-preserving. Leo was in good hands, and their mom was out of reach, at least for the time being. There wasn't much of a role for him here. Gail's arrival would guarantee that someone he could trust was nearby while he did what he could to find out what had happened.

He didn't actually suspect much, of course. He was acting more from professional paranoia, or perhaps habit born of witnessing bad things. But it would keep him busy, and perhaps on the edge of the double emotional tar pits represented by Gail and his family's plight.

Besides, there was always the nagging possibility that this had been more than a simple car accident.

**littledk:** Marvel's really better at selling incredibly random merchandise

**kay:** Yeah. They sell Marvel perfume

**littledk:** . . . WHAT

**littledk:** see, DC should really get on this. I'm sure they have better-smelling super-heroes

**kay:** Hee. Yes. Exactly.

**kay:** I mean. Do *you* want to smell like the Hulk?

**littledk:** ewwww

**littledk:** clearly they need to make Hal Jordan perfume

**kay:** Clearly!

**kay:** Drives the ladies NUTS!

**littledk:** Warning: May Cause Spontaneous Subconscious Puberty.

**kay:** *giggles*

**littledk:** I can't believe it. they make Spider-man perfume, and the fanboys STILL

don't smell better
**kay:** Well. You've never smelled the perfume.

# CHAPTER 4

It was snowing in a Bing Crosby sort of way
— fat, lazy, photogenic flakes that, in the
end, wouldn't amount to much. Under
normal circumstances, it was the kind of
weather that Joe loved to stand in, designed
for kids to catch snow crystals on their
tongues.

Except that he was no longer a kid, and
was staring at a scene where no sane parent
would let any child run free. He was standing in an auto graveyard on the eastern
reaches of Thetford Township, a few miles
north of where Leo went off the road,
confronting a long, low wall of precariously
stacked cars, piled like absurdist bricks and
extending from one edge of the property to
the other.

The snow cover had softened some of the
visual carnage, but there wasn't much hope
for the raw materials — a virtual billboard
of the crushed, sharp-edged, broken detri-

tus of an all-consuming industrial juggernaut. It was a vision only enhanced by its otherwise bucolic surroundings. All around the yard, gently vanishing into the blur of falling snow, were tree-crowded hills, fields, and forestland.

This section of the Connecticut River Valley was absurdly pretty, slicing between New Hampshire and Vermont, and decorated with covered bridges, backwater bays, and cow-sprinkled farms. The background of ancient mountains behind the massive, undulating, dark river told a tale of humanity's struggle with nature, since both these weather-beaten New England states had eschewed their peaks for the water's edge and turned the river into a commercial highway for over two hundred years, luring pioneers, aboriginal and white, who had forged far inland and upstream for reasons benign and not.

Held up against such a portrait of heritage and beauty, not even a car graveyard stood much chance of becoming a significant eyesore.

"Who're you?"

Joe turned at the voice coming from the low building to his left. A man had appeared at a door haphazardly cut into the sheet metal siding. He was bearded, long-haired, and dressed in the standard-issue green uniform of mechanics and road crew workers everywhere, complete with name tag stitched above his breast pocket. The man was labeled "Mitch."

Joe pulled his badge from his pocket. "Police. I was looking for a car brought in last night. A Subaru."

"That's sealed up. Can't get to it. Sheriff's got the key."

That's one of the things Joe had wanted to hear. It seemed Deputy Barrows was efficient as well as accommodating. "You ever get a look at it?" he asked.

Mitch shook his head. "I wasn't on. You here to pick it up? The boss wants it gone. It's taking up space."

"The sheriff not paying you?"

"Sure, but we're not a storage unit. We got work to do. We need the bay." He waved at the picturesque falling snow, adding, " 'Specially in this shit."

"Won't be much longer," Joe reassured him with no basis whatsoever. "Who's the boss?"

"E. T. Griffis."

Joe had turned toward his parked car, getting ready to leave, but he faced Mitch again at this. "E. T.? No kidding."

"You know him?" Mitch asked.

53

"Everybody knows him."

Mitch cocked his bushy head to one side. "Everybody local. That you?"

Joe smiled before heading back to his car. "Used to be. I'll tell the sheriff to get that car out of here soon."

Joe continued up the road. It had been a poignant and disturbing journey so far — from the hospital, to the crash site, to where the car was stored, and now on to the family farm — perhaps exacerbated by the very beauty he'd been admiring earlier. The familiar name of E. T. Griffis commingled with his sentiments to form a curious mixture of comfort and pain. One generally revisited one's place of upbringing for support, not to wonder if it might become the watershed where everything falls apart.

Because that was a distinct possibility: His entire family was so small that the present situation had the potential of leaving him all by himself.

The mention of E. T. also served to highlight what few degrees of separation there were within Vermont's scant population. A small, square man with blunt hands and a manner to match, E. T. had been a near mythological fixture in the greater Thetford area for as long as Joe could think back. He seemed to own at least a piece of every rough-edged business around. And his impact on Joe hadn't stopped with nostalgic memory — years earlier, Joe had also arrested his youngest son, Andy, for a crime committed in Brattleboro, revealing an abrupt fragility to E. T.'s aura of indomitable feudal lord.

Joe could sympathize. He had received such reversals himself over time, starting as a young man, when he lost his seemingly indestructible father. After that, life had never seemed quite so secure, and the more of it he'd seen, from combat to police work to the vagaries of the daily grind, the more he'd been confirmed in his skepticism. His wife had been taken by cancer; colleagues had died in the line of duty; Gail, years ago now, had been raped and forever transformed. His personal experience had not been lacking in drama, nor his emotional wariness left wanting for evidence. That a local monolith like E. T. Griffis had begotten a son who would later end up a jailbird was mere proof of the futility of denying humanity's clay feet.

Joe Gunther had become a student of hard knocks. As he approached the homestead, he was under no delusions that life would suddenly surprise him by cooperating.

The farm was less than it had once been.

In fact, it wasn't a farm at all anymore. Much of its land had been sold off to neighbors to retire debts and establish a nest egg. But the core remained, and certainly its appearance was unchanged. All his life, Joe had learned to come up the winding drive and trust that his heart would beat easier. Even now, despite its inhabitants being in the hospital, the place still lent him hopefulness by simply standing strong.

Ostensibly, Joe was here to feed the cat, turn off the lights, check the doors, and do whatever else hadn't been considered by two people thinking they'd be out for a couple of hours. In fact, he discovered that this housekeeping applied more to himself. He took his time wandering through the rooms, absorbing the scents and scenery that had populated his upbringing, and tried to position his thinking to accept whatever might be coming. He didn't want to be pessimistic, but he did want to be prepared.

He stood, finally, in the living room, his mother's center of operations. There was a docking station of tables and a desk laden with reading material, a phone, a recently added only-the-basics computer, all facing a large, empty-eyed TV set. Only her wheelchair was missing to make it complete, and it looked barren as a result. He used the opportunity to remember to check on the wheelchair's welfare in the back of the ruined car. When Mom woke up, she'd be clamoring to get back here and tend to her piled-up projects.

Gail had arrived at the hospital about an hour earlier, carrying two briefcases and clutching a cell phone as if it were a lifeline. She and Joe had hugged awkwardly before she moved directly to his mother's bedside to gently stroke the old lady's hair and murmur her greetings. Joe had left shortly thereafter.

He sighed, shook his head, and went back outside into the falling snow. Visiting the farm had been useful emotionally, but his instincts told him it was time to get busy. It rarely paid to linger and ponder overmuch.

Outside the door, under shelter of the roof's overhang, he pulled out his phone, taking advantage of the farm's exposure to the New Hampshire hills across the river, and their cell towers. He dialed a number in Burlington, in Vermont's far northwest corner.

"Office of the chief medical examiner. This is Suzanne."

"Hi, Suzanne. It's Joe Gunther. I was wondering what you might have found out about that John Doe we shipped you — the damp, bald one."

Suzanne laughed. "For that, you want the chief. You really got to her this time."

In part, Joe was glad to hear that. He and Beverly Hillstrom went back a long way and had developed, he believed, a possibly unique relationship, cemented last year when, after he'd broken up with Gail and Beverly had been left by her husband, they spent a single night together. In theory, a terrifically bad idea. In fact, the best thing that could have happened to either of them. It had cemented the trust they shared, and had granted each a brief respite in which to reassess their lives. In Beverly's case, she'd been able to reconcile with her husband; in Joe's, the night with her had allowed him to better distance himself from Gail's departure.

They had never referred to that encounter since, but the nominal formality that had existed before had been replaced by something much warmer and more valued.

"Joe," she said when she came on the line. "You usually let me put them in the cooler before you chase me down with questions."

"I'm sorry, Beverly. I've got nothing with this guy. I hope it's all right."

"Of course," she said. "I just finished up. But keep your fingers crossed for good tox results, because I didn't find a thing — aside from a run-of-the-mill drowning, of course."

"Nothing?"

"Not a scratch or a bruise. And his organs are in the same condition. I wouldn't call him a health nut. He clearly didn't make a point of exercising, and his personal hygiene could have stood improvement. But all his parts and pieces were working fine."

Joe thought back to the man's clothing, which had seemed unremarkable to him. "You think he was a bum?"

Hillstrom's response was immediate. "More like he was heading down the social ladder. He struck me as a man who lives alone and doesn't get out much, or lives with someone who doesn't care that he only bathes occasionally. For what it's worth, and based on a theory I would never share with anyone else, I think he was pure middle class. And from the style of his clothes and their present condition, I'd guess his fall from grace dates back less than a year."

"What theory?" Joe asked, intrigued, remembering only now a frayed pant cuff and the worn heels of the man's shoes.

"Toenails," she said flatly, adding, "which I will deny if you quote me."

"You guess their social class from their nails?" he asked, taken by surprise.

"Something like eight times out of ten, I'm right," she told him. "It's hardly rocket science, but the worse the toenails are, the worse is the decedent's economic situation. This clearly only becomes useful when a person's other outward indicators are conflicting, as with a bum dressed in a fine suit. Which," she added, "is a little of what you've got here — a man on the skids, but whose toenails reflect a regular, if nonprofessional, attention to personal appearance. Do with it what you will."

He laughed, shaking his head at the phone. "You don't have much to worry about there. I won't touch that with tongs. I appreciate it, though. And I will wait for the tox."

"Speaking of which," she said, "we did do the standard alcohol test on him — the prelim. He'd had maybe a couple of beers, that's all."

"Anything distinctive in his stomach?"

"No, I'm sorry. He ate too long prior to death."

Joe stared sightlessly at the mesmerizing blur of snowflakes falling before him, lost momentarily in thought. Beverly knew him well enough to let half a minute go by.

"Okay," he finally said. "I can't thank you enough."

"You already did," she said, and hung up.

He punched in Sammie Martens's number.

"Anything new?" he asked after she answered.

She knew he was in business mode, and kept to it for the moment. "Zilch. I expanded and double-checked the VSP canvass of the area, went over where we found the body with everything from a metal detector to a thermal imager, and ran the guy's prints through AFIS, which admittedly only rules out major crimes — and only those that've made it into the database. Still, he's not there. I'm now working on the theory that he was dropped from a plane, wearing a parachute, and that we should be out hunting for a used-parachute thief. How're you faring?"

"Nothing. I just called the ME. Waste of a dime. Isn't a mark on him, inside or out. If your jumping-from-an-airplane idea is right, he didn't even die of a heart attack. She called it a run-of-the-mill drowning."

"But the tox is still pending," she stated.

"Right," he agreed. "It's the only straw we have left." After a pause he added, "Well, maybe not entirely. Circulate his picture to all the motels in a ten-mile radius. He might not have been a local."

"Got it," she said, and then asked, "How's the family?"

"Leo's a wreck but awake. Mom looks fine but won't wake up."

Sam was clearly nonplussed. "Wow. That sounds bad."

Joe pursed his lips. "Could be," he admitted.

"What're you going to do?"

He hesitated. "About what?"

"You going to stay up there to be with them?"

That, of course, was at the heart of what was gnawing at him. "What's it sound like if I say I'd rather be down there with you guys?"

"Like you think they're in good hands and that you're already getting stir crazy."

"I'm not really," he conceded.

"What, then?"

He was less sure of himself here. "I'm sort of poking into this."

She instantly took his meaning. "The accident? You think something's funny?"

"I just want to rule it out. Leo said he thought it was the car, so I'm having the sheriff look into it."

Sam kept with him. "Like the brakes?"

"He didn't say. Just that it wasn't the road conditions. He was a little out of it."

"So it could've been a blown tire?" she asked doubtfully.

Joe shrugged, standing all by himself. "I don't know. I haven't seen the car yet."

He was greeted with dead silence. They both knew how many cars went off the roads in New England in the winter — and how many of those accidents were the result of sabotage. Even Joe had never heard of a single instance.

"Leo knows cars," he added lamely.

"He service this one himself?" she asked, following a more rational line of thought.

"No. Mom wouldn't let him."

He could almost hear Sam switching gears with her next comment. "If I were you, boss, I'd stay up there a little longer. Get this car thing out of your mind one way or the other. You come down here to play with us now, you'll only drive us nuts thinking about it."

He nodded, knowing she was right. "All right. Thanks for the advice."

She laughed. "That's a first. I don't think I've ever done that for you before."

He joined her. "Don't sell yourself short, Sam. You have no idea what an influence you are. Keep Willy from burning the place down till I get back."

"Roger that."

Joe closed the phone, reviewing his situa-

63

tion. Sam was right, of course, and perhaps wiser than she knew. He was between a rock and a hard place emotionally. The John Doe needed his full attention, but to ride shotgun with Deputy Barrows on a doubtlessly futile case would keep him busy, near the hospital, and out of his team's way.

He stepped out into the snow, which, as expected, had tapered off to just a few desultory, drifting flakes, and scuffed down the path between the house and the barn, enjoying kicking through the fresh crystalline cover and sending it flying into tiny swirls of white.

At the barn door, he fumbled with the clumsy hasp and put his shoulder to the door, swinging it open on groaning hinges, just wide enough that he could slip inside.

It was a typically cavernous barn, open in the middle, soaring up to half-seen rafters high overhead, and surrounded by long abandoned animal stalls, now filled with junk. Joe groped for the old-fashioned light switch and turned on a bank of haphazardly placed fluorescent tubes that dangled from the cross beams. Leo was an impatient and practically minded electrician.

Joe smiled at the scene: a virtual car park of dusty vintage vehicles, some of them dented and scratched, none of them cov-

64

ered. Leo loved them and collected them for the memories they evoked and for the hours he could spend tinkering with them. He wasn't the least bit interested in museum-level preservation. He drove these things when he could get them to run, and he didn't mind if they got dinged now and then. It was a casual man's casual love affair.

Joe shook his head and switched off the light again.

Christ, he hoped they got home in one piece.

**Goth Gurl:** hi
**Jiminy:** how are u
**Goth Gurl:** great u
**Jiminy:** same - how u like the snow
**Goth Gurl:** it sucks
**Jiminy:** why
**Goth Gurl:** cause i dont want to shovel
**Jiminy:** well don't
**Goth Gurl:** u tell my mom that
**Jiminy:** ok i will
**Goth Gurl:** u will what tell my mom
**Jiminy:** i will tell her that u won't shovel
**Goth Gurl:** k - u like to shop
**Jiminy:** yeah why
**Goth Gurl:** that is like my favorite thing
**Jiminy:** ok
**Goth Gurl:** u like shopping for clothes
**Jiminy:** yes
**Goth Gurl:** kool - o what u doing now
**Jiminy:** nothing

# CHAPTER 5

Deputy Sheriff Rob Barrows was a compact man, as if whoever created him had run out of room at the last minute and sat on him before snapping him shut for delivery. He was in no way fat but seemed, from head to foot, as bunched up as a clenched fist. This was in total contrast to his manner, which Joe found almost gentle. Joe's wild guess was that Barrows would be a good man in a bar fight, and perhaps not just for his musculature.

They met the following morning back at E. T. Griffis's car yard, where, as they emerged from their separate vehicles, they were greeted by the hirsute Mitch, who didn't look as though he'd changed a molecule of his appearance since Joe first laid eyes on him.

"Back, huh?" he said as Joe came within earshot.

It was an inarguable comment, which Joe

didn't bother contending.

Barrows, however, didn't hesitate, shaking hands, introducing himself, and even pulling a Dunkin' Donuts bag out of his marked cruiser and offering them coffee and doughnuts all around, apologizing for not knowing their particular tastes.

It proved to be no obstacle. Mitch and Joe filled their hands and voiced their appreciation. Rob's gesture was all the more thoughtful because of the kind of day it had become — crystal clear and bitterly cold, where even breathing in sharply hurt your nostrils.

As their host put it, leading them toward the warmth of the garage, "Colder than a well digger's pecker."

Given Mitch's appearance, the garage was predictably strewn about with cast-off debris. In fact, Joe had rarely seen worse. The whole interior looked as if a metallic glacier had burst through the far wall, with the only efforts at reclamation being a narrow path and a couple of small semiclear oases directly before the two closed overhead doors. Mitch led the way into its midst with the practiced ease of an archaeologist navigating a dig he'd known for decades, which, in fact, he may have.

Barrows explained as they went, "This is

one of the few secure places we have for vehicles around here. The sheriff's got a contract with Griffis."

Mitch reached a door on the far wall, indistinguishable from its neighbors aside from the large padlock barring its use.

"It's all yours," he said, stepping aside. "Let me know when you're done." He pointed at Joe. "And like I told him, the sooner we can get this bay back, the happier the boss'll be."

"I'll let him know, Mitch," Rob tried soothing him. "Shouldn't be much longer."

Mitch shambled back into the garage's gloom while Rob pulled a set of keys from his pocket and selected one for the padlock. "We have the only copy," he said. "Maintains the chain of custody."

Joe nodded, having figured that out for himself. In addition to the lock, someone had signed, dated, and attached crime scene tape across the doorjamb, which Rob broke through as he twisted the knob and pushed back the door.

"Like maybe I told you on the phone yesterday, we don't usually do this — secure a car after a ten-fifty — not unless there's been foul play." He stepped inside and hit the lights. "And for all the crime tape and lock, this chain of custody wouldn't hold up in court. I didn't do this till after you called me. Before then, it was just in the yard where the wrecker dumped it. Sorry."

Joe brushed that aside. "Doesn't matter. You said you'd give it a closer inspection. Were you able to do that?"

He was no longer looking at Barrows, being distracted by the familiar car, bent and sagging as if exhausted, standing in what was clearly the garage's paint room — as pristine and bare as an operating theater, and almost as well lighted by a double bank of color-balanced fluorescent tubes. Having just emerged from the clutter behind them, Joe found the contrast startling — and the sight of the car dismaying.

Barrows picked up on his mood, saying softly, "I meant to ask, Agent Gunther: How're they doing? Your family, I mean."

Slowly, Joe turned away from the car, where, in the glaring light, he'd just seen some of his mother's blood on the passenger seat. "They're hanging in there, Rob. Thanks. And call me Joe."

Barrows nodded. "Right." He gestured toward the car. "I checked it out about an hour after we talked."

He crossed over to a control panel mounted to the wall, and pushed an oversize button. There was a loud whirring sound and a slight trembling underfoot before the car began hovering into the air on a lift. Once the tires were at about eye level, Barrows took his hand off the button, returning the room to its otherworldly quiet.

He then removed his flashlight from his duty belt and crooked a finger at Joe. "I think I found out what happened," he said, leading the way underneath the battered car and switching on the light.

Once Joe joined him, he pointed to a spot inside the crumpled right front wheel, which was frozen at a grotesquely unnatural angle. "See that?" he asked.

Joe squinted at where the light's halo was holding steady. He was struck by how much debris was clinging to the undercarriage — souvenirs of its trip down the embankment.

"That's your tie rod," Barrows was explaining. "Or what's left of it. It's missing the nut that holds it in place. As soon as that sucker drops off and the arm goes free, you lose your steering."

Joe paid closer attention, now clearly seeing and understanding the mechanics involved. "Christ," he muttered. "Seems an iffy way to hold something that important together. Don't the nuts work free all the time?"

"They're usually locked in place with a

cotter pin," Barrows told him significantly.

Joe cast him a glance and raised his eyebrows.

His guide kept talking. "Of course, cotter pins can break, or rust off, or be forgotten during reassembly. If that happens, it's just a matter of time before the car's vibrations or hitting a good bump make the nut do what this one did."

Joe nodded thoughtfully before suggesting the obvious. "But that's only true if the car's old enough to have that rusty a cotter pin, or if the tie rod end's been worked on by somebody."

Both men fell silent before Barrows supplied the requisite rejoinder: "And in theory, this car's too new for either one."

Joe returned to studying the broken part. "Well, you never know. We should check out the car's repair history. Leo always had the same folks work on it — Steve's Garage in Thetford Center."

"Huh," Barrows grunted.

"What?"

"Coincidence is all," the young deputy explained. "Steve's and this place are owned by the same person."

Joe straightened, glancing his head against the car frame and instinctively ducking back down, although he hadn't incurred any

72

damage. "E. T. owns Steve's? I didn't know that."

"That and a dozen other outfits. You just don't see his name on the door too often. Old E. T. likes his privacy. You know him?"

"Yeah — I grew up around here. Arrested his son once."

Now it was Barrows's turn to be surprised. "Andy?"

"Yeah. Down in Brattleboro."

"You know he's dead. Killed himself."

Joe stared at him. "My God. He was just a kid."

But Rob was studying the damaged wheel again. "E. T. was really broken up about it, and Dan went ballistic. You know Andy's brother?"

Joe nodded. "Used to be a hothead."

"Still is. Tore up a local bar when he heard Andy'd died. Spent the night in jail. That's how I know."

He reached out and touched the car's undercarriage with his fingertips. "I bet your name was mud in the Griffis household that night."

Joe frowned at the comment. "What're you saying?"

Barrows shrugged. "I've lived here my whole life. The Griffis clan makes things personal, which can definitely be good news, bad news. They're great if they like you, but they got a lot of money and know a lot of the wrong people if they don't."

Joe gestured at the car overhead. "And you think one of them did this because I busted Andy?"

But Rob shook his head. "I'm saying they wouldn't forget who you were if they blamed you for his death."

"What's the scuttlebutt?" Joe demanded, growing angry.

Barrows remained placid. "That's what I'm saying. I haven't heard a word. I didn't even know about you and Andy." He slapped the tire hanging by his head. "You asked me to take a closer look, remember? So, I'm not the one saying the Griffis bunch is after you. But if you're thinking this was done on purpose, I'd sure have an idea where to start digging."

Norma Wagner peered up from her crossword as the motel's front door set off the quiet chime behind her counter.

"Good evening, sir. Are you checking in?"

The man on the threshold looked as if she'd just asked the one question he hadn't been anticipating. He glanced around the empty lobby nervously. "Yes."

Norma smiled, both at him and to herself.

He was a decent enough looking guy — trimmed beard, not too fat, okay clothes — but homely. A work mouse, as she'd come to consider men like him — processed forms in an office building, went to the movies once a month, ate at the local Bickford's on Friday, and had a wife he'd grown so used to, he barely knew she existed.

And now, she thought to herself, this one was in the big city — or whatever Brattleboro might be considered. She watched him check the lobby a second time before hesitantly approaching her counter. Instinctively, after fifteen years in the motel business, she checked his left ring finger. The indentation of a wedding band was there, but the actual item was missing. *Ah,* and he was stepping out, as well.

Norma blended her satisfied laugh into her official greeting. "Welcome to the Downtowner, sir. Do you have a reservation?"

"No." He spoke barely above a whisper.

Of course not, she thought, eyeing the small overnight bag he kept clutched in his hand.

"That won't be a problem. We have plenty of room at the moment. How many nights will you be staying?"

"Just one."

But what a night, she imagined vicariously, typing into her computer, at least in *his* wildest hopes. She wasn't faulting him. She'd been married for twenty-five years to a man she saw as little as possible. She hoped this round little guy was going to have the night of his life.

"And how will you be paying tonight?" she asked.

He pulled out a billfold and laid three twenties on the surface between them. "Cash."

"Cash, it is," she said cheerily. "Do you have Triple A or another type of discount?"

He cast down his eyes even farther. She was starting to feel bad for him and wanted to get him into that room before he changed his mind and bolted.

"Not to worry, sir. That'll be forty-three ninety-five, with the businessman's discount. My treat."

He looked up partway at that and managed a weak smile, although his beard made it hard to see. "Thanks."

She placed a registration card before him. "Not a problem. If you could fill this out, we'd sure appreciate it."

As he put pen to card, she added, "And if I could have a credit card for both our security and any additional incidentals, that would be great."

He stopped and looked at her straight-on for the first time. Nice brown eyes. "I don't have a credit card."

Right, she thought. No more than you have a nose on your face. But, again, he was looking twitchy to her, so she cut him some slack. "That's all right. It'll be my job if you mess up, though, so you better promise to be good."

That broke eye contact. His gaze dived for the card before him again. God, she was having way too much fun with this poor bastard.

She decided to cut him loose with her final zinger. Smiling broadly, she collected the finished registration card and asked, "Two key cards or one?"

"Two, please."

*Yes*, she forced herself not to say aloud, instead handing over the keys while she glanced at the card he'd filled out. "Your room's at the end of the corridor, to the right of the vending machines. Have a nice night, Mr. Frederick, and thank you for choosing the Downtowner."

He nodded quickly and moved away. She watched him, the small bag still tight in his fist.

And have the night of your life, she mused again. Glad I could help.

**Julia:** Okay, to get the idea, you should sort of think of the Wizard of Oz.

**Cat:** ok.

**Julia:** There's a woman scientist, a butch team leader, a big-hearted archaeologist, and an alien guy with a snake in his stomach.

**Cat:** yes. simple. is he gonna do something about the snake?

**Julia:** Oh, he doesn't have it anymore.

**Cat:** oh ok.

**Julia:** It died, and he couldn't get another one in time, so he's on a drug now that mimics what the snake did for him.

**Cat:** ohhhhhhh of course

**Julia:** So now he's only like an alien because he has a gold brand on his forehead.

**Cat:** oh that guy! ok. i know which one he Is.

# CHAPTER 6

"Hi, sweetheart."

Joe opened his eyes without otherwise stirring, a habit born on the job, where catching a nap, sometimes with coffee still in hand, often made it possible to keep going for hours more.

But he was sitting empty-handed in his mother's hospital room. Across from him, she was looking at him, her head turned at last on that white pillow.

He smiled at her. "Hi, yourself. How're you feeling?"

He rose and crossed over to her, sitting on the edge of the bed and taking her hand up in both of his.

"Woozy," she conceded, adding after a moment's consideration, "Thirsty, too."

He reached for the pitcher by the bed and poured out a cup of water, fitting a straw to it and holding it so that she could draw a sip.

She emptied half the cup before setting her head back. "Good Lord, that hit the spot."

"How's your head?" he asked her.

"Fine. What did I do to it?"

He pursed his lips slightly, concerned. "You don't remember the crash?"

Her response set him at ease. "Oh, yes. Well, most of it. I remember the snow crashing against the windshield. I thought it would break. But that's about it." Her eyes suddenly widened and she gripped his hand. "Is Leo all right?"

"He's fine," he soothed her. "Banged up a little, too, but on the mend."

She closed her eyes. "Thank God. Poor boy."

Joe smiled at that, considering the man's age. The door to the room opened, and a nurse stepped in, smiling. "So," she said brightly, "you decided to join us, after all? I would have, too, with a good-looking son like that hanging around."

Joe's mother narrowed her eyes as she scrutinized him. "How long have I been like this?"

"A few days, Mom," he told her, bending quickly to kiss her cheek. "We've been keeping you company in shifts. You just missed Gail. She had to go back to Montpelier."

"Oh, my," she reacted, her cheeks pinking up, as if she was embarrassed at being caught napping too long.

The nurse set about checking her vitals and asking her questions. Joe rose and crossed to the window. The surrounding trees had maintained their thick mantle of snow in the windless cold and so now were almost hard to look at in the sun's glare.

"Mr. Gunther?"

He turned at the nurse's voice.

"The doctor will be wanting to check your mom out. If you'd like to take a small break and maybe grab a cup of coffee, now would be the perfect time. She'll be in good hands, I promise."

He smiled at the roundabout, practiced verbiage. "You'd make a good bouncer." He reached out and touched his mother's foot. "You have fun with the doc. I'll go torture Leo a little. Tie a knot in some of his tubing."

"You're an awful child," she told him, but he could see that he'd hit a nerve with the mention of tubing.

"Never claimed otherwise," he said, adding, "I'll be back with a report card."

That, as it turned out, was going to be a bit tricky, assuming the news was to be upbeat. Leo was still in intensive care, was in fact still hooked up to multiple tubes and wires, and, if anything, was in slightly worse shape than when Joe had seen him last.

He remained coherent, however, though only barely.

"Hey, Joe," he said weakly as his brother came into view by his side.

"Hey, yourself. Got good news: Mom just woke up. They're checking her out, but she seems fine. Just needed to sleep it off."

Leo closed his eyes briefly with relief. "Jesus." He then tried to move his hand to grasp Joe's, but grimaced and failed. Joe took his fingers in his own and gave him a squeeze. "Relax, Leo. It's going to be fine. All that's left is for you to get better."

Leo nodded quietly, taking his time. Joe noticed a tear building up in the corner of one of his brother's eyes. He reached out and wiped it away.

"I don't know," Leo said, so softly his words were almost lost in the whir of the surrounding equipment.

Joe leaned over to be near his face when he whispered. "Leo, you've got to do this. It's not like I have any spare brothers, and Mom'll make my life hell if you kick the bucket. Stop thinking of yourself, for Christ's sake."

Leo smiled slowly. "You are a son of a bitch."

Joe kissed his bristly cheek. "I love you, too."

His brother sighed and gave a halfhearted nod. "Okay. What about the car?"

"The nut on the tie rod went," Joe said, hoping that made sense.

Leo's eyes widened. "No shit? How the hell would that happen?"

"You had it serviced lately?"

"Yeah, but not for that. It's too new. The tie rod ends should be factory fresh."

"You bring it to Steve's, right?" Joe asked. "Exclusively?"

His brother nodded, beginning to fade.

"You ever have problems with them?"

Leo didn't respond immediately. Joe bent close again, not wanting to miss his chance. "Leo?"

"No problems," Leo mumbled.

Joe straightened back up. That would have to be it. He placed his palm flat on Leo's forehead and told him, "Hang in there. Mom's fine. That part's over. But we need you back, okay?"

He thought he could feel his brother nod agreement under his hand, but it was too slight a gesture to trust.

Their mother was discharged later that day. Joe had remembered to salvage her wheelchair from the trunk of the shattered Subaru, and used it to roll her out of the hospital and into the cold New England sunlight. As they cleared the overhang of the main entrance portico, she tilted her head back and let the sun hit her full in the face.

"God, that feels good."

Joe was relieved by the gesture. She'd refused to leave without first visiting Leo, and the sight of her last born, rigged up like a science experiment, had clearly shaken her. But she'd spoken to his physician in detail and had been told of a probable, though long-term, full recovery. Joe hoped that had helped with the worst of her concerns. But he wasn't sure. She hadn't spoken until hitting the sidewalk — she was, after all, of hard-core Yankee stock, a people who were not cold, as was their weather and their reputation, but who were indeed prone to self-containment. By instinct, people bred and brought up among these ancient mountains didn't speak of their feelings and didn't pry after those of others. For that matter, he hadn't asked her outright himself.

She worked at being upbeat during the drive home, insisting on stopping by the market to pick up a few things she thought he'd enjoy, and chatting about everything but the accident and her broken son. Joe let her find her emotional bearings, which, he sensed, would only really fall into place once they reached home. He therefore wasn't surprised when she quieted as he topped the same rise in the driveway that had similarly affected him the day before. He did, however, reach out as he stopped the car before the house, and squeeze her hand.

"He'll be fine, Mom. We'll see him through it."

She turned to him then, her eyes glistening. "He wouldn't be there now if he hadn't taken me to the movies."

Joe actually laughed as he leaned over and kissed her. "You probably saved his life. He would've been driving at twice the speed with some bimbo in one of his favorite wrecks. Tell me I'm wrong."

She smiled despite her sadness. "He doesn't carry on as much as he claims. But I suppose you're right."

Joe hadn't told her about the missing tie rod nut.

■ ■ ■ ■

They spent much of the day getting used to each other. Joe hadn't been at home without Leo in more years than he could recall, and he had a hard time gauging between too much together time with his mother and too little. She and Leo were like an old married couple, working on instinct, memory, and habit. Joe had only the first to draw on, and that was dulled by their both thinking of the missing member of their small company. He had to ask her about lunch, to discover if and when she napped, whether she could handle the bathroom on her own, what her rhythm was for reading, watching TV, and moving about in pursuit of various errands or tasks.

For her part, of course, he appeared like a fish out of water. He did nothing like his brother, had little here that belonged to him or would occupy him for long, and knew even less about the house's organization.

Still, they managed, mostly with humor, sometimes with reservations, and were clearly relieved when the doorbell rang.

At that moment they were both in the kitchen, where she was giving him a crash course on product geography, as he mentally termed it, struggling to retain how she liked her groceries organized.

More to the point, since dinner was looming, they'd also been discussing the upcoming meal. Sadly, Leo was the house's primary cook — Joe had no such talent, being of the opinion that all food should come packaged and ready to eat, preferably unheated — and it was becoming clear that the kitchen was where their cordiality might collapse.

"Who would that be?" Joe asked, the sound of a doorbell being a rare thing in a farmhouse.

"Maybe one of the neighbors," his mother suggested, "seeing we were home and knowing my son was about to poison me."

Joe moved toward the door. "Just trying to broaden your mind, Mom. We came out of the caves eating with our fingers. Sandwiches are an homage to a cultural heritage."

"We came out of the caves eating other people, period," his mother corrected him. "Go see who it is."

The other oddity, of course, was that the doorbell belonged to the front entrance, which almost everyone knew to ignore in favor of the kitchen door, around to the side, where the car was parked at the bottom of the wheelchair ramp.

As a result, Joe was expecting either a salesman or a Bible thumper as he opened the door.

Instead, there was a tall, slim, long-haired woman, looking both expectant and nervous.

Joe stared at her in astonishment, his hand frozen on the doorknob and his mouth half open in a generic greeting he didn't deliver.

He knew her, but not from around here. It was from a case a couple of years ago, when they'd met in Gloucester, Massachusetts, and he'd interviewed her in her capacity as a local bartender. She'd been helpful, aiming him toward someone who proved useful later on, but more importantly, in giving him a single kiss after a conversation laced with a subtle and meaningful subtext. That gesture had filled his head with thoughts, questions, yearnings, and possibilities that he'd retained ever since. By then, he and Gail had begun their slide away from each other, if only in small increments, and the woman now standing before him had loomed as an occasionally comforting fantasy to ease the transition.

But he'd never called her, had never thought of her except at odd moments, and had certainly never expected to lay eyes on her again. He didn't even know her last name.

At his stunned befuddlement, her nervousness yielded to an embarrassed smile. She stuck her hand out. "Joe Gunther . . ."

"Evelyn," he blurted, interrupting her.

She wrinkled her nose, the smile expanding. "You remember. I never figured how that got out. It's my real name — Evelyn Silva — after my grandmother." She added with a laugh, "But I don't like it much. Wasn't too crazy about her, either. Most people just call me Lyn."

He was still processing her appearance. Names could come later. "What are you doing here?" he asked, the host in him hoping it didn't sound too hostile, while the cop wondered if maybe it should.

"I read about your family's accident in the paper," she explained. "I wanted to see if you needed any help."

He stared at her. "In the Gloucester paper?"

She shook her head, her cheeks flushing. "No, no. The *Brattleboro Reformer.* I live in Brattleboro now. I moved."

"Who is it, Joe?" his mother asked from behind him.

Joe stepped aside to reveal his mother rolling up to them. Lyn broke into a wide smile.

"You're all right," she exclaimed. "They said you were in the hospital." She hesitated only a moment and then took one step forward and stuck her hand out. "I'm Lyn Silva, Mrs. Gunther. I'm really just an acquaintance of your son's, but I wanted to see how you were doing."

Joe's mother looked at her son. "I'm freezing. You're heating the whole state." Then she smiled brightly at their unexpected guest and shook hands. "He's still in training. I'm happy to meet you."

Joe removed his fingers from the knob as if it had been electrified. Like most locals, he was usually compulsive about open doors and drafts. He reached out and gently steered Lyn across the threshold. "I'm sorry," he said. "Wasn't paying attention."

"Come into the living room," his mother said, preceding them. "We have a fire going in the woodstove. Where are you from, Miss Silva?"

"Brattleboro now," Lyn told her, entering the cluttered, homey living room, adding, "Oh, I *love* this room. When was the house built?"

"Eighteen-thirties," Joe told her, bringing up the rear. "And we haven't done much to it since, except for the modern amenities."

He studied the back of their guest as if

she might suddenly pull a gun. He kept retrieving fragments of the one time they'd met, and coming up with only good memories. She was a single mother of a then twenty-year-old girl, a bookkeeper by day and a bartender at night, and at the time, at least, she'd been genuine, smart, sexy, and remarkably appealing — just as she appeared today.

But what was she doing here? When they last parted, he'd felt they had forged a definite connection, one that he would have pursued in Gail's absence. He'd even thought of locating her after his breakup, but had been stalled by both geography and a general emotional inertia.

On that level, therefore, he was astonished and pleased to see her again. But at his core he remained a cop and, as such, wary and watchful. Once the social niceties were dealt with and he found a quiet moment, he planned to inquire about the details behind this visit.

His mother parked her chair in her docking station of tables before asking, "What brought you to Brattleboro? And did I overhear that you came from Gloucester?"

"Yes, ma'am," Lyn answered. "I was a barkeep there, and I just bought a bar in Brattleboro — I found it through the Internet, if you can believe that."

"And how did you two meet? Have a seat in that armchair."

Joe glanced up at that question, trying to read between the lines. His mother's face was cheery and her eyes bright, but he knew her well and had clearly heard the interrogator's edge in her voice.

Lyn sat carefully in the old leather armchair. "Your son came to Gloucester to investigate a murder — a man who lived over the bar where I worked." She looked over at Joe with a smile. "He sat at the end of my bar drinking Cokes for a couple of nights before he said anything, just watching the crowd. It was fun seeing him study people." Again she reddened slightly, adding, "Including me. He's quite an observer. And when we finally did talk, he had me remembering things I didn't know I could." She touched her forehead with her fingertips. "You had me close my eyes and slowly redraw the scene in my head, detail by detail, until I could see that guy you were after — the one with the scar on his hand. Did you ever catch him?"

Joe nodded. "We did, thanks to you. It was a good description."

With her reminiscence, he, too, was recalling that trip, and how he'd spent those many hours, in part surveilling the crowd she served — and in part admiring her.

"That must have been fascinating," his mother interjected. "I've never actually seen Joe at work. But what are you doing way up here? Brattleboro's a long drive."

Lyn laughed. "I know. That must seem a little weird. No, I promise, I had to be up here anyhow, to get some supplies for the bar — I'm totally renovating it — and like I said, the newspaper was full of what happened. I figured I'd kill two birds with one stone."

"But how did you find the farm?" Joe asked.

Her expression brightened. "That was good, huh? I knew the accident happened near here; I figured you must live nearby, so I asked around. I felt a little like Dorothy asking directions to Oz — 'Could you tell me where the Gunthers live?' Good thing your last name isn't that common. The young woman at the Mobil station knew all about you. Is your brother named Leo? The paper just said he was your brother."

Both her companions burst out laughing.

"Sorry," Joe explained. "Leo's pretty popular with the local ladies."

"Especially those who are supposedly interested in cars," his mother added.

Lyn nodded in comprehension. "She did seem to know him pretty well."

"He's also the local butcher," Joe continued, "which adds to his appeal. Not," he said quickly, catching a warning glance from across the room, "that he isn't also a very skilled and professional guy. I don't want him to sound like a stud or anything."

The source of the glance explained, "The two of them have this running gag about Leo and his women. I can attest to his being more of a braggart than a practitioner. Either Joe doesn't know or won't admit it, but his little brother is a virtual homebody."

"How is he doing, by the way?" Lyn asked. "The paper said you were both in serious condition."

"Mom was in a deep sleep for a couple of days," Joe told her. "But she woke up good as new. Leo's pretty beaten up. He's conscious and can talk, but he's in the ICU. He's getting better, though."

This part of the conversation created an awkward silence, which prompted their hostess to push away from her tables and offer, "Anyone for tea or coffee?"

Both Lyn and Joe asked for the latter, allowing the old woman to escape to the kitchen and her own thoughts.

In her absence, the two of them remained

silent, not looking at each other, groping for something to say. In Joe's case, the inhibition was compounded by a wary curiosity struggling with his pleasure.

Lyn spoke first. "I'm sorry I barged in like I did. I didn't really expect anyone to be here. I just sort of yielded to impulse." She finally looked up at him. "When you opened the door, I couldn't believe my luck, but your mom being home just makes me embarrassed. This is not when I should be here."

"Not true," he said candidly. "I'm sorry I was such a dope at the door. I figured I'd never see you again."

She nodded silently, back to studying the rug.

"Not that I didn't want to," he added.

That brought her head up. "Really?"

He thought back to one of the few short conversations they'd shared in Gloucester, when, prompted by his observations of her at work behind the bar, she'd admitted to being at once forthright and shy with others, especially men.

"The reason we met may have been a little offbeat," he understated, "but it left a lasting impression. A really good one."

He was tempted to expand but resisted.

She smiled slightly, more with her eyes

than with her mouth. "Yeah," she said. "For me, too."

**SNOWGIRL:** how old r u?

**THUMPER:** 18. U?

**SNOWGIRL:** 14. feel lik 100

**THUMPER:** im sorry. Bad day?

**SNOWGIRL:** bad life

**THUMPER:** me 2

**SNOWGIRL:** y?

**THUMPER:** sister died. Luvd her a lot

**SNOWGIRL:** so sorry

**THUMPER:** U?

**SNOWGIRL:** sucky mom, pissy x-bf

**THUMPER:** He brok up with u? Y?

**SNOWGIRL:** same ol, same ol

**THUMPER:** Guys dont get it

**SNOWGIRL:** u do?

**THUMPER:** U want a hug, he wants sex. Rite?

**SNOWGIRL:** ya

**THUMPER:** I get it.

**SNOWGIRL:** ur cool

# CHAPTER 7

Steve's Garage, unsurprisingly, wasn't far from where Leo had his butcher shop in East Thetford. Suitably for a small village, the garage, unlike Mitch's car-corralled, straightforward cinder-block house of wrecks, was of evolutionary design, having begun life as a small barn. That said, it still wasn't quaint or neat. Rather, like so many of its brethren across this pragmatically minded state, it was a place where labor overruled aesthetics and where, if you needed to place an engine block temporarily in the dooryard, on top of two truck tires, you did just that.

Joe arrived as a passenger in Rob Barrows's cruiser, playing a role somewhere between investigator and representative of the injured party. They'd agreed beforehand that Barrows would do the talking, although, as a strategy, that would have been considered less than a fig leaf by any competent lawyer. But such were the agreements occasionally made by rural cops sniffing around the edges of barely definable cases.

The ambivalent tone was about right for Joe, who was beginning to feel that limbo had become a near permanent state. His mother's advancing years and frailty, his brother's precarious physical condition, Gail's proximity and yet distance — she'd called that morning to get a report — and now the reappearance of the very appealing, previously unavailable Lyn Silva, had all helped to make him feel totally easy about trespassing into an investigation based on a lost nut and involving two relatives.

Not that he minded Lyn resurfacing. She'd departed for Brattleboro shortly after finishing her coffee, but what she left behind — which Joe even heard in his mother's voice afterward — was a suggestion of positive intrigue. Not a bad thing, all other things considered.

The two men swung out of the car and eyed the garage's bland frontage, buttoned up tight against the cold.

"D'you call ahead?" Joe asked.

Barrows stayed watching the building. "I thought we'd surprise 'em."

It didn't take long. In most rural areas, it

is less a door knock or a ringing bell that draws attention from inside a building — simply showing up usually does the trick. Sure enough, moments later the wooden door under a hand-lettered sign reading "Office" opened, and a small, narrow man in a soiled baseball cap and a T-shirt stepped partway out.

"Rob," he said neutrally.

Barrows didn't move. "Barrie," he answered loudly enough to carry across the distance.

"How're ya doin'?"

"Good. You?"

"Great."

Barrie looked from one of them to the other. Barrows allowed the silence to stretch out, forcing the mechanic to ask, "So, what's up?"

Only then did the deputy approach the building, Gunther in tow. Rob smiled as he drew near, sticking his hand out in greeting, abruptly offsetting his slightly threatening initial tone. Joe took note of the tactic and didn't offer to shake.

Rob jerked his thumb in his direction. "Barrie McNeil, this is Joe, from the Vermont Bureau of Investigation." He and Rob had agreed beforehand to use his last name discreetly, if at all.

For a split second, McNeil froze. Enough time had elapsed since the Bureau's inception for the initials "VBI" to carry an ominous meaning among those who might have reasons to care.

McNeil forced a small smile. "Just keeping the deputy company?"

Joe looked him straight in the eyes. "No."

Rob picked up the cue. "So, Barrie, we were wondering. There was a car crash a few days ago — the Subaru on Route Five?"

Barrie was already nodding. "Leo's car. He all right?"

"He's a mess. In the hospital. Intensive care."

"Damn."

"Yeah." Rob pointed at the doorway Barrie was filling with his slight frame. "You want to let us in?"

McNeil bobbed his head and stepped backward awkwardly. "Oh, yeah. Sure. Come on in."

They entered a waiting room of sorts, certainly a room with three mismatched office chairs lining a wall, facing a card table with a pile of ancient and bedraggled magazines strewn across its surface. There were posters hanging about advertising young, semi-clad women holding automotive products, and rows of shelves sagging under stacks of oil filters, brake pads, boxed spark-plugs, and the like. It was all beyond a restorative cleaning, aside from the gleaming spare parts themselves, and all illuminated from a single slightly flickering fluorescent light overhead, whose plastic enclosure showed off the shadows of generations of dead insects. An open door to the side revealed the garage proper and a car with no wheels, perched high atop a lift.

The entire place was uncomfortably hot, explaining how the T-shirted Barrie had so easily loitered within the open doorway without complaint.

"Barrie," Rob began, strolling around the room, looking at the posters, "tell us about tie rod nuts."

Barrie hesitated, again nervously switching his attention from one of them to the other.

"They hold the tie rods together?" he guessed.

"Just like that? You screw 'em on and they hold on tight?"

"Pretty much . . . There's a cotter pin."

Rob turned to face him, as if responding to a poke in the ribs. "A cotter pin? Why?"

"So it don't back off. Is that what happened to Leo's car?"

Rob tilted his head to one side. "Is it?"

Barrie pursed his lips, clearly not wanting to flunk whatever test this was.

"Probably, if it failed. That happens," he said tentatively.

"A lot?"

"No . . . Sometimes."

"What about Leo's car?"

McNeil scrunched up his face in confusion. "Jesus, Rob. That's what I just asked."

"And what did you come up with, Barrie? Could the nut have come loose in Leo's car?"

McNeil snatched his baseball cap off and passed his palm across the top of his head several times. "No . . . I mean, it *could* have, but I don't see why. This is all fucked up, Rob. What do you *want?*"

Rob leaned forward at the waist for emphasis. "I want to know about Leo's tie rod, Barrie. Talk to me."

Barrie slapped his hat back on and extended his arms out to both sides, saying loudly, "I don't *know* about his fucking tie rod, Rob. I never touched it."

Barrows let a slow count of five tick by before he stepped back and said pleasantly, "Geez. You seem awfully worked up about something you never touched."

Barrie didn't answer, but he'd gone paler in the process.

"Okay. Cool," Rob resumed. "Let me take a look at Leo's service records on that car. Maybe we can clear this whole thing up here and now."

But it didn't work. Barrie's face shut down. "No can do. Not without a court order. Boss's orders. That computer is, like, sacred."

"Griffis?" Joe asked, unable to stop himself.

McNeil looked at him as if he'd just stepped into the room. "Yeah. I let you do that, I'm outta here. Like that." He snapped his fingers. "That's, like, his biggest rule."

Rob looked vaguely offended. "You're shitting me. Why would the old man get all cranked up about a bunch of car repair records?"

But now it was Barrie's turn to turn the tables. "I'm not talkin' about E. T.," he said. "Dan's the boss."

Once more, Joe couldn't stop himself. "*Dan* owns the garage?"

"Yeah, for a coupla years. Old E. T. gave him a bunch of stuff. Passing the light."

"Torch," Rob said sourly.

Barrie stared at him, back on firmer ground. "Whatever."

Joe asked, "Why did Dan slam the door

on the records? You guys get sued or something?"

Barrie shook his head. "Nope. He just
came in after he made boss, and said there
was gonna be some tightening up around
here, and that's when he gave the order."

"What else did he change?" Rob asked,
looking around at the decor to see if he'd
missed some subtle improvement.

"That was it."

Rob glanced at Joe, received a barely
perceptible shrug, and told Barrie, "Okay.
No problem going the legal route. In fact,
even better. Keeps things clean. We'll get a
warrant."

"Does Dan use the computer much?" Joe
asked.

"All the time."

Rob moved toward the door to leave, but
Joe paused to add a final recommendation:
"You probably heard on TV how once data's
entered into a computer, it never really
disappears, right?"

Barrie clearly had no idea what he was
talking about. "Yeah," he said without conviction.

"You want to think about that. Something
happens to this one, we'll come looking for
you to find out why, regardless of who
monkeys with it."

The two cops left the building and walked back to Rob's cruiser.

"Nice, with the computer," Rob said as they settled inside. "Maybe he won't squeal to his boss."

Joe grunted. "Could be. If I were him, I'd solve the problem by throwing the damn thing into the river. Not that it matters. We'll never find a judge to allow us into it, anyhow."

Rob nodded without comment.

"Too bad we can't find that nut," Joe mused.

His companion glanced at him inquiringly.

Joe explained further, "It might have tool marks on it — something we could match to a wrench or something in there." He pointed his chin toward the garage. "Enough PC for a search warrant, given that Barrie said he never touched the nut."

Rob's expression began to lighten. "But that's possible. I mean, it's a reach. But it is possible."

"What? Find the nut?" Joe was incredulous. "There's two feet of snow out there. And who knows where it fell off?"

"Could be right near the crash site," Barrows said. "That's how it works sometimes — the nut falls off and the rod follows, slambam. There's no waiting. Not often, but when it does, it's immediate. The nut could be within a hundred feet of where they went off the road. Closer, even, if we're really lucky."

Joe was catching a fragment of his colleague's enthusiasm, but he still couldn't ignore the odds. "Be more likely to find a fresh flower in all that snow."

Rob smiled. "Can't find a flower with a metal detector, and the sheriff's got two of them. Plus," he added, holding up a finger, "a small crowd of teenage wannabe cops from the high school who love doing police work — our official Explorers troop, complete with uniforms. It wouldn't cost the department a dime to set them to sniffing around."

"The sheriff would go along with that?" Joe asked, finally gaining on the idea.

Barrows laughed. "You just watch."

Late that night, having missed the dinner hour, Joe found himself standing in the kitchen, scrutinizing stacks of cans in one of the cupboards.

"What are you looking for?" his mother asked from the door.

He turned and laughed. "Busted. I heard the TV. Didn't want to bother you. I know it's getting late. I was looking for some Spam or something."

Her eyes widened. "*Spam?* I should be visiting your graveside, the way you eat." She rolled farther into the room, heading toward the fridge. "I'll make you something. Leo's gotten me lazy. Time I got back into cooking. How about an omelet? I'll throw in some ham, tomatoes, maybe a little cheese?"

It was a more than acceptable compromise. Joe kept little in his own fridge except milk and mayonnaise, along with a few jars containing substances he couldn't identify. Eating was something he did out of hunger, drawing few distinctions between a doughnut and a salad. It used to drive Gail insane.

He settled down at the kitchen table to get out of his mother's way as she expertly traveled the room.

"What's the latest on Leo?" she asked as she worked, her voice self-consciously nonchalant.

He smiled at her. "As if you didn't know. I did just come from there, though. I think he's looking a little better. He certainly has more to say, which isn't pretty. I figure in a week, the nurses'll kill him and that'll be the end of it."

She gave him a dark look, which he knew

not to take seriously.

"He's got company, by the way," Joe added.

"Who?"

"Cops. I found a state trooper there tonight, just visiting, and Leo said there'd been others. Word got out, and guys from a bunch of departments are dropping by, just showing support. They even started a guest book you can see next time you're there."

She nodded once, visibly moved. "That's very sweet."

"It's a small world I work in," he told her. "And cops are pretty sentimental. What did the doc tell you on the phone?" he then asked, knowing she'd called.

"That he's past the worst of it but has a long way to go." She cracked an egg into a bowl and put the shell down beside it, sighing. "I keep wondering if all this will change things."

He reached out and patted her hand. "One step at a time, Mom. Leo's pretty irrepressible. He'll have some physical therapy afterward, and you might be taking more care of him than he ever did of you for a while, but I'm guessing he'll be back in full form by the end."

She nodded and broke another egg. "What did you learn about the accident?"

He raised his eyebrows. "How did you know I was looking into that?"

She looked up at him. "I would be."

Good point, he thought. Part of the reason he'd turned out the way he had was because she'd trained him to be curious about everything and everyone.

"A piece of the car fell off," he said. "That's what messed up the steering. The sheriff's department is going to see if they can find it tomorrow, using metal detectors."

She kept working, whipping the eggs in the bowl, her eyes down and her voice neutral. "That seems like a lot of work."

He shrugged. "I've teamed up with one of their deputies, Rob Barrows. He says they have an Explorers troop that are all eager beavers. Won't cost them a cent."

Again she nodded. "Laura Barrows's boy. He was in the MPs in the Army. Got out three years ago. A nice man."

"Yeah. Seems so." Joe was watching her carefully, knowing something was brewing.

After a small pause, she added, "If you know the accident was caused by something falling off, why do you need to find it?"

*Ouch,* he thought. Too smart by half. "Just to make things neat and tidy."

She stopped whipping and fixed him with

111

a baleful look. This one he did know to take seriously. "Joseph."

He pushed his lips out in defeat. "You're good, Mom. If I knew how to scramble eggs, I'd trade jobs with you."

"I wouldn't wish that on the rest of humanity," she told him. "What's going on?"

He studied the tabletop for a couple of seconds, pondering his response. "Truth? Maybe nothing, and I'm not pulling your leg. It's just that the piece I mentioned shouldn't have fallen off a car as new as the Subaru."

"What else?" she asked.

"That's it. I told you it was probably nothing."

She frowned at him. "You were the same way as a child. You could never just spit it out. Parts fall off of new cars, too, Joe. All the time. What are you not telling me?"

Joe repositioned his chair, crossed his legs and arms, and reconsidered his strategy.

"Cops are professional paranoids, Mom. You know that, right? It keeps us focused and it keeps us safe. It also makes us look under the bed, even when we know there's nothing there."

She kept studying him, the eggs temporarily forgotten.

"So," he resumed, "two members of a

cop's family get injured because a relatively new car falls apart, you gotta wonder why, especially when that car is serviced by a business belonging to E. T. Griffis."

She nodded, satisfied at last, though not happily so. "Ah."

"You knew about Andy?" he asked.

"Yes. Poor boy."

"Well, I didn't. Barrows just told me. When did it happen?"

"Late this summer. He hanged himself."

"I heard E. T. and Dan took it hard."

She seemed to notice the bowl before her for the first time, gave it a couple of last swirls with the whisk, and set to work on dicing up a piece of ham. She spoke as she worked.

"Dan confronted me in the grocery store afterward."

*"What?"* Joe leaned forward in his chair.

She put her knife down briefly for emphasis. "I'm only telling you this because I assume you'll hear it from someone else, and I don't want to explain why I kept silent. It's the worst part of living in a small community."

"What happened?" Joe demanded.

"Essentially nothing. He just came up to me in the grocery store when I was there buying a few things — Leo had gone across the street — and he let me know he was unhappy with the way things had turned out."

Joe let out an angry laugh. "Oh, right. I bet that's the way he phrased it. Come on, Mom. What did he say?"

She was back to cutting up the ham. "It was unpleasant and said in the heat of the moment."

Now he was the one merely staring in silence.

She let it drag on for almost a minute before finally conceding, "He said we'd be sorry. That we'd pay for it."

Joe rubbed his forehead. "Great. Did you know E. T. handed Steve's Garage over to Dan?"

That stopped her in mid-motion. "No," she allowed.

Joe sat back and thought for a few seconds. "What was the reason given for Andy doing himself in?" he then asked in a calmer voice.

"The most I ever heard was that he was having problems, whatever that means." She looked up from her task and then asked, "What did you arrest him for?"

Joe smiled bitterly and shook his head. "For something I couldn't prove he didn't do."

"He *didn't* do?" she parroted.

"It was a burglary. The store owner interrupted it and was injured in the process — an older lady. She didn't see who hit her, but she saw a car driving off afterward, tires squealing, and got the registration. It belonged to Andy, and when we went by his place to talk to him, the tools used in the break-in were right there in plain sight and were later matched not only to the marks left on the lock of the place he rifled, but to a blood smear belonging to the woman."

"That sounds pretty strong," his mother suggested.

"On the face of it," he agreed. "My problem was that he'd never done anything like that before and there was nothing in his private life to explain why he would — except for having a loser brother who happened to be facing what his type calls 'the Bitch.' "

Her eyebrows shot up. "I beg your pardon?"

"That's the habitual offender label that can turn a standard sentence into a lifetime in jail. The SA will slap it on you if he's had enough of giving you second chances, and I happen to know that Dan was nose to nose with it big-time back then. I couldn't prove it, but I always bet Dan was in Brattleboro when all this happened — that he'd done the job and convinced Andy to take the fall because he'd get off light."

"Three years doesn't sound light."

Joe didn't argue with her. "It was an election year, the SA had been accused of being too easy on criminals, the old lady was a charmer, complete with bandaged head, and did I mention that Andy copped to having done it? According to statute, he was looking at fifteen years. I figured — and I swear this is what Dan sold him, too — that he'd get a suspended sentence and probation. But that's not how the SA saw it, and for some reason, the judge let it fly, too. It was pure Russian roulette on Andy's part, with five out of six chances of being lucky."

Joe sighed heavily, remembering his irritation at the unusual outcome. "That's what upset me when you said Dan had confronted you in the grocery store," he added. "If Andy's death does have anything to do with my quote-unquote sending him to jail, then Dan better not look into any mirrors, 'cause he won't like what he sees."

"But you don't know any of that for sure," she half asked.

There he had to concede defeat. "No."

The pager on his belt began vibrating quietly. He groaned and removed it from his belt and saw Sam's callback number on the display, along with the message, "ASAP."

"I better answer this," he muttered, getting up.

"A problem?" she asked.

"Don't know. It's Sam." He moved toward the door.

"Joe," his mother said, stopping him.

He crossed back over to her and kissed her forehead. "Don't worry, Mom. We'll figure this out." He pointed at the bowl. "You better hold off cooking that till after this phone call, though."

He went into the living room to give both of them some privacy, more from instinct than any notion that his mother needed shielding.

"Hi," he said to Sam after she'd picked up the phone. "What've you got?"

"Sorry to bother you, boss, but we found another dead guy with no ID and no obvious signs of what did him in, just like the first. This one's in Brattleboro."

Joe felt his stomach rumble. He'd stop at a gas station for a sandwich on the way.

"I'll be there in an hour."

**Bordfem:** hi
**csawurm:** your cute
**Bordfem:** thanks
**Bordfem:** asl
**csawurm:** 23 male vermont
**Bordfem:** kool - 14 f vermont
**csawurm:** whoa your 14?
**Bordfem:** is that bad
**csawurm:** Im pretty sure thats jailbait - you look older in your pic
**Bordfem:** well its my school pic
**csawurm:** what school?
**Bordfem:** brattleboro middle school
**Bordfem:** u there
**csawurm:** yep
**Bordfem:** u want to chat
**csawurm:** yeah but I have to go soon
**Bordfem:** k
**csawurm:** bye youngin

# CHAPTER 8

Joe paused on the threshold, completely clad in a Tyvek jumpsuit, and surveyed the room. What crossed his mind immediately was less the scene before him — a motel room remarkable only for its blandness — and more the fact that the dead body draped across the foot of the bed didn't seem particularly unusual.

Being in situations like this, whether they were homicides, suicides, or undetermined, had by now become a habit.

There were four others in the room ahead of him, all dressed as he was. The smallest of them turned as he closed the door behind him.

"Hey, boss," Sam greeted him. "You made good time."

He nodded in response. "Still no ID?" he asked.

"He might as well've been dry-cleaned," another of the figures answered, turning to

119

reveal himself as Lester Spinney, Sam's exact opposite in both height and demeanor — he, laid back and tall; she, high strung and diminutive. Standing beside each other, they looked like an antiseptic comedy act. The two other detectives, both on their hands and knees, worked for the Brattleboro PD. One, surprisingly to Joe, who had spent decades in that department, he knew only slightly, and not by name. The other, by contrast, was Ron Klesczewski, the chief of detectives, anointed by Joe on his departure, and a close friend. The first man did no more than glance in Joe's direction before resuming work, scrutinizing the rug inch by inch. Ron, for his part, leaped up and shook hands like a long-lost relative, making Joe realize guiltily that, in fact, they hadn't seen each other in months, despite their having offices one floor apart.

After pleasantries — and apologies — Joe looked into the bathroom to his right and the open closet door immediately beyond it, making sure not to step off the ribbon of butcher paper laid down from the doorway to the far wall for scene preservation. Both areas appeared untouched, all the way down to the toilet paper end still folded into a point.

Ron caught the meaning of his survey.

"He did check in," he reassured him, "but paid cash."

"No luggage?" Joe asked.

"Supposedly a small bag. If so, it's missing," Lester suggested.

Joe stepped deeper into the room. The body lay facedown on the made bed, fully clothed. The TV was off, the lights on, the curtains drawn. Aside from the dead man, the room looked ready for rental.

There was a knock on the door, and Alan Miller stuck his white-hooded head in. "Okay to come in? I'm all decked out."

Joe looked to Ron, who was the nominal lead investigator until or unless he ceded control of the case to the VBI.

"Good by me," he said. "I want to see what he looks like."

Alan stepped inside cautiously, lugging his metal equipment case. "Any idea who we've got?"

"None," Sam told him. "What you see is everything. I checked his back pockets already, since they were staring at me, but so far, nothing. Feel free to do the honors."

"No weapon?" Miller persisted.

"We don't even know if he was murdered," Lester volunteered cheerfully. "Could be a natural."

"Or another parachutist," Sam muttered darkly.

Miller looked at her doubtfully but didn't ask for an explanation. Instead, he opened his case on the butcher paper, extracted a camera, and took a few shots that would later accompany the body to the ME's office in Burlington. Beverly Hillstrom liked seeing what her customers looked like in place.

He then began carefully examining the body, first by simply placing his gloved hand on its abdomen to feel its temperature, before moving to the hands, arms, and legs to check for stiffness. A vague rule of thumb had it that rigor mortis takes some twelve hours to reach its peak, before a body's flaccidity begins reasserting itself. But everyone in the room was experienced enough to know that such rules were notoriously unreliable.

"Okay to move him?" he asked.

Klesczewski nodded, and Miller rolled the body onto its back, farther up onto the bed. A gentle sigh escaped its lungs as it settled into its new position.

They all studied the man's face, as if expecting him to deliver a name. He was about five feet ten, on the edge of going fat, dressed in jeans, a chamois flannel shirt, and sneakers. He had thick, curly hair, a narrow, neatly bearded face, and absolutely nothing to say to any of them.

To satisfy Sam, whose habits he knew all too well, Miller checked the decedent's front pockets first. "Nothing," he announced.

The rest of his examination came to about the same conclusion. Clothing was opened and shifted, but not removed — again according to the ME's wishes — but no wounds, telling tattoos, or interesting artifacts surfaced. Whoever this was, he remained, for the moment, simply a corpse in a motel room.

They'd been told in the middle of Miller's procedure that the funeral home had arrived for transportation. The body was, therefore, eventually sealed in a heavy plastic bag and handed over to the hearse and its police escort, leaving the original team alone in the room.

In the momentary silence following their host's departure, Joe scratched his cheek through his Tyvek hood, feeling claustrophobic. "How many key cards did he request at the desk?"

Sam and Ron exchanged glances — a throwback to when Sam was also on the local squad. Lester picked up the hint and moved to the phone, made a quick call, hung up after asking the same question of the clerk, and reported, "Two."

"That's interesting," Joe said. "How many cards did you find here?"

"None," Ron admitted in a monotone, adding, "I should've thought of that."

"Call me a pessimist," Joe then mused, "but I'm guessing our buddy didn't die of natural causes."

Sam paced the short distance to the far wall and came back again, staying on the brown paper but agitated by the same oversight Ron had owned up to. "Okay. Let's put it together. He checks in, presumably looking for anonymity . . ."

"And for love," Lester added.

"Right. But no sooner has he entered this room than his date arrives and whacks him somehow, stealing all his stuff, including both key cards."

"He arrived alone?" Joe asked.

"Yeah," Lester answered. "We did get that much. I had the manager get hold of the night clerk for a positive ID and a short interview."

"Then why the two cards?" Joe asked again. "Wouldn't you just tell your date what room you were in and open the door when he or she knocked? Or maybe leave the second key at the desk? Why ask for two and then take them both into the room?"

There was no answer from any of his colleagues. Joe tapped the wall beside him. "Any neighbors?"

"One," Ron answered. "The other room's empty. And that neighbor didn't hear a thing."

"How did he get here?"

"That's another thing," Lester said. "We don't know. Every car in the lot's accounted for. He didn't list one on his registration card."

Joe made another survey of the room, standing still and scanning slowly in a circle. At the end, he said, "One of you is meeting someone in a motel. You want it nice and anonymous — no real names, no credit cards, an out-of-the-way place. How do you set it up?"

As usual, Sam spoke first, after only a momentary hesitation. "I either call the other party with my room number after I check in, or I tell them to ask at the desk."

"Right," agreed Lester, catching the spirit of Joe's question. "But we already ruled out that he used the phone, and if you're trying to be secretive, you don't then tell that other party to ask at the desk. You tell him to come straight to the door. Plus, this guy took two key cards. He could've just left the second one at the desk, if that was the plan."

"How does the visitor know what door to go to?" Sam challenged.

"A signal out the window?" Ron mused. He stepped around his subordinate, still working on the rug, and opened the curtains. The room had a full view of the parking lot.

"Or a sign outside the door," Sam suggested. "Even a large piece of blank paper would do, Scotch-taped in place."

"Maybe the second key card itself," Lester added, "stuck in an envelope."

He walked to the door, opened it, and scrutinized its exterior surface, aided by a penlight. The others watched him, his nose almost touching the door, until he finally paused, brushed the area before him gently with his latex-gloved fingertip, and announced, "There was some tape here, recently enough that the residue's still tacky."

Joe was nodding all the while. "So our person of interest gets here, opens the door himself to avoid the noise of a knock or the risk of nonadmittance, then what?"

"Kills our guy," Lester said immediately, adding just as quickly, "but how?"

In the meantime, he left the door, crossed

126

to the desk, opened the drawer, removed the cardboard folder he found there containing writing paper, a cheap pen, some postcards, and a single envelope. Holding up the latter, he said, "Two postcards, two sheets of paper, one envelope."

"But no Scotch tape," Sam said. "He either brought it with him or just used the glue on the envelope flap to hang it on the door."

"Suggesting some DNA transfer from tongue to envelope to door," Joe mused.

"Yeah," Lester agreed. "But from the victim, so who cares?"

"Right," Joe conceded before waving his hand in a semicircle. "So, possibly apart from the envelope, nothing's disturbed, the dead man's clothes were neatly tucked into place, and there wasn't a mark on him." He paused to address Ron's detective. "You find anything yet?"

"No, sir," he answered.

"And," Joe concluded, "we found him lying across the bottom of the bed, facedown."

"As if stretched out for a nap," Lester said.

"Or passed out," Sam proposed. "You take a nap, you position yourself properly; you use a pillow, take off your shoes. Plus, you don't even go there if you're waiting for someone. The adrenaline's pumping. Naps don't come into it."

The four of them contemplated what all that might mean.

"Be a bummer if the ME said it was a heart attack," Lester said.

Joe smiled, knowing the unlikeliness of that. His response went to the crucial point none of them had yet addressed. "The real bummer would be if *both* our dry-cleaned John Does turned out to be naturals. This is number two, after all."

Sam grunted softly. "Christ. I hope they end up with something more in common than this."

"Like the same poison?" Lester asked.

"I don't know. Anything."

"No local connections to the first one yet?"

"No," she said gloomily. "We're still asking around."

"We might have to ask for some help there," Gunther suggested. "Get the newspaper involved, especially if this fellow turns out not to be from around here, either. You know: 'Have You Seen This Man?' Run them both. And if that fails, go wider, reach across New England. There's got to be somebody who'll recognize at least one of them. What was the name this one used at the desk?"

"R. Frederick."

Gunther laughed.

"What?" Ron asked.

He held his hand up. "I don't know. It just flashed through my mind — R. Frederick, Ready Freddy. Wonder what the 'R' stood for."

"You serious?"

Joe shrugged. "I don't know. I guess not. It's possible, though. You check into a motel for illicit purposes, maybe you're feeling playful. Anyhow, doesn't matter. We have to do this by the numbers, even if it turns out he used his real name. BOL, canvass, AFIS for the fingerprints, the whole smorgasbord. And we need to figure out how he got here — train, bus, cab, hitchhiking."

He paused to address Ron. "Anything you need from us?"

Klesczewski shook his head. "No. We're okay. We'll do a forensic vacuuming later, maybe use the luminol. Since the Bureau's paying, the sky's the limit, right, even though it's a motel room and guaranteed to give us too much and therefore nothing at all?"

Joe raised his eyebrows. "That mean you're giving us the case?"

Ron bowed slightly. "With our compliments. We're drowning in work right now, the budget's hemorrhaging, the chief's on the warpath, and Sam and Ron were telling me you might be working a related case anyhow. It makes sense."

"Then our wallet's your wallet," Joe told him. "And thank you. You going to want the crime lab at all?"

The state forensic lab usually did such work, traveling to assist almost every department in Vermont. But not all of them. The bigger PDs liked to lay claim to being just as good on their own. Brattleboro had been known to go either way.

"I think we got it," Ron said. "We'll keep you posted."

Joe headed toward the door. "Okay, then, I'll leave you all to it."

In the hallway outside, he began climbing out of his Tyvek suit, leaning against the wall for support. Sam had followed him outside.

"Thanks for coming down. I hated bothering you. How're things up north?"

He hesitated, one foot in the air, and pursed his lips, trying to pay the question its due. "Complicated," he finally said.

She tried reading between the lines. "Medically?"

"Not really, although Leo's not out of the woods." He resumed removing the overalls, continuing, "I'm helping the sheriff's office look into the car crash."

"You're kidding me," she exclaimed.

He shook his head. "I'm not saying there's anything to it — not necessarily. But I have some questions."

He held his hand up as she opened her mouth, her eyes wide. "Sam, that's all I've got right now. If I hit on anything, you'll be the first to know. In fact, you'll probably have to take the case over 'cause of my personal involvement. Right now I'm just sniffing around."

He bundled up the white suit and shoved it into a transparent bag for disposal. "You could do something, though, come to think of it," he admitted.

"Shoot," she answered.

"Run down what you can about Andy Griffis. I don't remember his birth date, but he was from Thetford originally. I busted him in Bratt a few years ago, and he committed suicide late this summer, so he shouldn't be hard to locate. Everything you can find."

She was already scribbling a few notes in her pad. "Got it. Reach you at your mom's?"

"Generally, or use the pager. And don't punch a case quite yet, okay? Off the books."

Joe stood on the sidewalk, his hands buried

131

in his coat pockets, looking across the street at the bar. It was a far cry from the place in Gloucester where he'd first met Lyn Silva, whom he'd known then only as Evelyn. That had been a notorious dive, well known to the local cops, and literally home to an ever-changing tide of anonymous people who lived on the top two floors in rented rooms that looked like jail cells. Included among those residents had been the dead man Joe had come down there hoping to interview.

This was a serious step up. A handsome, elaborately carved sign over the door advertised "Silva's," the bay windows to either side of the door had been framed with nicely worked wooden casings in the style of a century ago, and he could see, behind the glass, tables placed on raised platforms to afford patrons a better view of the street.

He crossed over and saw a paper sign on the door reading "Not open yet, but hold that thought."

He paused at the foot of the three steps leading up, startled at how well that phrasing reflected his own situation. His attraction to Lyn was not at issue, nor was her clear interest in him, despite his wondering at that good fortune. What was stalling him was old baggage — his age, his past with Gail and its lingering emotional fallout, his near miss at losing his mother and Leo. He was gun-shy and unsure and more inclined to pulling in than to exploring a new relationship. His one night with Hillstrom had been a defining moment, though in large part appreciated precisely because it had no future.

Proceeding through the door ahead of him could be much more than he wanted to handle right now — if ever again.

"Does he dare?" came from behind him.

He turned around sharply, struck as much by the wording as by the voice. Lyn Silva stood in the street, carrying three precariously balanced cardboard boxes, a half smile on her face.

"I serve Coke, too," she added.

He wondered if her opening line, as insightful as it had seemed, had in fact meant something more mundane. It was possible, given the Coke follow-up, but he'd learned not to sell her short. Her canny instincts about people — including herself — had struck him all the way back in Gloucester. She was just as possibly allowing them both a little leeway.

"Looks like it's really coming along," he said blandly, instinctively reaching for the top two boxes of her stack.

She nodded, glancing up at the sign. "I

was about to ask if you wanted to come in, but if you don't now, you'll be stealing my stuff."

Almost surprised, he looked down at what he'd just taken into his arms. "Sorry. That was a little —"

"Much appreciated," she interrupted. "Come on. It's open."

She cut around him and led the way, bumping the door open with one slim blue-jeaned hip.

The interior was warm and smelled of old wood and leather, with a scattering of tables and upholstered stools paralleling the long bar stretching into the gloom ahead. The room was narrow, high-ceilinged, and deep, with an unusual balcony high and to the back, overhanging what seemed fated to become a small stage for musicians. The decor largely consisted of more wood detailing, old mirrors, and framed photographs and portraits, some of which were still propped against the baseboard. There were also several dartboards.

"Just dump those on the bar," she told him, doing the same. "*Would* you like a Coke? I'm about to have one. Long day. Take your coat off."

He pulled over a stool and settled down as she circled the bar to get to a small fridge tucked under the counter near the cash register. "Lucky you have a thing for Coke. I had a deal with the Pepsi distributor until we got into a fight, so I dropped them for the out-of-town Coca-Cola dealer. Not that I've gotten the equipment and supplies yet, so we'll see. Anyhow, I keep a few basics on hand, just in case. Be crazy not to have anything except water, even if the place isn't officially open."

She quickly crouched and extracted two cans of soda from the fridge in one clean movement, reminding him of how habituated she was to this environment. Looking around again at the boxes and the gentle disarray, he thought this might be like visiting a magician backstage, before the curtain rose and the lights blocked out all but the main attraction. He recalled sitting at the end of the bar in Massachusetts, admiring how she simultaneously worked the clientele while balancing the multiple tasks of her profession — taking orders, pouring drinks, making change, washing glasses, refilling nut dishes, keeping the bar top clean and free of clutter — all without missing a beat. And by Vermont law, all bars had to serve enough food to supply at least 20 percent of overall sales, so he knew she had the basics of a kitchenette somewhere, as well.

She popped the tabs on both cans simultaneously and poured the contents into two ice-filled glasses she'd conjured up, seemingly out of thin air.

"Lime?" she asked.

He laughed at the automatic request dovetailing so perfectly with his line of thought. "No, I'm fine. Thanks. How long till you open?"

She took a long pull on her own drink and looked around, as if at a museum exhibition under construction. "Couple of weeks, tops. It's been an amazing haul — just filling out paperwork for over a month, for one thing. Inspections, license applications, tax forms, contracts — none of which had anything to do with the actual work of painting, sanding, buying furniture and fixtures, rigging the sound system, you name it. And there's still a ton of piddly stuff left. But most of the heavy lifting is done. I can see the light at the end of the tunnel."

"It must be like reaching a life goal," he suggested. "Being able to work for yourself."

By now she was leaning with the small of her back against the counter behind her. "I wouldn't go that far. It is just a bar. But it's nice to be out of Gloucester. I was way too long in that place."

He smiled and suggested, "Things look

good after a few years, but maybe for all the wrong reasons?"

She nodded. "Yeah, exactly. A bunch of habits you start thinking are a life." She gave him a thoughtful look. "I have you to thank for waking me up, at least partly."

He was genuinely surprised. "Me?"

"That night we met at the end of the pier, after my shift. You were looking for the guy that killed poor old Norm, so you bought me a lobster roll and a milkshake to butter me up — you probably don't even remember that."

"Sure I do," he said, his own memory being much sharper than she could know.

"Well, call it the right gesture at the right time. I don't know," she mused. "But that hit me right where it counted. Made me think how I was about to make a really big mistake and probably take a huge step backward."

He looked at her inquiringly.

She frowned and stared at the floor for a moment. "I'm not making much sense. You remember seeing a kind of slimy guy at the bar earlier that night — long hair, tattoos?" she asked. "You commented about him — how I gave him a free drink to make him look good to his buddies."

"Kenny," he said.

Her mouth dropped open. "You remember his name?"

His face reddened. "I might've been a little envious."

She touched her lips with her fingertips, assessing this revelation, which he now wished he'd withheld.

But her conclusion set him at ease. Her face softened and her shoulders slumped slightly. She stepped up to the bar and laid her hand on his. Their faces were close together as she said, "You had nothing to worry about."

He didn't know what to say.

"I kissed you that night to thank you for being nice to me," she explained. "But there was more. I had almost decided to make a play for Kenny, even though every bone in my body told me I shouldn't. You woke me up."

"With a lobster roll?"

She laughed and stepped back, accepting his offer of humor to regain her balance.

"That's when I decided to pull up stakes. Coryn, my daughter, was out of the house and on her own; I'd saved up enough money to make a new start. It was time. When this place came on the market, and it was in your hometown, I couldn't believe it. The coincidence was too much to ignore."

"Like a sign?" he suggested.

She made a face. "I don't believe in that junk. But I wasn't going to ignore it, either."

"Christ," he told her, waving a hand around at the clutter, "I'm going to feel pretty bad if it goes belly-up."

"It won't," she said simply. "I did my homework, too. I'm not a total romantic."

"But a bit of one."

"Yeah," she conceded after a pause. "I guess." She was silent before adding, "That's why I drove up to Thetford to find you, after reading about the accident. I wasn't really going shopping."

"I wondered," he admitted, sitting very still.

"I did want to offer any help I could," she said quickly. "I meant that. Still do. But I suppose I wanted you to know I was in the area, too, for what it was worth."

"A lot."

She'd been staring into the middle distance at that point, but his rejoinder made her look at him directly. "Really?"

"Yeah," he said simply.

She pursed her lips. "Wow. I thought for sure you'd already have someone in your life . . ." She abruptly held her hand to her forehead. "Hold it. That came out wrong. I mean, not that you wouldn't, but that if you don't, that I wouldn't be —"

"I don't," he said, hoping to end her embarrassment.

Her face was by now bright red. "Okay. Sorry. I'm not a stalker or anything."

"I know."

"I just — what with the bar being in Brattleboro, and what I said about your getting me to leave Gloucester — sort of — well . . . it just seemed stupid not to get in touch somehow."

Now it was his turn to stand up and at least lean in her direction, since the bar was between them — the very safety barrier she'd once told him was a blessing for most barkeeps. "I'm glad you did, Lyn. It means a lot to me. Kind of a right time, right place thing, if you know what I mean."

"Those aren't too common, right?" she asked, taking a half step toward him.

"So they say."

They stood there for a few seconds, seemingly frozen by in-decision, before he finally moved back, undraped his coat from the back of the adjacent stool, and said, "Well, I've got to get back north."

"Oh, sure," she said, leaving her post and heading back around the end of the bar to meet him. "Give your mom my best."

He was close to the door, moving reluctantly, slipping his coat on. "I'm glad you came up when you did, when I was on the sidewalk."

She reached him and laid her hand on his arm. "You've got a lot on your mind right now."

He nodded silently, welling with emotion that he'd been suppressing for days.

"That's okay," she said. "I'll be here." She took his hand, removed a pen from her breast pocket, and wrote a phone number on his palm. "That's my home. Call anytime. I mean it."

He opened the door with his other hand, letting in a sharp sliver of cold air. "I will."

He quickly leaned forward, kissed her on the cheek, and let himself out.

**RadMan:** so wut u do for fun
**Suze:** soccer and shop
**RadMan:** ur parents strict
**Suze:** there assholes
**RadMan:** oh why
**Suze:** cause they r
**RadMan:** i drive
**Suze:** i cant no licens
**RadMan:** so wut do u like to chat about -
 do u have any wishes
**Suze:** yeah i wish i had a car
**RadMan:** why
**Suze:** so i could drive ya
**RadMan:** well i got a car
**Suze:** can i have it
**RadMan:** only gfs can use my car
**Suze:** so what does that mean
**RadMan:** u really want my car
**Suze:** for real
**RadMan:** what do i get then

# CHAPTER 9

"Oh, please. Parole and Probation? You have got to be shitting me."

Sammie Martens sat back in her chair and studied the ceiling without response, well used to her colleague's harangues, which, for him, passed for humor.

"Those guys are such cowboys. Not even cops, for Chrissakes."

Willy Kunkle looked across the small office they all shared, to see what effect he might be having. "Run around like they own the place," he added for good measure.

She didn't move, refusing his bait despite the temptation he was clearly counting on.

"Not to mention there's not a rule they don't break."

He saw her face crinkle in pain, as she absorbed this last crack. She straightened, put her elbows on her desk, and studied him as if he'd just emerged from a test tube. "What did you just say?" she asked, caving in at last.

He smiled at her innocently. "Not that I have a problem with any of that. When do we leave?"

She groaned and got to her feet. "Now." She pointed at his withered left arm, an appendage he usually kept anchored to his side by shoving its hand into his pants pocket. "Why didn't you join *them* after you lost that thing, instead of coming back to the cops?"

He rose, too, and joined her at the coatrack near the door. "You and I weren't an item back then," he explained. "I had to come back to irritate you."

"And that's changed now that we are?"

He patted her butt on his way to grabbing his parka. "Yeah. 'Cause now you love it."

She headed out the door. "You are such a jerk."

He laughed and followed her into the overheated second-floor hallway of Brattleboro's municipal building, where the VBI had a one-room office for its four regional agents. "So, what's the deal?"

"With P and P?" she asked. "We gotta interview Dave Snyder about one of their ex-parolees — someone named Andy Griffis."

"Griffis?" Willy commented, following her

144

toward the stairs. "He's dead. What do we care?"

She half turned to respond, "How did you know that?"

He poked her in the small of the back. "You gotta keep up, girl. Plug into the gossip."

Say what you might about Willy Kunkle — that he was irascible, disrespectful, impolitic, and prone to cutting corners — he was still a cop's cop and made an art form of knowing everything about everybody who'd ever had a run-in with the law. He had an encyclopedia in his head about the people you'd never want to invite home.

As if to prove the point, he added, as they headed down the stairwell, "He was Gunther's case from when we all used to work downstairs. He hung himself."

Downstairs meant the Brattleboro Police Department, where Willy had also once been a detective. Of their squad, only Spinney had come from outside.

"Hanged himself," Sam corrected.

"Whatever, and you didn't answer the question."

"Joe asked me to look into Griffis because of the car crash that put Leo and his mom in the hospital."

Willy reached out and grabbed her arm to

slow her down. "Whoa. I thought that was an accident."

"It is on paper," she answered, still walking toward the door to the parking lot.

"Meaning what?"

She shrugged. "Not sure. He didn't go into details. Just asked us to get what we could on Griffis."

Which vagueness, of course, only appealed to Willy's sense of balance. "Cool," he said as they stepped outside.

In the town of Brattleboro, Parole and Probation was housed in what used to be a bright pink chocolate factory, adjacent to both a popular restaurant and a stunning view of the confluence of the West and Connecticut Rivers. It was wrapped in greenery and appointed with enough small architectural details to make it look like an Italian villa designed by someone who had never traveled overseas.

To many observers — and many in law enforcement — the setting and history of this halfway house for the unfortunate was apt for both the town and the state in general, given Brattleboro's and Vermont's reputation for being less than draconian in their treatment of the legally wayward.

That said, the facility's interior was pretty

standard office building, and nothing about its layout or the attitude of its occupants implied any coddling of the clientele. This was immediately demonstrated by the receptionist behind the bullet-resistant window when Sam and Willy walked in — especially after she caught sight of the latter and leaped to a reasonable conclusion.

"Sign in and have a seat."

Sam smiled brightly and flashed her badge. "Understandable mistake. We're here to see Dave Snyder."

The receptionist reacted with a deadpan "Don't sign in and have a seat."

Snyder, when he appeared a couple of minutes later, was a small, intense man with a hard handshake and a ready smile, who ushered them down a tangle of narrow hallways, up a half flight of stairs, and finally into a truly minute office with not even an air vent for circulation, much less a window. So much for the Italian villa.

The three of them conducted a facsimile minuet getting seated without bumping into each other, after which Willy, with his usual grace, opened up with a small conversational ice breaker.

"Christ. Either somebody really hates you or you need lessons on sucking up."

Snyder laughed. "I spend about an hour a

day in here. It's actually kind of restful. And nobody ever bothers me."

Even the walls were blank, completely free of pictures, calendars, or a bulletin board.

"Go figure," Willy agreed.

Snyder fired up the computer monitor on his desk and addressed Sam. "You wanted to know about Andy Griffis?"

"Yeah," she told him. "He was arrested by the Brattleboro PD, but then we let him drop off the radar — until we heard he'd committed suicide, of course," she added quickly, addressing Snyder's look of surprise.

He nodded. "I was going to ask if you knew." He waved a hand at the screen. "Well, I don't know. To be honest, the guy who actually handled this case is gone, so I'm pretty much the tour guide here. I never met Griffis. What're you after?"

Sam took pity on the man, since she was in much the same boat, given Joe's vagueness. "Tell us the overall first, then maybe we can get more specific."

Snyder slowly began scrolling down and reading, highlighting his findings in a descriptive monologue. "Okay. Let's see. Wow. Talk about no luck — first-time offender and he goes straight to jail. Oh, okay. I get it, kind of. Proprietor gets hurt during a burglary, and she's an old lady to boot. Media must've been all over that. Still, tough for him. Got five to ten with all but three suspended. Bet he wasn't expecting that."

He hit a few more commands and moved elsewhere within his database. "Started out jail in Springfield," he resumed, "then got moved to St. Albans. Indicators are he was generally compliant and cooperative. In her notes, the prison case worker mentions a depressive period toward the end, basically lasting till he was released. Don't know what that was about. Probably just bummed. Our interactions with him afterward were routine. He got a job working up north first, around Thetford. His family has a bunch of businesses there. Says here he was a mechanic. Wasn't long before he headed back to Brattleboro, though, which is how we wound up with him. According to this, he said things weren't working out in Thetford. That happens often enough, where the family shakes out after one of them comes back from inside. Maybe that's what happened here."

He started reading more carefully, his own interest growing. "We picked up his check-ins," he resumed, "which he seems to have met. His conditions weren't too onerous —

pretty much the usual. Oh, I was wrong; he did miss a check-in, right at the end. After that, nothing. He was found hanging from the crossbar in his apartment closet after he failed to show up at work two days in a row."

"He leave a note?" Willy asked.

"Doesn't say here, but that's no surprise. We get notification of a parolee's death, but the local PD and the ME's office have the actual details. You'll have to ask them."

"Any mention of close friends?" Sam asked.

"There's a Beth Ann Agostini," Snyder read. "Her name pops up in the last few months. Lives on Canal." He quickly scribbled her address down on a pad, adding, "Or used to. These folks move around a lot."

"That's it?" Willy asked incredulously.

Snyder was almost apologetic. "Yeah. Griffis wasn't adjusting all that well after he got out, but he kept within our guidelines." He sat back and studied them. "He was a probationer, not a parolee. That would've put him on a tighter leash. But on probation, as long as you check in and don't get caught doing anything foolish, you're part of a big pool of people. It's easy to fall through the cracks."

He passed his hand through his hair

abruptly, his frustration showing, and added, "We get a lot of flack for trying to keep people out of prison, or letting them out on conditions too soon and too easily. But, believe me, it ain't high school, and some of these younger guys get really screwed up. Always drives me nuts when people go on and on about more jail cells and tougher sentences when they have no clue what they're talking about."

Sam and Willy didn't respond, both of them just staring back at him.

Snyder smiled awkwardly. "Sorry. Guess that was a little overboard. No offense, I hope."

Willy dragged out his response, making a mockery of it. "Naaaah."

Sam pulled out a subpoena she'd secured just to be on the safe side. "Any chance we could have a printout of the case notes?"

As if defeated by some inner debate, Dave Snyder merely placed the subpoena on his desk and set to work at the keyboard.

Leo remained in the ICU, looking increasingly reduced by his standing retinue of monitors and IV hangers clustered around like skeletal mourners. And now he spent all his time asleep.

"I thought he was getting better," his

mother said softly, sitting in the waiting room, her shoulders slumped.

Leo's primary physician crouched down before her wheelchair to better make eye contact, a gesture Joe appreciated. His name was Karl Weisenbeck, and so far, he'd been attentive, honest, and compassionate, seeking them out more often than they'd asked for him over the previous few days.

For Joe, the man's soothing presence was doubly welcome. Not only had Leo's downturn come as a surprise, but so had Gail's unannounced return. In fact, Dr. Weisenbeck had been talking to her alone upon their entrance, creating in Joe's mind an awkward jarring, as if he'd accidentally walked in on something inappropriate. Given the multiple emotions he was then balancing, the addition of this unusually loaded one had been a shock.

Not that her being here was a bad idea. The greeting between the two women had made that clear, reminding him of a loving daughter and mother after a long separation. Now, especially given Weisenbeck's announcement of Leo's reversal, Joe had to concede that his mother's coping ability was strengthened by Gail's presence. Over the years, these women had become close friends, driving home Joe's occasional sensation of being the odd man out.

None of which mattered at the moment, he forced himself to remember as he leaned forward to hear the doctor's explanation.

"It's a delicate time for your son," Weisenbeck was saying. "As you know, he suffered initially from a collapsed lung and flail chest, which is a breaking away of an independent part of the rib cage. The lung issue we resolved pretty easily, but the combination is what made it so difficult for him to breathe, and why we were helping him out with the nasal cannula at first. Unfortunately, the extent of his injuries has now led to what we call shock lung, or more technically, post-traumatic respiratory distress."

There was a small, almost indistinguishable intake of breath by his elderly listener, which prompted the doctor to take her hand in his own before continuing.

"Leo was no longer able to oxygenate his blood on his own, Mrs. Gunther," Weisenbeck said. "Which meant that we had to put him on a respirator."

She nodded slightly. "I understand."

But he wasn't done. "I wish that were the extent of it, but I'm afraid there's more. As a result of the multiple bone fragmentation, Leo's also suffering from fat embolization. This has affected his brain function, among other things, which is why he's asleep for the moment."

She began to ask a question, but he gently held up a finger in order to keep going. "I know — for how long? Right?"

She nodded silently.

"I'm not sure," he answered. "We are treating him with blood thinners and steroids and time, and we are monitoring him every second of every day. I came to work at this hospital because of its level of patient care, Mrs. Gunther, and I've never been disappointed with my decision. I will do everything in my power to make sure that will be true for your son as well. Leo is a strong, resilient, middle-aged man. That is a huge plus in his favor."

There was a long, painful lull in the conversation before her voice rose quietly into the silence. "Will he be okay?"

Weisenbeck leaned forward and squeezed her fingers again. "He's resting. You will hear the word coma. That's true, also, but it's not necessarily a bad thing. Our bodies are much more intuitive than we doctors in knowing what to do and when. You went through much the same thing when you came to us, remember? Your body needed rest, and so it went to sleep for a while. Better than what any of us could have ordered."

Joe's mother took it in like the psychological medicine it was meant to be, but then asked pointedly, "What dangers is he facing?"

He hesitated, gauging his best approach while looking her straight in the eyes. There seemed to be no breathing in the room.

"He is walking right at the edge. He is susceptible to stroke, pneumonia, and pulmonary embolus, as well as catheter-induced sepsis and several other threats. I will not pretend that it's not a long list." Here he added emphasis to his voice and intensified his gaze. "But I must stress with the same honesty that my optimism outweighs my fears.

"In the end, though," he added, slowly standing back up, "we all just have to wait and keep our hopes up." He smiled as he concluded, "While we watch him like the proverbial hawk. Okay? When he begins to come around — and I stress *when*, not *if* — the initial first signs will be neurological. He will most likely first respond to pain stimuli. His breathing will also improve as the ribs begin to knit, increasing his body's oxygen saturation, and that, in turn, will help clear out the fat emboli and allow him to emerge from the coma."

By now he was looking at them all, as if

addressing a class. They all instinctively nodded.

"Great," he said. "Now. Would you like to come in and spend a little time with him? I'll have one of the nurses help you out." He glanced regretfully at Gail and Joe. "I'm afraid we're only letting one person in at a time for the moment, mostly just because it gets so crowded otherwise."

Joe was already holding his hand up. "Not a problem. We knew about that. We'll be right here, Mom," he added, patting her on her narrow shoulder.

She looked around and up at him, her smile belying her concern. "I won't be long."

"Take your time."

They watched her through the window overlooking the ICU as a nurse helped drape her in a gown and fit a sterile mask over her face in preparation for the visit. In the distance, Leo remained as still as a mummy, white-clad and corralled.

"God. What a nightmare," Gail murmured.

"Could be better," Joe agreed.

She glanced at him. "You believe him?"

He kept staring through the window. "What's not to believe? He said Leo's walking on the edge of a cliff."

After a momentary silence, Gail said, "I've

been trading e-mails with your mom. She says you're looking into the crash."

He pressed his lips together, considering how to respond. There was a time when his reaction would have been immediate and open.

Gail instantly interpreted the hesitation. She'd always read people well. "That probably wasn't something she should have told me," she said quickly.

"No, no," he then said. "It's not like it's a secret. Sure as hell the people we're asking know about it. I just wondered why a relatively new car would fall apart like that. That's really all it is for now. The sheriff's department is helping me out. I'm not even officially involved."

She nodded. "I thought maybe he'd just hit some ice."

It was a leading question, but this time Joe played along. "A tie rod nut worked loose. Without it, the wheel pretty much does what it wants. It happens. I just want to make sure that it happened by accident."

"How do you do that?" she asked.

That felt like pressing, and he resisted her, his reasons at once professional and very personal. "Well, like I said, I'm trying to keep my nose clean. The deputy handling it owes me a call on that very subject. He's pretty good around cars, it turns out."

He still hadn't made eye contact with her, instead studying his mother being wheeled up to his brother's bed. But he was also consciously aware of Gail staring at him from the side, in search of some reaction.

"How're you doing?" she finally asked softly.

He glanced at her quickly and then nodded toward the scene before them, using it to dodge the true meaning of her question. "I've been thinking about the old lady lately, wondering what'll happen after she dies — Leo, the farm, all the rest. I never saw this coming."

This time Gail was the one who remained silent, prompting Joe to seek out her reflection in the glass. She was no longer looking at him, but her sadness radiated like heat.

Damn, he thought. This is too hard.

He glanced at his watch. "Speaking of the sheriff," he said, his voice loud and bluff in his ears, "I ought to hook up with him. Find out what he's got new, if anything. Could you handle Mom? Drive her back home, maybe?"

"Sure," Gail said softly, still not turning. "Happy to."

Joe patted her shoulder once and left the room, relieved and frustrated, both.

He found them out on Route 5, standing like a line of bird hunters at a shoot, except that they were all standing in a snowbank, looking down instead of skyward, and dressed alike in dark blue pseudo uniforms decorated with glaring white sheriff's patches. Barring a couple, they were all boys, mostly thin and gawky, sporting hair that looked painfully short in the cold weather. Slightly back of them was Rob Barrows, watching for traffic as much as giving guidance to the two of his teenage Explorers who were actually manning the metal detectors.

Joe pulled over by the side of the road and got out of his car.

"Any luck yet?" he asked.

There was a shout from the most distant detector handler.

Barrows smiled at the timing. "Guess we'll find out." They began walking together down the line. "We'd be due," he added. "We've been out here almost three hours, finding enough scrap metal to open a business. Slow going."

They reached the young woman who'd shouted out.

"What've you got, Explorer Ferris?" Rob asked in a clipped tone.

The girl stiffened slightly as she barked out, "A signal, sir. Pretty strong."

"Show me."

With her companions looking on from both sides, Ferris swept her instrument across the top of the snow by the edge of the road. They were about a half mile away from where Leo had gone off.

The detector began signaling loudly as she hovered over a marked defect in the white crust at their feet.

"Does look like something went in there," Barrows commented quietly. He turned to another of the Explorers. "Drury, get in there and carefully open up a channel going to the bottom of that hole. Take your time."

They watched as this second teenager got to his knees and slowly began digging into the snow, removing great handfuls in his gloves and dropping them behind him onto the roadway.

"Matthews," Barrows ordered, "you and Johnson go through what Drury's dumping there. Run the detector over it. Make sure there's nothing hidden inside."

Joe watched the deputy gradually engage more and more of his team until almost everyone had a job and felt useful in some fashion.

Fifteen minutes later, one of the kids helping Drury held up his gloved hand. "Got something, sir."

Barrows took it from him and showed it to Joe. It was a nut.

Joe looked up at the eager faces crowded around him, discipline having caved in to enthusiasm. He showed them the small piece of metal and spoke in a loud voice.

"You've done some great work here today. I thank you, and the Bureau thanks you. When I get back to the office, I'll make sure you all get officially recognized for your efforts. This is a terrific example of how some police work, maybe a little dull at first, pays off big-time in the end. Thumbs-up to all of you."

He poked his own thumb into the air, feeling only slightly foolish, comforted by the obvious pride and pleasure he saw in their faces.

Leaving the Explorers to pack up the equipment and trade excited one-liners, Rob and Joe walked back to the vehicles. Barrows held the nut out in front of him as they went.

"You can definitely see tool marks on it."

"You sure that's it?" Joe asked, hoping not

to sound too doubtful.

Barrows gave his signature easy smile. "No. It's not like Subaru stamps every nut it uses. But what're the odds? It even has fresh grease on it. I'd bet that alone might connect it to your brother's car. Amazing what forensics can do these days."

He carefully dropped it into a small evidence bag he'd extracted from his coat pocket. "In any case," he added, "I am sure it's enough to get into Steve's Garage with a warrant."

Willy Kunkle pulled out his cell phone and responded in his standard professional manner.

"Yeah?"

"It's Scott." To Willy's total lack of response, the caller added hesitantly, "McCarty. You know . . ."

He did. McCarty was one of his many snitches. "So what?"

"Well, so I got something for you."

Willy stopped in mid-stride at the edge of the parking lot behind the municipal building. "Oh, right," he said scornfully. "Like I'm going to waste more time with you."

"No, no," Scott pleaded. "Don't hang up. It's about the guy you're looking for, one of the ones in the paper — 'Do You Know

Either of These Men?' Well, I do. I mean, I don't, but I know who does."

"Who?"

There was a telling pause on the other end of the line. Willy's grip tightened on the phone. "Listen, you little asshole —"

"Okay, okay," Scott interrupted him. "Meet me at the town garage in an hour. I'll have my man there and we'll do business."

"*Business?* After all the crap you put me through last time? That officially made you one of the worst informants I got," Willy blew up. "You owe me this as a freebie."

But Scott demurred, taking his time before answering, "I'm sorry you feel that way, Detective, especially since this is such a big deal — two dead men, big mystery, police at a standstill. Be a shame if you don't know what I know."

Willy scowled. Like it or not, he had to take a closer look at this. "And how much is what you know gonna cost me?"

The answer was instantaneous. "Hundred bucks."

As was Willy's. "Fuck you." He hung up.

He stayed where he was, phone in hand. It rang a minute later.

"Seventy-five," Scott said. "I gotta split it with —"

Willy hung up again without a word.

This time, it took three minutes for the phone to ring again.

"Fifty," Scott said in a flat voice. "After that, I don't give a shit."

Willy believed him. "See you in an hour."

In fact, Willy drove to the meeting place immediately, to stake it out. Brattleboro's town garage was on Fairgrounds Road, just beyond the sprawling rebuilt high school. The road was on the edge of town, not heavily traveled, not overly well lighted, and the "garage" itself was actually an assemblage of buildings — storage sheds, equipment units, repair bays, and the like, all affording a wide choice of shadowy hiding places.

Just to be on the safe side, Willy was going to make sure he was the first to take advantage of that.

Brattleboro is not the kind of town that harbors ambushes. There are no drive-by shootings, few muggings; murders crop up once every few years on average. The police largely respond to calls involving people they've come to know personally over time.

None of which mattered to Willy Kunkle.

Willy was not a Brattleboro native, or a Vermonter, or easily influenced by peaceful precedent. He was a recovering alcoholic, a recovering Vietnam-era sniper, an ex-NYPD cop, and a man whose crippled arm — the ironic gift of another sniper — stood as more of a symbol than an actual disability, since it certainly didn't slow him down on the job. He was hard-bitten, paranoid, short-tempered, and intolerant.

Of course, as Joe Gunther — his defender against every law enforcement bureaucracy so far — might have put it, he was also insightful, intuitive, hardworking, driven to perfection, honorable, and faithful. *And* a total pain in the neck.

He was also a born survivor, convinced by everything he'd experienced so far in life that you could never be too suspicious of, or too careful about, people.

As an example of this, he parked his vehicle unobtrusively in the high school parking lot and walked almost invisibly toward the town garage complex, eventually blending into its crosshatching of shadows until he could no longer be seen.

And there he waited.

As it turned out, he waited for quite a while, since Scott McCarty, not atypical of his ilk, was only vaguely aware of time. Nevertheless, he finally drove up in an exhausted Toyota sedan, slithering to a stop on worn summer tires, and killed the engine in the middle of the complex's dooryard, leaving his headlights on to play across the mashed and rutted landscape of ice and dirty snow created by countless truck tires.

He had someone sitting beside him.

As Scott pushed at his door to get out, he found that it only opened a foot. Through the gap, a cold and muscular hand reached in and grabbed him by the neck.

"You're late, you little shit." Still jamming the door with his leg, Willy called out to the passenger, "You, beside him — move a single muscle and you're dead. Ask Scott."

Scott nodded nervously. "He's not kidding, Benny."

"What's your name?" Willy demanded of the passenger.

"Benny Grosbeak."

"And I'm supposed to believe that?"

"It's true. My parents were hippies and changed their last name."

"Why're you here, Benny?" Willy asked.

Benny opened his mouth, but Scott spoke up first. "That's what I —"

Willy tightened his grip, making him gasp. "Shut up."

Benny hesitated. "Scott told me about some money."

"How much?"

"Twenty bucks."

Willy laughed. "What do you know, Benny?"

Again the pause, followed by "I saw that man."

"The one in the paper?"

He nodded.

"Which one?"

"The bald guy." That was the floater, found in the stream.

"Where?"

Now Benny was freer to talk, the truth being out. "At the motel where I work. I'm the night clerk."

Without prompting, he gave Willy the name of the place, on Brattleboro's Putney Road, about a mile from where the other John Doe had been found at a far better motel. Willy liked the coincidence. He opened Scott's door wide with his knee and leaned into the car, so he was face-to-face with the occupants. "Benny and I are going to step outside," he said. "You are going to stay here, waiting for your money, right?"

Scott nodded again. It was only then that Willy unlocked his fingers from his informant's throat.

Willy glanced over at Benny, his voice almost gentle. "Okay, Ben, why don't you climb out and stretch your legs a bit? I want to ask you a couple of more questions."

167

Benny complied and Willy circled the car to join him, escorting him until he was beyond earshot of the car. He then positioned the young man with his back to the vehicle, so Willy could see, over his shoulder, Scott's pale face through the windshield.

"Sorry about the rough stuff," Willy began. "Scott and I have a history. I gotta pretend to be the tough guy."

"You do a nice job."

Willy laughed. "That's good. I like that." He reached into his pocket and extracted a twenty-dollar bill, using Benny's body to hide the gesture from Scott. "This is something extra for your efforts. Scott'll give you what he owes, so you might want to keep this between us."

Benny palmed it and slipped it into his pocket. "Thanks."

"No sweat. You help me; I help you. Tell me about the bald man."

"Not much to tell. He came in one night about a week ago and paid cash for a room. One night."

"Any car or luggage?"

"An overnight bag. Small. He told me he came in on the bus, so no car."

"How many key cards did he ask for?"

Benny smiled slightly. "Two. That happens a lot."

"Did you ever see the other party?"

Benny shook his head. "Nope. And that was it. I took the money, had him fill out the form, and gave him the keys. Never saw him again till that picture was in the paper."

"What was his name?"

"I don't remember." His eyes widened at Willy's instantaneous reaction. "Honest," he added urgently.

Willy softened his expression again. "He say where that bus came from?"

"No."

Willy kept his voice conversational. "Why didn't you call us?"

Benny looked embarrassed. "I was going to. That's what I told Scott when he said we could get paid for it."

"You know he's a schmuck, right?"

"Yeah, I guess. I'm sorry."

Willy shook it off. "Don't worry about it. Tell me your full name, your date of birth, where you live, and your phone number."

Benny did as he was told, Willy listened intently, memorizing the details until he could write them down later — a trick he'd developed from not always having a free hand.

"Okay. You wait here while I have a few words with Scott. You did good, by the way. Next time come to me direct. You can still get paid and you don't have to get fouled up. Right?"

"Yes, sir."

Willy left him there and tramped back to the car, leaning once more into Scott's face. "Twenty out of the fifty you're screwin' me for?"

Scott grimaced. "I'm just trying to make ends meet."

"And he's not?"

"He's got a job," Scott complained.

Willy pulled the money out of his pocket and dropped it on the other man's lap. "Fifty-fifty. Be a man. I take care of you for doing nothing. You take care of him for making you twenty-five bucks. Plus, I don't tell him you were about to fuck him over."

Scott opened his mouth to protest, but Willy silenced him with a quickly raised hand. "You did tell him you'd split even money, didn't you?"

"Yeah," Scott admitted sullenly.

Willy straightened, still looking down at him. "Then do the right thing, like I said. For once in your life."

Scott nodded, already leafing through the bills, dividing them.

Willy whistled at Benny and gestured him over. "We'll probably be back in touch, Mr. Grosbeak. Don't go on any trips without letting me know, okay?"

Benny nodded and got back into the car.

Willy stepped back, his hand still holding Scott's door open. "Twenty-five bucks for each of you — not too bad. Don't forget your seat belts."

Scott gave him a sour look as he started the engine. "Yeah — whatever."

Willy laughed and let them drive off.

**CanadaBoi:** so who's all home with you right now?

**Becky:** younger step brother

**CanadaBoi:** oh wheres ur parents ?

**Becky:** working

**CanadaBoi:** and your stuck babysitting

**CanadaBoi:** that must suck

**Becky:** only until 5

**CanadaBoi:** what time is it now?

**Becky:** 415

**CanadaBoi:** oh its 3:17 here

**Becky:** were r u again

**CanadaBoi:** im in canada

**Becky:** i thought u were in california

**CanadaBoi:** oh no

**Becky:** how far is that from vt

**CanadaBoi:** to far if ya ask me

**Becky:** lol

**CanadaBoi:** sarah baby what are you wearing right now

**Becky:** clothes

**Becky:** lol

**CanadaBoi:** lol

**CanadaBoi:** im wearing black silk boxers and a rad shirt

**CanadaBoi:** red**

**Becky:** i got to run bye

**CanadaBoi:** ok

**Becky:** chat later

**CanadaBoi:** im gonna add you

**Becky:** k

**CanadaBoi:** later baby

# CHAPTER 10

Barrie McNeil looked as if Rob Barrows had just spoken in Chinese. "What?"

"This is a search warrant," Rob repeated, shouldering him out of the way to enter the garage and allow access to Joe and four more deputies. "Look, it's not really your problem. This is your copy. Call the boss or whatever lawyer you have on tap. They'll know what it is. Meantime, we'll get to work." Barrows paused to add, "Unless you want to argue the point and be arrested."

Barrie raised both dirty hands in surrender, one now filled with the slightly crumpled document. "No, no. Knock your socks off. I don't give a shit. Dan will, though, and I will call him. Or my ass is grass."

"Go for it, then," Rob recommended before unleashing his team to find what they were all looking for.

The warrant covered any tools that might

174

have been used to remove the now infamous tie rod nut, and any documentation, electronic and not, pertaining to the servicing of Leo's car. That latter part sent Rob and Joe directly to the decrepit-looking computer nestled in the corner of a cluttered and paper-strewn office.

Barrie, seeking whatever privacy he could amid the invasion, went to a phone in the service bay wall to call Dan Griffis, a task his body language clearly indicated he didn't relish.

Rob gingerly pulled out the lopsided, duct-taped office chair parked before the computer, and, after studying its seat for both springs and foreign matter, settled in to address the filthy keyboard.

"Jeez," he said softly as Joe pulled over a folding metal chair to join him. "Good thing they're building these things to resist wear and tear."

He shuffled the mouse under his right hand to illuminate the screen. A desktop surfaced with a cluster of different icons, spread out like colorful confetti. He'd barely double-clicked the first one when the office door banged open and Barrie appeared on the threshold.

"He is *really* pissed," he announced. "And he's gonna be even more pissed when he sees you guys on that thing."

"You talking about Dan?" Rob asked without looking over his shoulder at him.

"Well, yeah. Who else?"

"How long till he gets here?"

"Three seconds, the way he sounded."

Rob sighed slightly, keeping at his task. "How long?"

"Ten minutes."

"Okay. Send one of the deputies in here, okay? On your way out."

Barrie hesitated a moment, translating both the content and the meaning of that last request. He then vanished, to be replaced by one of Rob's team, an older officer with mostly gray hair.

"What's up?"

This time Barrows turned to face the man. "We're about to be visited by Dan Griffis, the owner."

"I know him," the deputy said in a near growl.

"Then you know what to expect. Keep him outside. Thanks."

Rob and Joe returned to the screen. Under the former's prompting, icon after icon began opening, revealing spreadsheets, correspondence files, financial records, inventory lists, and more, some of which was clearly recreational, such as games, and certainly one of which was password locked.

"What do you think?" Joe asked his guide when they hit that one.

Rob worked the keyboard harder, uncovering what he could about the file. "It's accessed a lot. I can tell you that much," he reported after a couple of minutes.

At that point they were disturbed by the sound of shouting from outside the building.

"That'd be Dan," Rob murmured, his eyes still on the screen. "You want to do anything about it?"

Joe straightened, considering the proposal. Initially, he saw no point. The man was worked up, he was being controlled by the deputies — or would be arrested — and discovering that Joe Gunther was part of the investigation would only be inflammatory.

That last detail made Joe get up, his own irritation finally rising to the surface. "Maybe I'll just say hi," he said.

Rob glanced at him, waiting a beat before smiling and saying, "Yeah. Why not? I'll just keep poking around."

Joe left the office, crossed the waiting room, and opened the door onto the frozen front parking lot — and two deputies bracketing a red-faced, spittle-lipped barrel of a man who was bouncing on the balls of his feet in barely controlled fury.

"Hey, Dan," Joe said from the door. "Long time."

The man froze in mid-expletive and stared at him. "Gunther?" he finally asked, his tone incredulous.

"Yeah."

"What the fuck're you doing here?"

"Assisting the sheriff's department."

Dan Griffis took two steps in his direction and was immediately closed in on by the two deputies, one of whom rested a restraining hand on his shoulder.

It was a defining moment — a split second when the entire course of the next few minutes rested with Dan and whether he chose to take that hand as a challenge to fight, or as the pacifying gesture it was meant to be.

As far as Joe was concerned, it was a no-loser, with his personal preference being for an old-fashioned piling-on. His famous self-restraint notwithstanding, Joe Gunther was feeling a slow, boiling rage deep inside. The mere possibility that his family had been threatened by this man was enough for Joe to wish him ill beyond a simple threat of legal action. In his youth, Joe had never hesitated to join a fight — a fact only rarely recalled by others now. But in this moment, had Dan offered even the slightest excuse, Joe was ready to try his hand in a nostalgic and perhaps soul-cleansing violent blowout.

But it wasn't to be. Right at the edge of letting loose, Dan took a deep breath and suddenly relaxed, giving Gunther a nasty smile. "You bastard. You know I'm still looking at the Bitch. One fuck-up and I get life." He gently slid the deputy's hand off his shoulder. "Well," he added, "no such luck. I don't know what you jerk-offs're cooking up, but I'm gonna get a lawyer and shove it up your ass."

"Asses," Joe told him. "Proper grammar."

Dan's eyes narrowed before he smiled again. "Right. You would know. Mister Straight-and-Narrow. Guess your brother's not so fancy, though. He have too much to drink before he tried killing your mom? Or did he do it for the inheritance? Must be driving him nuts waiting for her to kick the bucket."

Joe could feel his face burning, despite the cold, but he remained silent, not trusting himself to use his voice. The older deputy, to his credit, spun Dan around and pushed him toward his pickup. "Go home, Dan," he said. "Let them do their job. You wanna call a lawyer, do it from there."

179

"You bet I will," Dan snarled at him, yanking the truck's door open. "And then I'll sue every last cop in this fucking department." He pointed a finger through his window at Joe, adding, "I'm also gonna make it my life mission to knock you off your pedestal, you preachy cock. You're gonna wish you were in intensive care instead of your faggot brother. You wait. You won't know what hit you."

Again Joe didn't react, although, by now, the initial onslaught of Dan's venom had dulled through repetition.

Dan Griffis gunned his engine and shot out of the garage's dooryard, his vehicle's back end slithering back and forth on the icy ground.

The three men watched him hit the asphalt beyond and squeal away, tires burning. The older deputy turned toward Joe. "We could nail him for that, just for what-the-hell."

Joe nodded, acknowledging the point, but answered, "I'd sooner save my ammo for when it counts."

"Yeah," the deputy agreed. "I see what you mean."

Joe stepped back inside and closed the door. He paused before rejoining Rob, for a moment's worth of privacy. Dan Griffis had always been a bully, a drunk, and a self-involved show-off, from the first time Joe met him, many years ago.

Unfortunately, despite the soothing adage that such people were forgettable, they were not, and their abusiveness mattered and cut deep. It was, in fact, their very careless aggression that caught the public eye and put them higher on the food chain of notoriety. They became a force not only because of the violence of their demeanor but because of the paradoxical respect society granted them as a result. People may admire a good man, but they will more often rally around a brute.

This depressing truth had been Dan's fuel his whole life, as it was for so many of his kind, and yet, whenever Joe encountered it, it rattled him still. He wasn't cynical enough, even now, not to find the insult fresh and disappointing every time.

Pulling his earlobe and sighing slightly, he reentered the office.

"Noisy," Rob commented. "He gone?"

"Gone," Joe told him, thinking, *but far from forgotten.*

Barrows pushed his rickety chair away from the desk and gestured toward the screen. Hovering in its center was the earlier rectangular warning advising the need of a password.

"We need to get past that," he said. "And I'm definitely seizing this computer and applying for a warrant. 'Cause from what I've been able to see, there's a whole lot more here than garage business."

**Matthew:** I have 3 brothers and 4 sisters

**SweetAngl:** sorry

**Matthew:** but 2 borthers n 1 sister dont live here

**SweetAngl:** thats good

**Matthew:** my twin sisters are 16 and my little sis is 12

**SweetAngl:** thats kool u have twins sisters

**Matthew:** its aiight

**Matthew:** 1 night i was drunk I went up into my sisters room to get a peak

**SweetAngl:** of what

**Matthew:** I was curious to what color her underwear was

**Matthew:** its a good thing she was sleeping in a skirt

**SweetAngl:** oh my

**Matthew:** she didn't wake up or nothing

**SweetAngl:** thats weird

**Matthew:** yeah i know

**Matthew:** so do you wear mini skirts alot ?

**SweetAngl:** sometimes

**Matthew:** how short do you usually have ur skirts

**SweetAngl:** 2 me knees

**Matthew:** nice

**Matthew:** you ever catch ur step dad checking you out?

**SweetAngl:** thats sick

**Matthew:** i just had to ask that

**SweetAngl:** why

**Matthew:** cuz step dads do check out there step daughters

**Matthew:** idk why they just do

# CHAPTER 11

"These places really do all look the same," Lester Spinney mused, pausing on the threshold and taking in the narrow view of the motel room before him — cheap dresser with TV, the foot of a large bed, nondescript drawn curtains, and two screwed-to-the-wall paintings.

Willy shouldered him roughly from behind. "We'll get you a postcard. Move it."

Spinney laughed and let his colleague push by. On paper, like oil and water, they actually worked together very smoothly, the one fleshing out the characteristics less obvious in the other. In practice, while Willy's intensity homed in on details and people like a laser beam, Lester's disarmingly gentle, hands-off style frequently supplied the more general view, along with access under a suspect's defenses.

He turned back toward the door, where the motel's manager was hovering nervously, still clutching his copy of the search warrant.

"Mr. Nelson," Spinney asked affably, "did you get a chance to check the records for the night in question?"

The manager, a short, round man with thinning hair and glasses, nodded energetically, eager to please. As well he might have been. Before coming over here, Lester had inquired into the Brattleboro police's knowledge of the place. His reward had been an outburst of laughter. This motel, especially, was a favorite stop-off for those wanting sex, drugs, suicide, or all three. As one of the detectives on the municipal building's ground floor had said, "They should charge a hell of a lot more for all the services they provide."

Mr. Nelson was apparently the doorkeeper of a true den of iniquity, although Spinney couldn't help doubting that he benefited from any of it.

During this brief musing, the manager pulled a crumpled sheet of paper from the inner pocket of his jacket and adjusted his glasses.

"Let's see . . . The gentleman checked in at eight forty-eight p.m., pretty late. No car, paid cash . . ."

Lester could see where this was going, and

interrupted, "You don't take a credit card imprint for security?"

Nelson chewed his lip once before admitting slowly, "No, sir. We found that sometimes made people nervous."

"I bet," Spinney said. "What name did he use?"

"N. Rockwell."

Lester grimaced. "Okay, that's weird. How did he get here if it wasn't by car?"

There again, the manager paused before admitting carefully, "I'm not sure he didn't have a car. He just said he didn't."

"And, of course, you never want to invade their privacy."

The manager allowed a small smile. "No, sir. Not sure I'd want to go there."

"How many key cards did he ask for?"

Nelson consulted his piece of paper. "Two," he answered.

"We heard the night clerk was Benjamin Grosbeak?"

"Benny — that's right."

"And the maid who cleaned up the next day?"

"Angela Lundy."

"Any chance we could get them here to interview?"

Nelson checked his watch. "It's midmorning. That shouldn't be too hard. They're usually up by now."

Spinney patted him on his bulky, soft shoulder. "That would be great, Mr. Nelson. If you could do that and report back to me, I'd appreciate it."

Nodding again and walking backward, Nelson began fading down the hallway. "Yes, sir, I'll get right on it."

Spinney watched him finally turn on his heel and walk away before he reentered the room to join Willy.

"Yes, sir, thank you, sir, if you please, sir," Willy growled from his position looking under the bed. "You know that little fuck is probably a pimp and a pusher both, right?"

"I'll be sure to ask him when he comes back," Lester agreed affably. "You find anything?"

Willy scowled. "What did he say the maid's name was?"

"Angela."

"Well, she sucks at her job. Looks like a toxic dump under here. If our boy did leave anything behind, it's mixed in with shit from half a dozen other people."

"I thought these beds were supposed to be built on platforms, so nothing got shoved underneath," Spinney said, getting to his knees beside his colleague and taking a glance at the strewn collection of assorted, albeit tiny, trash that gleamed in Willy's flashlight glare.

Willy cut him an incredulous look. "God, you live in a dream world. This is a dump. People're lucky the sheets are changed between customers."

Spinney got back up and crossed to what passed for the room's desk — actually a table with a drawer supporting a lamp and a microwave, both bolted down. He opened the drawer.

"Like you said," he announced, "not as fancy. No folder or postcards, but there's an envelope and a few sheets of paper."

Willy sat back on his heels. "Did I hear Nelson say the guy got two key cards?"

"Yup."

Willy nodded, his thoughts paralleling Spinney's. "Something else to ask Angela." He got up. "Help me move this."

The two of them shifted the bed away from its wall-attached headboard and slid it across the carpeting until it was jammed up against the dresser. The contrast between the open floor and what they'd just exposed was startling — gray with dust and whatever else had filtered down from the mattress, and pocked with the debris that Willy had discovered earlier.

"Gross," Spinney murmured.

189

There was a gentle knock on the door. Spinney opened it to face Nelson, who looked apologetic. "Sorry to interrupt. You wanted to know about Benny and Angela?"

"Yeah," Lester said. "They coming?"

"Should be here in about ten minutes."

Nelson did his usual disappearing act. Spinney closed the door again.

"I might as well take Benny," Willy told him. "I made sure he was well treated last time."

"Works for me," Lester said vaguely, studying the ground again. "How do you want to process this?"

Willy shrugged. "Probably doesn't make a whole hell of a lot of difference. The room's been used and abused Christ knows how many times since our guy was here. I think we're just looking for anything interesting."

Spinney got to his knees and pulled on a pair of latex gloves, as much for his sake as to preserve any evidence. "Okay," he said simply, and set to work.

They went slowly, using flashlights, and even a magnifying glass that Willy carried despite the Sherlock Holmes cracks he routinely gathered. The edge of their search area, mirroring the footprint of the bed frame, was the richest in findings. People either dropping things or simply kicking them under the bed had resulted in a three-sided swath of items ranging from rubber bands, to candy wrappers, to condom packs. There were, in addition, a straw, a dirty napkin, several pills, a desiccated french fry, and, of course, a single sock.

In the midst of this treasure hunt, where a muttered conversation played background to each discovery, first Willy and then Les was pulled away by the arrival of the two interviewees. Benny Grosbeak, who was happy to see Willy again, told him little new, beyond that N. Rockwell had seemed nervous and evasive, somewhat new to the skid row life, and made no calls using the phone in the room. Benny had found him so bland, in fact, that he'd become memorable, making his reappearance in the newspaper all the more startling.

Angela Lundy, the maid, told Lester that when she'd entered the room the following morning to clean it, she barely found anything to do. The bed was still made and the trash empty. The toilet and shower stall hadn't been touched. She conceded that, in general, she only cleaned or straightened what most obviously needed attention, and she stared at him blankly when he asked whether she ever went into the desk drawer to check on the stationery supplies. She did

say that she found only one of the two issued key cards.

Les didn't bother asking about her technique for cleaning under the bed.

But, despite the time the two men spent
in Rockwell's former quarters, neither of
them had a single eureka moment. In fact,
the more they collected, the less they
thought they had anything of worth.

Until Willy, with his magnifying glass, suddenly hunched over, his nose two inches off
the carpeting.

"What've you got?" Spinney asked.

"Hand me the tweezers," Willy answered
him.

Les watched as his partner painstakingly
extracted something minute and dropped it
carefully into a small glassine envelope,
which he then handed over for scrutiny.

"Can you figure it out?" he asked with a
knowing smile.

Lester held it under the glare of his
flashlight. Inside the envelope was a single
brightly colored dot, much like a piece of
confetti, looking as if it were made of
plastic. Remarkably, however, it had numer-
als stamped across its miniature surface.

Lester straightened as if pricked by a pin.
He knew he was looking at a serial number,
and he remembered seeing this kind of tiny

item before.

"Holy cow."

Willy's smile broadened. "A Taser tag, right?"

Tasers, the well-known electrifying alternative to a baton or a shot of pepper spray, had a feature few people knew about. Along with the twin wire-trailing barbs that flew from the device upon being fired, each Taser cartridge contained a cluster of about forty tiny confettilike plastic flakes, or "tags," that were stamped with the cartridge's unique serial number. The logic was that every Taser could thus be traced to the person using it — a handy detail when and if it came to conducting a postshoot analysis.

The fact that every police officer knew that his or her Taser shot, like the bullets from a gun, could be traced back to the shooter was supposed to be a deterrent to reckless acts of abandon.

Or, as just possibly in this case, any acts of criminal mischief.

Lester stared at Willy in astonishment. "Damn. Here's hoping that where there's a number, there's a name." He waved the small envelope between his fingers. "This should be interesting."

Willy, however, in keeping with his darker outlook, had already gone beyond such a prize. He frowned and nodded slightly, before suggesting, "Yeah, and where there's a name, there might be a cop. 'Cause whoever shot it knew enough to pick up all but this one tag — and why."

Sammie Martens watched from her car as the teenage woman she was waiting for left the restaurant after closing, waving to her fellow employees and adjusting her coat against the cold winter breeze. It was almost midnight.

Beth Ann Agostini — Andy Griffis's former girlfriend — was on foot, despite the weather and the lack of sidewalks on Route 9 beyond West Brattleboro. She didn't live far away, true — in an affordable-housing complex only a mile down the road — but any pedestrian travel was quasi-suicidal, given the speed and accuracy of some of the late-night motorists out here. Still, Sam knew that Agostini took this route every night and was probably an expert at keeping an eye peeled for traffic.

Either way, it wasn't a relaxing walk, especially after a long day. Which was exactly what Sam hoped to have working to her advantage. She'd done her homework, as usual. Beth Ann didn't like the police much, had had her run-ins with them over the years, but, according to Sam's informant, had yet to become too hard-bitten.

If approached correctly.

As Beth Ann reached the halfway point across the restaurant's broad parking lot, Sam put her car into gear, turned on her headlights and casually drove up alongside the woman.

Agostini looked over her shoulder warily.

Sam had already rolled her window down. "Hey. Beth Ann?"

Agostini's response was guarded. "Yeah."

Sam stuck her hand out the window for a shake. "Samantha Martens. I'm with the Vermont Bureau of Investigation."

Reluctantly, Beth Ann took the hand in her mitten and gave it a limp tug before letting it drop.

Sam stopped the car and got out, still talking. "I'm sorry to bother you. I was just hoping you might be able to help me out with something."

"What?"

"I want to learn a little about Andy Griffis."

"He's dead."

As was the tone of her voice.

"I know," Sam admitted regretfully. "I was sad to hear about that. Would you mind if we talked a bit? I'd be happy to buy you a cup of coffee, or at least drive you home."

A sudden gust of cold wind made the girl hesitate. "What's to talk about?"

"I was wondering what was happening in his life towards the end. You two were close. It must've been a real shock when he died."

Beth Ann shook her head, staring at the ground.

"You still miss him, I bet," Sam suggested.

"He was a nice man," Beth Ann said simply.

Sam reached out and touched her arm gently. "Let me drive you home."

Beth Ann looked into her face, saw nothing but sympathy, and finally nodded. "Okay."

Sam waited until they were both settled in the front seat of the warm car before she asked, "Would you like me to treat you to a coffee somewhere? Or a piece of pie?"

That drew a tired smile. "Ugh. Food doesn't do much for me right now. Not after all day in there." She gestured toward the restaurant.

Sam laughed. "Good point. I hadn't thought of that. You probably just want to take a load off. I'll drive you home and get out of your hair as fast as I can."

"Thanks."

Sam pulled out of the parking lot and

headed west. "How long had you and Andy known each other?" she asked, wondering if the ice had been successfully broken between them. She was struck once more by her companion's lack of curiosity. Sam had long ago found that most people of Agostini's background were used to being questioned by authority figures and were generally, even if listlessly, compliant.

Beth Ann was looking out the side window. "A few months. We met at a bar. The only two people who didn't want to be there."

"You were with friends?"

She nodded. "Yeah. Him, too. We joked about that later, how it was like we had a radar for each other. He said we should form a group called Loners Anonymous, except that nobody would show up for meetings."

Sam laughed. "That's good. He sounds like a funny guy."

Beth Ann turned toward her, and Sam feared she might have put her foot in it. But the girl had understood her intent. "He was sometimes, when he was feeling up. But it was hard to tell. He could be real uneven."

Sam paused before suggesting, "That must've been tough."

"It had its moments."

"What was he like when he was down?"

"Quiet, mostly. He never got violent or drunk or anything like that. That's where the loner thing kicked in. He would go off and be by himself."

"At his apartment?"

She nodded in the darkened car. "Yeah. Did you ever see that place?"

Sam was surprised by the question. "No."

"It was weird. Like a cell. You know he was in prison, right?"

"Yeah, I read that."

"Well, his apartment looked just like that to me. I only went there once. Never again."

"Did you ever talk about it with him?"

"The time I visited, I did. I mean, I said something like 'Wow, this sure is empty,' or something. I didn't actually tell him it looked like a jail cell. But it did — bare walls, a cot, almost nothing in it."

"How did he react?"

"He looked around like he'd never been there before, and then he said, 'I like it this way. Makes me feel safe.' It was weird to me, 'cause I had just the opposite feeling about it. I felt totally cut off from the world in there, like it was a spaceship or one of those explorer balls they drop into the ocean with people inside."

Sammie nodded, entering the apartment

complex parking lot. "His record says he was only in jail for three years," she stated. "I wonder if he was that way before."

But Beth Ann shook her head emphatically. "No. It was prison that did it. That was a bad time. He said it changed everything. When he was in the dumps, that's all he talked about, how it ruined his getting along with his family, or being comfortable with other people. I had to be real careful what I said to him afterward, 'cause he would, like, almost disappear right in front of me." She paused before adding, "That's when he'd go to that apartment. I was never sure what to do then. Wait for him to come back or go after him and try to get him out."

She leaned forward in her seat and pressed her hands against her eyes. Sam pulled into a parking space and placed her palm on the other woman's back. Beth Ann wasn't crying, but she was silent for a long time.

Then she said through her hands, "I feel like I could've stopped it. I just didn't know what to do."

"It's not your fault, Beth Ann," Sam said softly, feeling a sudden kinship. "I live with a man who gets down like that, and disappears into himself to work through it. And I'm not always sure he will."

Beth Ann looked at her gratefully.

"Really?"

"It's tough. And lonely. They get so lost, they can't see you standing right in front of them."

She was nodding. "That's it. It was so frustrating. I couldn't make him understand that it didn't need to be that hard."

"My guy has a lot of ancient history to fight," Sam said. "What was Andy wrestling with?"

Beth Ann's straight and simple answer caught Sam off guard. "He was raped in prison."

"Jesus," she muttered, remembering not just what Dave Snyder had said about Andy's lapse into depression partway through his jail term, but how Andy hadn't been able to stay working for his family in Thetford afterward.

"He couldn't get over it," Beth Ann said softly.

Sammie stared out the window thoughtfully, reflecting on what had happened to Leo's car.

"He may not have been the only one," she said.

**Bart148:** what do u do 4 fun?

**AnnGee:** not much. U?

**Bart148:** u hav a bf?

**AnnGee:** yeah

**Bart148:** u dont hav fun with him?

**AnnGee:** sometimes

**Bart148:** what kind?

**AnnGee:** u know

**Bart148:** tell me

**AnnGee:** stuff. movies. music

**Bart148:** u sound bored

**AnnGee:** a little

**Bart148:** u super tite with him?

**AnnGee:** no

**Bart148:** u could do better

**AnnGee:** I lik that

**Bart148:** me 2. maybe we could make that happen

# CHAPTER 12

Joe stuck a finger in his ear and pressed the cell phone tighter to the side of his head. "A Taser tag?"

He was standing near the entrance of the hospital cafeteria, unsure if cell phones were as taboo here as they were elsewhere in the building. In any case, it wasn't working very well.

Sam was telling him, "Yeah. Willy found it in the first guy's motel room — Norman Rockwell. Lester's calling him Wet Bald Rocky so we can tell him apart from Dry Hairy Fred. Anyhow, we called the company and traced the serial number on the tag to a shipment of Taser cartridges sent to the Burlington PD."

"You saying a cop Tasered Rockwell?"

A group of people, laughing and talking loudly, passed by, burying Sam's response. Joe had come both to depend on cell phones and to hate them with a passion, especially since reception across most of Vermont was rotten.

"What?" he asked.

"I said all we know is that the cartridge was sent there. I have no idea who ended up with it. Maybe it was stolen."

Joe pulled out his notepad and pen, cradling the phone awkwardly. "Okay. Give me the serial number. I can shoot up to Burlington and find out."

Sam complied before asking, "You at the hospital?"

"Yeah."

"Is everything okay?"

"He's hanging in there."

"What about the car? You find what you were after?"

"Yeah. Now we're looking into a computer we found at the garage. I'm going to the sheriff's department next to find out what they've got."

"Well," Sam said after a small pause, "good luck."

"Thanks," Joe answered her, adding, "Nice job on the tag."

"Let's see if it means anything first," she cautioned before hanging up.

Joe dropped the phone into his coat pocket with a sigh of relief.

"Everything all right?" his mother asked

from beside him.

He looked down at her, her face upturned from her permanent perch in the wheelchair, and he bent over to kiss her cheek. "Yeah. I just have a brain teaser cooking in Brattleboro — seems to be getting weirder."

"Was that Sammie?" she asked.

"It was," he admitted, surprised. "How did you know that?"

She laughed. "I'm your mother. I've been watching how you react to people your whole life."

He joined her. "Good thing, too. Keep me flying straight."

She squeezed his hand. "I do what I can. It's not difficult." She gestured toward the cafeteria. "Did you get enough to eat? You didn't have much."

"I'm all set," he answered her, stepping behind her chair. "You ready to go back up?"

"Yes," she said, and faced forward, but in that one short word, he clearly heard her sadness. Leo remained inert, attached like a chrysalis to his attending instruments. Dr. Weisenbeck was still counseling them not to be alarmed, but Joe could tell that his mother was tiring of hanging in limbo.

He leaned in over her shoulder as he pushed her down the hall. "What do you say we catch a movie?"

"In the middle of the day?" she asked, startled.

"Why not? We could both do with a break."

He wheeled her over to a small bookshop off the hospital's central hallway and found a newspaper, after which they pored over the movie ads, found a comedy she'd heard about, which started in under an hour, and headed out into the parking lot after collecting their coats from upstairs and checking in on Leo one last time.

It was a bittersweet outing for both of them, playing hooky for each other's sake, not really absorbing what flickered across the screen, and yet acknowledging the moment's nostalgic richness. Only rarely had Joe and his mother ever done anything social together without Leo. He was always the glue that united them for such occasions. Now, in the movie theater, there was the lingering guilt, not only of enjoying themselves behind his back but of practicing their own companionship in his absence, as if hedging their bets against his survival.

They barely spoke on the way back to the hospital afterward.

There, they split up, returning to their separate jobs, Joe to Burlington, and his mother to her vigil. Before they parted, however, she took hold of his sleeve and gave him a long look.

"Don't keep too much of this inside, Joe. It doesn't do any good."

"I'll be okay."

"You're all alone now. If Leo doesn't make it, it'll get worse."

He thought of her in the exact same terms, of course, but couldn't utter the words.

He didn't need to. She added, "It's not the same for me. I have my own world, and not much more time to worry about anyhow. But you, now with Gail gone . . ." She hesitated before asking, "How's Lyn?"

He straightened, surprised. "Fine, I guess."

"When did you last see her?"

He reddened slightly. "I visited the bar she's setting up a couple of days ago."

She nodded and smiled. "Good. She likes you very much, and I think you could do a lot worse."

He laughed to cover his embarrassment. "I gotta go, Ma."

But she didn't let go of his sleeve, not quite yet. "You like her."

He let the smile fade from his face and considered her implication for a moment, before admitting, "Yes. I do."

The drive to Burlington was under ninety minutes from the hospital in Lebanon, New Hampshire, and cut through one of Joe's favorite scenic corridors — a meandering diagonal across the state's famous Green Mountains. It was a trip he'd made a thousand times since the interstate was laid out in the 1960s, and it took him by the front doors of both his organization's head-quarters in Waterbury and, just southeast of there, the capital city of Montpelier, where Gail now lived full-time.

In the past he would have at least consid-ered stopping by both places, but since, technically, he was still on leave, and, emotionally, he had no reason to see Gail, he stayed on the road. But he couldn't avoid pondering the latter situation, especially in light of his mother's parting words. He'd been struck, not just by her concern for his happiness — all the more touching when she was so distracted by Leo — but by her apparent openness toward Lyn Silva, whom she barely knew.

His mother and Gail had been the best of friends and, he presumed, still were. That she could supportively even consider his segue toward Lyn was an act of love he

207

doubted he could have made in her place. But his mother was made of strong stuff and clearly had enough heart to encompass the inevitable changes that both time and people dished up. That included the possibility of Leo's dying — and, certainly, that Joe might find happiness with someone new.

In that way, his mother and the snow-clad, sun-bleached, timeworn mountains he was passing by were not dissimilar. Both were old, stalwart bastions of tradition and place, around which Joe had found it wise to base his values. He was no stuck-in-the-hills galoot, ignorant and distrustful of the world's offerings and mishaps. But he had come to recognize the wisdom — at least for him — of admitting his roots and honoring their more admirable customs, of which his mother represented the best.

It was of some comfort to him to reflect on this and to draw strength from it as he considered the possibilities, good and bad, that seemed to be looming before him.

The chief of the Burlington Police Department was Timothy Giordi, the son of a small-town cop who had babysat Tim by driving him around in his patrol car. Tim was the first to concede that he might as well have had a police blood transfusion at birth, given all the chance he ever had of considering a different profession.

Fortunately, he was very good at it and looked as if, like his father before him, he'd struggle to stay on the job until the day he died, even if it meant as a school crossing guard.

He and Joe had been friends for more years than either could remember, which had made Tim's the first name Joe considered when Sam revealed the possible source of the Taser cartridge.

The PD's home was a thirty-thousand-square-foot converted factory building dating back to the twenties, half of which had once subsequently housed an auto dealership. It was also the largest, most up-to-date station house in the state, located a few hundred feet from Lake Champlain and bordering a city park — a testament to the hustle and political savvy of those who had preceded Tim Giordi as chief.

Giordi came out personally to collect Joe in the reception area, shaking his hand and patting his back as if he were a long-lost uncle returning from the wilderness.

"Damn, Joe — the field force commander of the Vermont Bureau of Investigation," he glowed. "That is truly the big time."

Joe laughed, looking around him as they

proceeded toward the back of the building. It was a white-walled maze of hallways, many of them without ceilings, since most of the partitions ended shy of the industrially trussed roof, allowing for a crisscrossing of exposed piping and electrical conduits high overhead. Joe felt slightly like a rat in a box, wondering when a huge pair of fingers might appear from just out of sight to pluck him from its midst.

"I don't know about that," he told his guide. "I bet you have three times my budget and manpower, not to mention the autonomy to play all alone in your own backyard."

Giordi aimed him through an outer office staffed with intense-looking people studying computer screens, and into a large room with curiously small windows overlooking the water below.

"Oh-oh," Tim said. "Do I sense a little chafing with political realities?"

Joe shrugged. "Not really. We have to play nice and give credit to the locals, including the state police, but that's only what we wish the feds would do when they come poaching, so I really can't complain. And it's a hell of a lot better than when we were brand-new, out of the box. Talk about cold shoulder."

Tim waved him to a chair near his large desk and sat in one like it nearby. "More than half your people came from the state police, didn't they?"

Joe nodded. "That helps a lot." He added with a smile, "Come to think of it, we got a couple of your guys, didn't we?"

"Yeah, you bastard. I meant to mail you a grenade for that. You want some coffee, by the way?"

Joe shook his head. "Not after that, I don't."

"What can I do for you, then?" Tim asked, getting down to business.

Joe pulled a scrap of paper from his pocket and handed it over. Tim recognized its contents immediately.

"I take it there's a punchline?"

"Stamped on a Taser tag. It — and only it — was under the motel room bed of a guy we found dead elsewhere, stripped of all identification."

Tim looked up at him. "The floater on that BOL you sent out a while back? No shit. I circulated his picture at every one of our shift briefings. Got nothing, of course. And you only found the one tag? You know there are supposed to be up to forty of these things in each cartridge."

"Meaning, whoever used it tried their best

to clean up," Joe agreed. "It got one of my guys wondering if maybe a cop was involved."

Frowning, Tim considered the scrap of paper a moment longer before placing it on his knee and stating, "I bet you're going to say you traced this serial number to us, right?"

"You have a cartridge go missing?" Joe asked.

But Giordi shook his head. "Not that I heard. Of course, I might not've been told, either." He got up, reached for the phone on his desk, pushed the intercom button, and asked the voice on the other end to join them. His demeanor had lost its earlier joviality.

An older woman appeared at the door thirty seconds later. "Chief?"

"Kathy, did we have a Taser cartridge disappear anytime recently?"

The woman glanced quickly at Joe, whom she didn't know, and immediately fell into professional mode. "I don't know, Chief. I'll get hold of Matt and have him report to you directly."

Giordi nodded. "Thanks. Right away."

She disappeared as Tim turned to Joe. "The shit just hit the fan there. We run pretty close herd on that kind of equipment, for obvious reasons, and Matt Aho, being the supply officer, is the go-to guy. If I were Kathy, I'd be telling him to put on a flak jacket right now."

But he was smiling as he said it, lessening Joe's apprehension about what might happen next.

A minute later, a concerned-looking young man showed up, a three-ring binder in hand.

"Something missing, Chief?" he asked.

Joe and Giordi got up as the latter made the introductions. "Matt Aho, this is Special Agent Joe Gunther of the VBI." Tim handed over Joe's note before continuing, "This belongs to a Taser tag. His people found it at a crime scene down south — a homicide. Apparently, it belongs to us."

Aho crossed over to a side table and laid his binder open. He began flipping through pages of equipment log entries. Finally, he stopped and ran his finger down the length of one particular sheet.

"Got it," he announced at last, his voice tense.

Both men leaned forward to see the line just above his index.

Aho explained. "Last month, three cartridges were issued to Brian Palmiter. He was on airport security then." Aho glanced at Joe. "Yours was one of them."

"Did he ever report it missing?" Tim asked.

"Not that I heard," Aho answered cautiously. "He sure hasn't asked for any more, which implies he didn't use them up."

"You said he was on airport detail then," said Joe. "Is he still?"

"I think he rotated off," Aho answered.

Tim crossed back to his phone and dialed a number. "Locate Brian Palmiter and have him report to my office right away."

He listened for a moment before responding, "Great. That's perfect."

He hung up and looked over at Joe. "Got lucky. He's in the building."

Giordi walked back to Aho. "That's it for the moment, Matt. Leave the log behind. I'll make sure it gets back to you ASAP."

Aho nodded to Joe and took his leave without further comment. In the next few minutes, Joe could imagine the air thickening with the murmurings spreading from just outside Tim Giordi's office door. He was all too familiar with how police departments were hotbeds of gossip, rumor, and randomly circulating tidbits. Long after this little mystery was resolved, people would be discussing what "really" happened, notwithstanding the chief's official explanation — and that would be only if the conclusion

214

was wholly innocent. God forbid if something untoward had actually occurred.

There was a knock on the open door, and a tall, angular man stood awkwardly on the threshold.

"You called for me, Chief?" he asked warily.

He was young, obviously not long on the force, and still looking slightly out of place in his uniform. Giordi brought him over to the table with the open binder. He gestured toward Joe as he did so, and repeated the introduction he'd made earlier to Matt Aho.

Not surprisingly, this only increased the concern plainly stamped on the officer's face.

"What Agent Gunther is trying to find out," Giordi explained, seeking the exact line on the opened page, "is the whereabouts of a Taser cartridge our records say was issued to you."

Giordi tapped on the entry with his fingertip. Palmiter bent at the waist hesitantly, as if expecting the entire binder to come leaping for his throat.

"Yes, sir," he said without meaning or understanding.

Giordi looked at him quizzically. "So, have you used or lost a Taser cartridge?"

Palmiter straightened, stung by the suggestion. "No, sir. I've never even fired one except in training."

His boss studied Palmiter's duty belt. "How many cartridges do you carry?"

"Two. I'm supposed to have three — one in place and two backups — but they only issued me two."

"When was this?" Joe asked.

The young officer pointed at the open page. "Then — when I was working at the airport. That's when I got Taser certified. I was issued the Taser and the holster." He tapped the weapon on his belt. "You can see where it's got places for two backup cartridges, but only one of them's full." He undid the Velcro flap on one of the compartments to reveal its emptiness. "I figured they'd run short or something," he continued. "And, to be honest, since there's not much action at the airport, I didn't see bothering them for extras."

He looked worriedly at his chief. "I hope I didn't screw up. I didn't think it was a big deal."

"Have you been down to the southern half of the state anytime recently?" Joe asked him.

"No, sir. I don't know anybody down there."

Giordi considered the binder thoughtfully

for a moment before nodding in Palmiter's direction. "Okay, Brian. Give me your Taser and get issued a new one. I want to hang on to yours for a while."

The chief waited until the door had closed behind his now very nervous officer. He hefted the plastic gun in his hand. "I'll have someone run the computer memory in this thing — find out when it was fired last. What do you think?" he asked Joe.

Joe made a face. "On paper," he answered, "either Palmiter is lying or Aho screwed up. But my gut tells me it's neither. Something else must've happened."

Tim pushed out his lips thoughtfully before murmuring, "Once you get me some more information about all this, I'm still going to put them both through polygraphs, just to be sure. What've you found out about your John Doe?" he then asked. "And do you know for sure a Taser was even used on him? They do leave holes."

"The ME has the body," Joe answered, crossing the room and considering the view of the park outside. "She told us there were no outward signs of trauma. We don't even know the cause of death yet, much less anything about the guy. Complete mystery. I'm seeing Hillstrom next, since I'm in town, just to kick the tires personally."

217

He turned to face his old friend. "Tell me about Aho and Palmiter."

Giordi raised his eyebrows. "Fair question, if a little painful. I'm not too crazy about all the possibilities here."

Joe held up his hand. "It's just a question."

"Aho, I've had with me for years. He's solid, dependable, never messed up before. He worked as a street cop before becoming the supply officer, also for this department. I know his family, and everything seems stable there, too. Palmiter, I don't know quite as well. The kid's only twenty-one and he hasn't been with us long. So far, so good, though. He gets good ratings from his sergeant."

He paused to run his hand through his short, graying hair. "I will tell you I'll be checking this whole thing out with the proverbial fine-toothed comb — and probably making some procedural changes, at least."

"You asked me what I thought," Joe said. "How 'bout you? Any idea how the cartridge left the building?"

Giordi looked a little hapless. "You know how it goes, Joe. We do the best we can. We have the usual bells and whistles, but a lot of people go through this building every hour of every day. How big is one of those cartridges? Half a deck of cards?" He frowned before adding, "I'll be shaking things hard to see what falls out, but don't be surprised — and for Christ's sake don't think I'm holding out on you — if, in the end, I've got nothing to show for it."

Joe again made an appeasing gesture before shaking Tim's hand and retrieving his coat from where he'd draped it over a chair. "Not to worry," he told him, heading out. "I appreciate both the help and the pickle you're in. I promise I'll be in touch, and don't worry too much until you have to. At least I know for sure where that little tag originated — whether that's relevant or not, we'll both find out."

Giordi shook his head. "Let's hope so."

**Mandi144:** Boring
**JMAN:** what do u lik 2 do?
**Mandi144:** Hang out. Try nu things
**JMAN:** I lik nu things. Lik wat?
**Mandi144:** Fool around
**JMAN:** kool. ASL
**Mandi144:** 14/f/Vermont - U?
**JMAN:** kool. 24/m/Mass
**Mandi144:** kool
**JMAN:** U dun that a lot?
**Mandi144:** Enuf
**JMAN:** All the way?
**Mandi144:** Sure
**JMAN:** kool

# CHAPTER 13

The office of the chief medical examiner, whose title was reduced throughout law enforcement to simply OCME, was located across town from the Burlington Police Department, in the cumbersome embrace of the awkwardly rebuilt Fletcher Allen Medical Center, Vermont's largest hospital and the home of the University of Vermont's nationally regarded medical school.

The OCME hadn't started here. As Joe first maneuvered through Burlington's dense traffic and then poked through the hospital's confusion of hallways and interlinked buildings, he recalled how Beverly Hillstrom had once kept an office down the block, above a dentist's office, and worked on her cadavers in the hospital's basement, not far from the loading docks.

It was a credit to her longevity, her efficiency, and her political prowess — not to mention a few friends in the right places —

that all that had been replaced with a clean, modern, highly professional workplace, albeit one hard to locate for the uninitiated.

Joe was certainly not among those, having been here dozens of times. As a result, once safely aboard, he was honor bound to spend a few minutes with whichever staffers he encountered on his way to Hillstrom's corner office, catching up on local gossip.

"I thought I heard your voice," Beverly Hillstrom greeted him when he finally reached her threshold. She stood and came around her desk to kiss him on the cheek, an unheard-of familiarity in the old days, when, for years, they had addressed each other formally, by title — an eccentricity she maintained with everyone else outside the office.

He surveyed her with a smile. She was perfectly squared away, not a hair out of place, her clothes unwrinkled and pristine — an image of uncanny precision enhanced by her dust-free, immaculate office. If he hadn't gotten to know her all-too-human and vulnerable side, she might have remained as scary as she appeared to almost everyone else. But she had granted him that access at one point, and while he understood that it allowed him no special liberties now, he was grateful that it had welcomed him into a highly restricted personal inner sanctum.

"You look great, Beverly," he told her.

She smiled, flushing slightly. "Well, I should. Life is good, both here and at home."

He knew not to pry, but that was happy news. Their single night of intimacy had been partly created by her husband walking out on her. Joe had since heard that the two of them had been working to mend that rift. Clearly, things were paying off.

She considered him seriously. "I heard about your family and the accident, Joe. How are things progressing?"

"As well as can be expected," he told her. "My mom is completely fine. My brother survived, which is saying a lot, but he's touch-and-go in a coma."

"I know it will sound trite," she said. "But if there's anything at all I can do . . ."

"I know," he interrupted her. "And I appreciate it. I promise, I will call if I need to."

She nodded once. "Good." She then brightened somewhat and changed the subject, moving them both to firmer ground. "A wild guess tells me," she continued, "that you're now going to try to upset my apple cart a little. You are here for at least one of your John Does, are you not?"

He laughed, as much at the comment's phrasing as at its content. Hillstrom was unique among his friends in her use of an almost textbook English. "I am, but I'm hoping it'll just help things along. We've discovered something that might tie in to the first one we sent you — the floater in the stream. Do you still have the clothes he arrived in?"

She nodded and moved toward the door. "We do, although we were about to ship them to the crime lab for safekeeping." She passed over the threshold and headed toward the lab in the back, speaking as she went. "So you're not here for the body at all?"

"I may be," he explained, "but I've got to start with the clothing."

"Ah. A mystery in the unfolding. I like a little intrigue."

She eventually took him to a wing off the autopsy room, beyond the coolers where, he knew from past experience, the two men he'd shipped her were still stored, and placed a couple of oversize plastic tubs on a nearby examination table.

"Brattleboro John Doe Number One, as we're calling him — or at least his personal effects," she announced, standing back.

Joe stepped up to the table and opened the tubs. Unlike when he'd first seen them, the clothes were now dry, though still soiled by some of the debris they'd picked up in the water.

By instinct, he started with the upper torso coverings, reconstructing the layering from skin contact to outermost garment, and then began poring over the fabric's surface, inch by inch.

Hillstrom finally yielded to curiosity. "What are you looking for?"

Gunther laughed. "Maybe nothing, but it was too interesting to pass up. We're pretty sure we found out where this guy spent his last night. He checked into a cheap motel with a small overnight bag, no car, paid in cash, and used a phony name — Norman Rockwell, in case you're tempted to change your John Doe."

Hillstrom wrinkled her nose. "Not the way this is going, I'm not. Rockwell deserves better."

"If it helps," Joe suggested, "my team's calling him Wet Bald Rocky, versus Dry Hairy Fred." He resumed his scrutiny. "Anyhow, we're playing with the idea that he met someone at the motel, which person then immediately rendered him harmless before transporting him to the stream."

Hillstrom was already nodding in comprehension, following where he was leading. "And it's the rendering him harmless that you're looking for? What did you find in that motel room?"

He paused to look over his shoulder at her. "You're good. It was a single identifying tag belonging to a Taser cartridge."

"A Taser!" she exclaimed. "But they work with wired barbs. I would have found skin defects on the body."

"Only if the barbs reached the skin," Joe explained. "They don't have to in order to work." He straightened, holding up the decedent's leather belt, adding, "They just need to close the circuit. By digging into something like this."

She came in close to see what he'd found. In the center of the belt's surface was a small hole with a minuscule jagged edge to it, as where a tiny barb might have left a tear upon being extracted.

"Oh, my Lord," she murmured. "It is possible, isn't it?"

He laid the belt back down. "It does connect. It would help if we found evidence of a second impact site."

She'd already grabbed hold of his upper arm. "Come here. Let's take a look at him, now that we know what we're after."

She led him to the storage cooler, which had two horizontal doors stacked one atop the other, and opened the upper one. A wash of cold air spilled out as she seized the edge of the drawer inside and pulled out a tray laden with the plastic-wrapped body of the man they'd found in the water days ago.

Quickly donning latex gloves, she expertly exposed the naked corpse, its torso pragmatically sewn back shut with a series of widely spaced stitches, and with Joe's help, she rolled it onto its side to reveal its back.

"That was the back of the belt, right?" she asked.

"Yeah," he said softly, already craning to study the blanched, fleshy surface before him. He touched the mottled body near its lumbar area. "Around here. If the shooter knew what he was doing, the second barb should have hit somewhere at or just below the shoulder blades."

"Here," she said, tapping the cold skin with her fingertip. "It's not an actual defect . . . more like a pimple."

She crossed the room to fetch a strong magnifying glass and applied it to the spot she'd found.

"That's it," she announced after a few seconds of study. "During an uneducated survey, it's nothing much to note. But with scrutiny, it's clearly not a pimple — more like a tiny burn."

Joe spread his fingers just above the body's back, measuring the distance between the lumbar spine and the small red dot. "About a foot and a half," he announced. "Which means the shooter was standing pretty close when he fired."

He returned to the pile of clothes to find some piece of clothing that might reveal a barb having been roughly torn lose. He found it in a tightly knit polar fleece vest — a mere couple of strands hanging loose from the fabric.

"Bingo," he said, bringing the vest back over to Hillstrom and holding it next to the cadaver.

"Lines up perfectly," she agreed.

She stepped back to consider him thoughtfully. "But what does that tell you, exactly?"

"Not much that's provable," he admitted. "It does suggest how to incapacitate a man in a motel room and then drown him fifteen miles away."

Joe drove from Burlington to Chelsea next, hoping to catch Rob Barrows in his office. He left the interstate at exit 4 and journeyed east through Randolph Center and East

Randolph to take the Chelsea Mountain Road up and over Osgood Hill. This was also a roundabout way to reach Thetford and New Hampshire beyond, and more reminiscent of the challenges the state offered its travelers a mere half century earlier, before most of them were seduced by the ease and comfort of I-89. These now less used roads were, by contrast, old Vermont to Joe's mind, set among a countryside as prickly as a porcupine's back with trees, and so encumbered with streams, ravines, and claustrophobic, pressed-together hills as to make progress before the advent of paved roads a quasi-heroic effort. Still, for all that, atop Osgood Hill, cresting a rise and emerging from the woods, he was abruptly rewarded with a sweeping view — long, curving fields, the sparkle of otherwise hidden water, and the solid massiveness of distant ancient mountains — and was won over yet again by his state's uncanny ability to both challenge and nurture those willing to carve out a living in its midst, while shaping them into something hardy, independent, self-sufficient, and sometimes a little cranky in the process.

Joe found Rob Barrows at the sheriff's headquarters in Chelsea, at the top of the northernmost of the village's two greens —

an eccentricity particular to the town. The sheriff's office was tucked behind the United Church of Christ, in a nineteenth-century redbrick building neighboring Court, School, and Church Streets — a trio of names simultaneously bland, comforting, and a little peremptory, as if the founders of the village had better things to do — and more land to grab — in the late 1700s than to linger here and apply their imaginations.

"Hey," Barrows said as Joe entered the officers' room, a small, cluttered space that served a variety of roles. "I thought you were going to give me a call, not actually make the trip."

"Nice day for it," Joe answered neutrally, choosing a chair beside Rob's desk. He did not go into how staring at his brother's inert form in the hospital for a half hour at a time was more than he could stand, even in his mother's company. "What did you get out of that?" He pointed at the equally blank-faced, remarkably filthy computer that they'd removed from Steve's Garage.

Barrows had been at his own console when Joe entered, and he now waved at his screen in explanation. "Just been following up on that," he said. "I got the software to get around the password. Hit pure gold. For one thing, he's cooking the books — the legit stuff is what we saw at the shop; the kickbacks and bill padding and bogus work claims are all behind the password. When everyone gets out of the hospital, I'd seriously recommend you get another mechanic."

Joe opened his mouth to respond, and to ask about Leo's car, but Rob was clearly building up steam and continued instead with "I also found out that somebody at Steve's has been filling his time with more than cars. I made a copy of his hard drive and transferred it to my computer so I wouldn't be tampering with evidence, but take a look at this."

He turned to the machine and began moving around from window to window, talking as he went. "Whoever's behind the password's been using one of the more popular chat rooms, in part looking for old car parts, but some other, much more interesting stuff as well."

He paused to cast a glance at Joe. "I won't bore you with all the computer geek stuff unless you're into that."

"Not me," Joe assured him, focusing on the screen. "But you said, 'whoever's behind the password.' You don't know?"

"I know Dan Griffis posted the profile using his real name, but technically, until we get more proof, he could claim somebody else did that to frame him. I just said what I did to be cautious, but do I think it's Dan? Sure. To be honest, old Barrie McNeil didn't look like he had the smarts to do more'n turn the thing on, if that.

"Anyhow," Barrows resumed, "I used a forensic software program we got to not only look at what he's been up to, but to read his supposed 'deleted' files, too. You can see he calls himself CarGuy — cute — and that he plays here a lot. I found more chats than I can shake a stick at, and most of it's recent."

The computer's cursor moved nervously across the screen, opening windows, closing others, almost as if it had a mind of its own, Rob narrating as it went along.

"A ton of this is pretty boring, so I went to the picture files as soon as I found a reference to a snapshot CarGuy wanted his contact to see. Worth a thousand words, right?" He laughed briefly as the computer burst forth with color photographs, primarily pornographic.

"So far, so good," he commented contentedly, "but not too surprising, either. Usual raunchy stuff. Until . . ." He paused while he scrolled to the right set of pictures. ". . . You get to this — it's what he was referring to in his chat."

He sat back to allow Joe a full view of several baggies of white powder, neatly arranged on a tabletop for their portrait.

"Heroin, I'm guessing," Rob announced. "I already cross-checked with the back-and-forth that led me here. CarGuy is dealing drugs on the side. I captured a whole conversation where he and SmokinJoe — whoever *he* is — set up a buy that took place two days ago."

Joe straightened and looked elsewhere to adjust his eyesight for a moment. "Did you . . . ?"

But Rob cut him off. "Get warrants for all this? Yep. Step by step, all the way down the line. I've been calling the SA as I go, making sure everything's legal."

Joe nodded. "Okay. That's all I was wondering."

Rob was smiling broadly. "There's more, of course. Other deals, other dealers, other pictures. I doubt our office'll get to play with any of it for long. Maybe the drug task force will want it, or even the feds — I'll let the sheriff duke that out — but it's a cool start, and I love that we're the ones who got it going."

He returned to the keyboard. Given Rob's high spirits, Joe felt bad that he was, by contrast, mostly disappointed. Nothing mentioned so far tied Dan Griffis or the garage to what had put Leo in the hospital.

"No connections to my brother's accident?" he almost murmured.

"Not yet," Rob admitted, his voice upbeat. "I did take advantage of all this to do a search for your mom's name, and Leo's — just to see."

Once more the cursor was leaping about, and text blocks of chat dialogue cut in and out across the screen, making Joe slightly dizzy.

"Like I said," Rob continued, "there's a huge amount of material here, and I doubt what I found'll be the last of anything illegal. I mean, even the porno stuff is likely to get us something. But I didn't hit on any of your names — except in the billing and service documents, of course."

Joe suddenly sat straighter in his seat. "Go back."

Barrows froze his hand. "Where?"

"Maybe one click. I saw something. One of the handles, or whatever you call them."

"Screen names?" Rob asked, moving back.

"Yeah," Joe said, pointing at the screen. "What's going on here?"

Rob paused to study the document before them. "It's a general chat room. Bunch of people all talking at once. You do this sometimes, like at a party, when you're looking for someone special. When you do, you can ask that person to kind of step away for a private chat, like you were going into another room, just the two of you."

"What's the topic here? Drugs again?" Joe asked.

"Nope, it's the other favorite. Sex."

Joe tapped the screen with his index finger. "What about this one? What's he after?"

Rob leaned forward and began studying the exchange, scrolling through the short and, to Joe, virtually incomprehensible one-liners where almost every word was reduced to its purely phonetic root, if not merely replaced by initials — for example, "LOL" for "laughing out loud." The dialogue before him now might just as well have been written in a foreign language.

"Ugh," Rob finally said, sitting back.

"What?"

"Well, it's sex, all right, but what that guy's looking for is young girls. There's a load of that shit on the Web. You see it everywhere. CarGuy's not biting, though, doesn't even address your man — different interests." He twisted around to face Gunther. "Why?"

"It's the name," Joe admitted.

Rob returned to the screen. "Rockwell? Where'd you run into that?"

"I don't know for sure if I did. I've got a John Doe case we're working on where all we've got for ID is the motel registration — N. Rockwell. I laughed when I saw it, because it reminded me of the painter." He pointed at the computer again. "Probably a big stretch. It's not that unusual a name."

Barrows was already typing, moving to another display. "Everybody has to register a profile with the chat room. It's a legal thing. They all lie, of course, but you're supposed to be able to check each other out if you connect. Most pedophiles pretend they're nineteen, or something." He laughed shortly and added, "Course, we lie, too, when we're trying to catch 'em. But the format is basically name, age, where you're from, what your hobbies are, and so on."

He paused so Joe could see what was before them. "Of course," he then added, pointing out a warning message, "there's always the flip side, too. They put a lock on their profile. We'd have to get a subpoena to open it, and, for that, a good reason to request one. Slim chance, given the innocuous language I saw."

Joe nodded, his enthusiasm undaunted.

Despite what he'd just said, he actually didn't think that the name Rockwell surfacing twice in odd circumstances was too likely. They had to be connected. "Going back to the chat where CarGuy was, too, can you tell if Rockwell does hook up with anyone?"

"Maybe" was the answer, as Barrows went back to work.

"Yeah," he said a few minutes later. "Looks like Mandi144 and he hit it off. They certainly go off together."

"And Mandi is . . . ?" Joe asked leadingly.

Rob broke away from the computer to give him a sour look. "Well, let's put it this way: She says right up front that she's fourteen in the general chat. I'm guessing your Mr. Rocky wasn't."

Joe nodded slightly. "My Mr. Rocky is also dead."

**JMAN:** U hav a pic or cam?

**Mandi144:** cams broke — howz this?

**JMAN:** wow. Hot

**Mandi144:** U have a pic?

**JMAN:** no. Im 6-1, tho. 170

**Mandi144:** no pic? How cum?

**JMAN:** I can get 1. Id lik u 2 see me

**Mandi144:** me 2

**JMAN:** Id lik u 2 do mor than that

**Mandi144:** me 2

**JMAN:** how old r u again?

**Mandi144:** 14. problem?

**JMAN:** not a cop?

**Mandi144:** lol. I look lik a cop?

# CHAPTER 14

Joe reluctantly turned away from the view outside. It had started snowing again, after too many dry days. He was of a mind that if you lived where snowfall was the norm, then it should come about regularly and heavily, satisfying everyone's worst fears. People were going to complain about it anyway — they should, therefore, have good cause.

He surveyed the small VBI office. Sam, Willy, and Lester were all at their desks, each occupied according to character — Lester on the computer, Sam sorting through case files, and Willy harassing them both.

"What handle do you use when you're chasing little girls online, Les?" he asked his colleague.

"Willy," was Lester's immediate response, to Sammie's appreciative laughter.

"Anything yet?" Joe asked Lester, who was in fact checking the BOLs they'd issued on both unidentified bodies.

Spinney sat back in his chair and shook his head. "Nothing. Guess we still get to call 'em Bald Rocky and Hairy Fred."

"It'll take all the fun out of it when we can't," Willy agreed.

"All right," Joe said, getting them back on track. "You all read my notes?"

There were a couple of nods and a muttered assent, none of them from Willy, of course.

"Well, in addition, I got a call this morning from Rob Barrows," Joe continued. "No big surprise; his boss is as excited about the possible drug dealing by Dan Griffis as he is totally uninterested about the possibility that Les's Bald Rocky is a sexual predator."

"Typical," Willy growled.

"I probably would've done the same," Joe conceded. "Predator cases are a bitch to sell, and this one's not even in his county. The drug case is a gimme. To be honest, I'm just as happy, given my personal connections to the Griffis family."

"That mean you're handing everything over to the sheriff?" Willy challenged him incredulously.

Joe tilted his head to one side noncommittally. "On the record? Sure. Off the record? I have Rob Barrows on speed dial.

By the way, since we're talking about it, there's been no evidence yet connecting Steve's Garage to my family's accident. Regular service records only, and nothing about tie rods. Looks like they had several layers of books, though, so it's still early."

He looked at Sam. "In the interests of full disclosure, I should also mention that I asked Sam to look a little beyond that interview the two of you did with Dave Snyder at P and P."

Willy let out a small bark of surprise as he stared at his girlfriend. "No shit? You didn't tell me that."

"Add it to the list," she tossed back at him.

"Now that a part of what happened to my family has become a formal case," Joe said, cutting off Willy's response, "I'd just as soon have everything out in the open. So, Sam, why don't you tell us what you found out."

"Not too complicated," she reported. "I chased down Beth Ann Agostini — we learned about her through Snyder — and she told me that Andy Griffis hanged himself because he'd been raped in prison. At least that's what it boiled down to. Pretty good reason for his family to be pissed at you," she added.

Joe considered that, not for the first time, and suggested, "If he told any of them."

Sam had no comeback, not having considered the possibility.

"I'm guessing nobody in law enforcement knew about the rape at the time, much less who did it?" he asked.

She shook her head. "I checked six ways toward the middle on that. Nobody knows who should know, and nobody's talking who might."

Joe squared his shoulders abruptly, as if shaking off a weight. "Okay. Let's put all that on the shelf for the time being. The other thing Rob Barrows gave me this morning was the name of a guy I'd like you, Lester, to contact directly." He quickly consulted a note lying on his desk. "John Leppman. A psychologist and computer geek out of Burlington — been working with the PD there and the state police, profiling Internet predators and making it easier to flush them out. Burlington's chief said Leppman was their go-to guy on this topic. I have his contact info here. Since it looks like we've stumbled into the middle of something having to do with the subject — at least for the time being — we'll be needing all the help we can get."

He glanced at the notes he'd scribbled down to help keep him on track. "Speaking of just that, let's look at what we've got so far. Two men without identity or background" — he eyed Lester and added — "Bald Rocky and Hairy Fred — both appear in town, both rent motel rooms, apparently to meet up with someone else, and both end up dead. We're pretty confident that one, at least, was immobilized with a Taser before being dumped into the water. The other, we don't know." He looked up at them to explain further. "After we found a small Taser dart hole in Bald Rocky's back, Hillstrom went over Fred, inch by inch. She found nothing similar. She now knows that Tasers don't necessarily need to pierce the skin in order to work, but they usually do, and it's pretty unlikely that you'd get two people in a row with minimal to no markings. My gut tells me that the Taser was used only once."

"He probably only had the one cartridge," Lester suggested, "since it looks like it was stolen."

"I got a question," Willy stated. "You still need a gun to shoot the cartridge. You can get both online. Why buy one and not the other?"

"Too early to know," Joe answered, "but it seems like we're dealing with a very careful guy. We've got to assume that both Fred and Rocky were acting on instructions when they checked into their motels. Too big a coincidence otherwise. And, you've got to admit, every detail was thought out, right down to the extra key being attached outside the room door."

"Plus, the fact that they both came on foot," Sammie commented.

Everyone in the room looked at her, drawn less by her words and more by the leading tone of her voice.

"What're you thinking?" Lester asked first.

"I'm not sure, but when you're talking about coincidence, that seems pretty big to me. Everybody drives around here."

"Bald Rocky's room looked like it might belong to a guy who rode a bus," Willy mused.

"Right," Joe agreed. "If maybe just recently. From his clothes and appearance, he seemed like a man heading down the social ladder, but not like he'd been that way for long." He recalled Hillstrom's appraisal of the man's toenails, but kept it to himself. "Hairy Fred's room was middle-class fare. Did you circulate both head shot pictures to the bus people?"

Sam nodded, adding, "Not to all the drivers, though. That'll take longer." As she spoke, she was pawing through the photographs they'd printed of both crime scenes.

She held up a picture of the man who had identified himself as R. Frederick — the body found in the more upscale motel. "Look at the back of his right shoe," she suggested, displaying it for all to see. "Just above the heel, on the leather."

Like trained pets, they all leaned forward in their chairs, including Willy. Lester was the first to notice what she was talking about. "It's worn from where he rests his heel on the floor of a car when he's pushing the accelerator. He drove a lot."

"Nice," Joe said. "Okay. Let's back up a bit. What you just said, Sam, about both of them arriving on foot. Why have them leave their cars behind?"

They knew what he was after — he'd been using this Socratic method for years.

"Identity," Lester chimed in first, just as Willy muttered, "Oh, for Christ's sake."

Lester forged on: "Our cars have everything about us — papers, fingerprints, DNA samples, you name it."

"You're saying Fred pulled a fast one," Sam said, her excitement building. "Disobeyed orders. Either stashed his car and walked, or just took the bus for the last leg of the trip."

"I'm saying," Joe expanded, "that we love our cars and we tend to bend the rules out of habit, especially if we're already breaking the law."

Willy said in a bored voice, "I already checked with the parking division downstairs. No abandoned cars in the last week."

"That still leaves a possible short bus trip," Sam countered.

Willy shrugged, but Joe followed up. "Issue a BOL to all municipalities within fifty miles. What we're after is an abandoned car in a lot or parking space near a bus depot or train station, maybe with out-of-state plates."

Sam began writing herself a note as Joe pointed at Lester. "I'm having Rob Barrows send you a copy of the hard drive we collected from Steve's Garage. Like I said, they'll be concentrating on the drug deal between CarGuy and SmokinJoe, but I'd like you to find out what you can about Rocky from that — retrieve what he said and who he said it to, or at least do the best you can."

Lester looked doubtful. "I'll give it a shot, Joe, but it may be slim pickings. You know that."

"Yeah, Barrows already warned me. But until we can either locate Rocky's computer or find whoever he was talking to in that chat room, we're reduced to grabbing whatever straws float by. Which includes John Leppman, by the way," he added as an afterthought. "If you can pull him on board sooner than later, he might be able to help you profile this guy, even with the little we get off the hard drive. Not to mention," he suddenly added, "that he might have a file with N. Rockwell already on it — this is his line of work, after all, and my guess is that a name like that is a whole lot rarer than Ready Freddy or all the other playful crap out there."

"Roger that," Lester acknowledged.

There was a momentary lull in the conversation, after which Willy asked, "Who do you want me to chew on?"

Joe pressed his lips together. "I haven't forgotten you," he finally admitted, adding, "but I'm of two minds about using you for what I'm after."

"Don't tell me," Willy said with a pitying smile. "It's the car thing up north, right? Your big family drama?"

Joe barely heard the tone in his voice, being so used to the man's unrelenting style. "It may not be only about me anymore, as the Rocky reference just made clear. Still, I won't deny I'd love to get to the bottom of what happened to Mom and Leo."

"Want me to torture Dan?"

Joe shook his head, not doubting for a moment that Willy could and would do it if properly encouraged. "Tempting, but no. Dan's too hot right now. Go after the old man — E. T. Cozy up to him somehow, get under his tent flaps. In his prime, there was nothing that moved in that whole township without his knowledge, and he ran his family like a full-bird colonel. That's changed. I need to find out what happened, and I'm too involved and too well known to do the kind of job you might. And I'm not just after the car crash — think more generally than that. Barrows could benefit from this, too, if you get lucky."

Willy's response was eloquent in its brevity. "Sure."

Volunteering to do the unorthodox was an easy response. What Joe sensed here, however — never to be publicly recognized — was Willy's implicit personal loyalty to him. That was a trickier trait for an avowed hard case to acknowledge.

Joe honored the message with a single nod of the head. "Thanks," he added quietly before addressing them all. "Okay, let's break it down into pieces, so nobody's stepping on anyone else's toes."

Joe parked his car on Oak Street, appreciat-

248

ing that the plows had kept the curbs clear, and got out into the still falling snow. This had turned into an old-fashioned snowstorm. Forecasters were calling for six inches by morning.

He paused by his car, looking up the street, noticing a few forlorn electric candles in windows, and the odd wreath or two on a door, left over from Christmas. This was familiar territory. Not only was it a major backstreet thoroughfare in a town he'd known since his days as a rookie, decades earlier, but he'd once lived a hundred yards to the south, on the corner of Oak and High, before he and Gail even met, when she'd been merely a successful local Realtor and he'd been a lieutenant on the detective squad.

The coincidence was ironic, since he had parked opposite Lyn Silva's address — a two-story, two-apartment Victorian rental. There was an argument in times like this, he thought, for a small world being just a little too tight for comfort.

He glanced up at the upper apartment, its lights blazing behind the soundless, shifting veil of falling snow. She'd given him her phone number, but he hadn't called ahead. For reasons he didn't ponder, he'd merely used the number to cross-index her address on the office computer and driven the one block from the municipal building.

Joe walked up the central path, already softened by the new snow, and climbed the broad porch steps to the front door. That led to a heated, well-lighted lobby with a carpeted staircase, which he climbed to the second-floor landing and an age-darkened oak door.

He pushed the doorbell near the knob and waited, a small part of him hoping no one would be home.

His reaction to hearing her footsteps approaching was hardly disappointment, however. As the knob turned and the door opened, he felt his heart beating as fast as a teenager's.

She smiled up at his slightly reddened face. "There's a sight for sore eyes."

His color darkened further. "Same for me."

She leaned in and brushed his lips fleetingly with her own, a gesture combining friendship with intimacy while overstating neither. "Would you like to come in?"

"Is that okay? I know I should've called."

She took his hand and tugged at it. "It's a pleasure. Plus," she added, looking at him over her shoulder as she led the way through what might once have served as a dining room, "I need a break. I've been spending so much time at the bar, getting ready, that I'm still living out of boxes here. It's a drag to be unpacking no matter where I am."

She wasn't exaggerating. The room looked like a shipping depot, with cardboard boxes alternating with loose bundles of crinkled newspaper and bubble wrap, piled up in almost every nook and cranny.

"Impressive," he said softly, half to himself.

But she heard him. She laughed, still walking toward the front of the large apartment. "It is bad, but you'll find out why in a second. There's method to my madness — at least, I hope so."

They reached the far wall of the cluttered room, and Lyn slid open a pair of double pocket doors to what turned out to be a spacious living room.

"This is why I took the place, even though the rent was more than I wanted."

It was a beautiful room, with hardwood floors and detailed window frames, a coffered ceiling, elaborate moldings, and gleaming antique fixtures. Along the narrow wall, under an intricate mantel, was a built-in wood stove with glass doors, currently alive with a robust fire. The warmth of it all, both physical and psychological,

251

surrounded them both in an embrace.

"Holy smokes," he said, looking around, reaching out to stroke the hardwood door frame beside him. "It's like a museum."

She groaned good-naturedly. "Yeah — of the wrong century, since all my junk is a museum to the eighties."

He saw her point. The setting was deserving of antique knick-knacks, overstuffed English furniture, and framed oil paintings. Her belongings, though attractive and comfortable-looking, clearly harkened to a different era.

"Maybe," he didn't argue, "but it's not like you have beanbags and cinder-block shelves."

In fact, she'd done wonders. With all packing materials banished to the room they'd just left, the furniture and rugs had been more or less permanently placed, over half the hangings were already on the walls, and even a few stand-arounds had been distributed along windowsills and shelves.

"You've made it feel like a home," he told her honestly.

Her smile broadened. "Yeah. That's what I was thinking. It kind of works." She waved with a flourish at an oversize armchair near the fire. "Have a seat. Would you like something to drink? Or maybe some tea?"

He hesitated, embarrassed that he'd come by unannounced and caused a commotion, but he yielded to her obvious good mood. "Sure. Tea would be great."

"Deal," she said. "Sit there. The kitchen's still a wreck, so it's better I go there alone. Be back in a sec."

He watched her vanish through a side door leading to a hallway. Suddenly alone, he eyed the armchair momentarily but yielded to taking a small tour of the photographs newly on the walls and lining the baseboards, still awaiting hanging.

Some were family pictures in which he thought he could see, in the freckled face of a laughing child, the woman he was beginning to know, surrounded by a tired-looking mother, two older brothers, and a dark-complected father with a thick mustache, rough hands, and a steady, unsmiling look to his eyes. The pictures, taken at picnics, a restaurant, and — one — on a small, weather-beaten fishing boat, were snapshots only, slightly blurry, the color fading, and, despite their careful mounting and framing, eloquent of an economically marginal existence.

Most of the newer pictures were of a different young girl growing up. She was accompanied by a handsome, distracted-looking man in the early shots only, and then alone or with Lyn. These mother-daughter shots tended to show Lyn with the watchful look of the novice photographer, wondering if the camera's self-timer was going to work — suggesting there was no one either behind the camera or in their lives.

Joe studied the ascent of the child through grade school and puberty, as caught on stage, in a cheerleader's outfit, at the high school prom, and at the desk of what looked like a newspaper office, where she was gazing perplexedly at a computer screen. She was a pretty girl with long hair, slim like her mother.

"That's Coryn," Lyn said from behind him.

He turned and saw her standing by the open door to the hallway, two mugs on a small tray in one hand — a practiced stance for someone used to delivering drinks and snacks to tables.

"She's very pretty," he said, crossing over to take the tray and set it on a coffee table between the armchair and the sofa, by the fire.

"Pretty," her mother agreed. "Also smart, stubborn, opinionated, and private. I love that child like nothing else on earth, but

I'm not so sure I'll ever figure out what makes her tick."

"Gave you some troubles over the years?" he asked.

Her answer surprised him. "Never. A completely even keel. Everybody kept expecting her to flip out, especially as a teenager, only because she was so steady, we all assumed she was building up for a huge blow. But it never happened. She's twenty-three now. I don't think it's going to happen."

Lyn sat in the middle of the sofa. Also on the tray were small containers of milk and sugar. "What do you take in your tea?"

He took the armchair opposite and chuckled at the question. "A little of both will work."

But she paused. "You're hedging somehow. How do you usually take it?"

"You're going to think it's like a bad Vermont advertisement. But if there's a choice, I put maple syrup in with the milk."

She immediately rose and headed back toward the kitchen. "I have some, right out in the open. Won't take a second."

She was back in almost that time, unscrewing a glass bottle as she entered. "This I've got to try. I love maple syrup, but I've never tried it in tea."

"Coffee, too," he said, adding, "but I may be alone there. Nobody else I know does that."

She sat again and prepared the mugs, smiling up at him. "You've got a sweet tooth."

He accepted the proffered mug. "Yeah, I've been told that." He took a sip. "Perfect."

She tried her own and nodded approvingly. "That's great. I wouldn't have guessed."

"Where's Coryn now?" he asked, settling into the armchair's embrace, enjoying watching her on the sofa.

"She works for some newspaper in Boston, learning the ropes and hoping for something bigger soon."

"The *Globe*?"

Lyn shrugged. "No — *that* she would've mentioned. I did ask her, but that's what I meant. She keeps her own counsel. For all I know, she'll be calling me tomorrow from the *L.A. Times.* I hope not, though. I would really miss her."

"You see a lot of each other?"

"Not as much as a mother would like, but we talk on the phone pretty often."

"Is she it for your family?" he asked, nodding toward the photographs.

Lyn gazed in that direction, as if the

subjects pictured had suddenly stepped into the room, which, after a fashion, they had. Joe kept his eyes on her. He had always enjoyed watching her, from the first time he'd seen her. She had a magnetic effect on him that he was only now beginning to appreciate.

"No," she answered quietly. "I have my mom and a brother, Steve."

"The other boy in the picture isn't a brother?"

She nodded slowly, still gazing off. "He was. He and my father died at sea."

He was taken aback, and felt badly for leading her there. "I'm sorry."

She turned toward him again, her expression sad but open. "I am, too. I loved them both, in different ways. José was wild and funny and full of beans; my father was just the opposite. A rock. I see a lot of Dad in Coryn — both of them so steady. Losing them pretty much kicked my family in the head. Steve and my mom never recovered."

"Where are they now?" Joe asked softy.

"Mom still lives in Gloucester," she said briefly.

He considered asking more but realized that either it wouldn't matter or that he'd find out later on. He hoped for the latter, if only because it meant some future for the two of them.

"Steve's in jail," she then added, almost as a challenge.

"Ouch," he reacted. "That's tough. I see what you mean — did all that start after the boat went down?"

She looked at him in silence for a couple of seconds, her mug cradled in her lap. "I guess that's right," she then said. "You're used to these sob stories."

She hadn't said it harshly, but he answered with care nevertheless, feeling his way. "They aren't sob stories, but I wish they were more rare."

She nodded silently and took a meditative sip of her tea. "I'm sorry," she murmured afterward.

"For what?"

"That all came out wrong. My dad and José died years ago, when I was still in my teens. It's not like it's fresh — or how Mom and Steve turned out. I don't know why I threw it at you like that."

"No damage done. We've got to get to know each other somehow. It won't always be just right."

"Is it right, though?" she asked. "So far? I don't want to come across as someone I'm not — including how I just showed up out of the blue."

"It feels right to me," he told her simply. "You said from the start where you stood." He laughed before adding, "And that it was basically nowhere in particular. I can live with that. I'm not without my own complications."

Her hand suddenly flew to her forehead. "Jesus," she said, "that's right. How are they doing?"

He smiled back at her, wishing that were the extent of it. "I didn't actually mean that, but they're fine, or at least Mom is, physically, and Leo is still stable."

"But she's taking it hard," Lyn suggested.

"They're very close," he answered.

She got that distant look back into her eyes. "So were Dad and José."

"It was a storm?" he asked after a moment of silence.

"Yeah. I almost wish it was something more dramatic, like in that George Clooney movie. But it was just run-of-the-mill, a carbon copy of all the other storms that kill fishermen year after year."

"Did they ever find them?"

"Not them, not the boat. Nothing."

He stared at the fire for a while, reflecting how much harder that must have made it for the survivors, never knowing for sure what had happened.

"God, what a life," he finally muttered.

"How come neither you nor Leo ever got married?" she asked after a while.

"I did," he answered, his eyes still on the flames. "A long, long time ago. She died of cancer. We never had kids."

"What was her name?"

"Ellen," he said, letting the name drift around inside his head like a childhood prayer, never to be forgotten. "I didn't feel like getting married again after that."

He finally shifted his gaze to her. "What about you and Coryn's dad?"

Lyn half smiled. "Nothing quite so romantic. We were no match made in heaven. Barely lasted three years. He stuck around for Coryn for a while after that; then he lost interest. Neither one of us has heard from him in years."

"You still have his photo."

She glanced across the room. "Yeah, well . . ." She left her thought unspoken.

Joe drained his mug, placed it on the coffee table, and stood up. "Guess I better get going."

She stood also. "You down here because of those two dead men I saw in the paper?"

"Yeah."

"Is it bad?"

He smiled slightly. "Right now it's just

confusing. Might get bad, though. We've only started digging."

She escorted him to the pocket doors and out into the cooler, darkened room beyond. "I open next Friday, if you're going to be around."

He cast her a look and draped his hand on her shoulder, enjoying the warmth of her through her shirt. "I can rarely make promises with my schedule, but I'd love to be there. What time?"

"I open at six, but things probably won't warm up till nine or later."

"You expecting a crowd?"

"God, I hope so. It would be a killer to have nobody show up on opening night. I've been spreading the word the best I know how, but in the end . . ."

He retrieved his coat from where he'd dropped it onto a nearby box, and opened the door to the landing before turning to face her. Now he placed both his hands on her shoulders. "You are so good at what you do, Lyn. I don't think you have anything to worry about."

She took advantage of his gesture to step into his arms and give him a hug. "Thanks, Joe. I hope you can make it, but I'll understand if you can't."

He leaned back enough to look down at

her. Under his open hands, he felt where her ribs came in to join her spine, just above her waist, and briefly imagined what it might be like to have only bare skin to explore.

"I'll try my best," he murmured, and kissed her, feeling her lips softening under his, then parting to let him in for the first time. His hands moved up her back, taking inventory, discovering that she wasn't wearing a brassiere.

He enjoyed her body being pressed up against his, and hoped this would eventually lead to where, he now realized, he was finally ready to go.

"This is nice," he said softly as they broke apart.

"For me, too," she whispered. "Come back whenever you want.

**JMAN:** U hav a bf?
**Mandi144:** no. had 1. loser
**JMAN:** Y?
**Mandi144:** 2 yung
**JMAN:** for wat?
**Mandi144:** wat do u think?
**JMAN:** u r hot
**Mandi144:** I feel hot
**JMAN:** wanna do something about it?
**Mandi144:** duh
**JMAN:** Where in Vermont?
**Mandi144:** Brattleboro. U?
**JMAN:** not far — Erving
**Mandi144:** kool. U sur Im not 2 yung 4 u?
**JMAN:** ur just rite

# Chapter 15

Willy slouched down in his battered pickup truck and pulled his soiled wool cap farther down above his eyes. Across the parking lot, barely visible under the single light over the bar's entrance, the famed E. T. Griffis, a bulky, big-bellied man in insulated overalls and unlaced snowmobile boots, slowly got out of a vehicle much like Willy's and shuffled across the hard-packed snow toward the door, greeting an exiting patron with a joke and a laugh before vanishing inside.

Willy bided his time, waiting for the second man to get into his car and leave, before entering the freezing night air himself and heading for the bar.

It was about what he was expecting — crowded, noisy, none too clean, and filled with the kind of people he'd come to see as extended family. For decor, the walls were lined with hubcaps, and the windowsills with empty bottles. The thin carpeting crunched underfoot with debris. It was the type of bar Willy had called home for years before realizing, at the very last minute — and with Joe's then much resented help — that he was facing an alcoholic's version of suicide.

He selected a spot at the end of the bar, near where E. T. had planted himself between two similar-looking men, who were still greeting him. They weren't effusive in style, reminding Willy of a pair of walruses congenially making room for one of their own, but there was an element of respect, as well. True, E. T. was visibly older than his mates, but, outward appearances notwithstanding, he was being awarded a muted homage for his elevated social status.

Willy wasn't surprised. Before he'd headed up here — he was in the Thetford area's primary workingman's bar — not only had Joe briefed him on E. T.'s history and neighborhood standing, but Willy had spent a few days on his own, soaking up all he could of the man's lore and legend. The resulting portrait had been familiar. In most communities, there was some equivalent of E. T. Griffis — a man who, through hard work, reputation, money, or a combination of all three, had established himself as an icon of some sort. Usually, this archetype was a man with working-class roots, an easy way with his peers, and enough money that when the occasional deserving local hit a rough patch, he or she might be eased through it by a loan or gift that never went advertised but was somehow made known. Willy, born and bred in New York City, where he'd also briefly been a beat cop, had first met these pseudo paternal types as neighborhood gang leaders or mob sub-captains, feeding as much off the social glow as off the fear that had struck its match. There had also been a few that might have been termed non-"connected," truly be-nevolent dons, but they had been harder to find, mostly because of the circles in which Willy had traveled.

Here, in Vermont, this latter, benign phenomenon prevailed, although Willy was still, all these years later, trying to suppress a natural suspicion that the likes of E. T. Griffis were treated as they were because of some hold they had over their cohorts and admirers.

Willy had acquired his cynicism the hard way.

The bartender, a thin, tall man with glasses and a blank expression, placed an unordered glass of what looked like scotch before E. T. and, then, paused in front of Willy.

"What'll it be?"

"Ginger ale."

The barkeep turned away without comment, but Willy caught the glances from those within earshot, including E. T. A stranger didn't come into a bar and order a soft drink unless he was a teetotaler, which wouldn't make much sense, or a cop.

The bartender returned thirty seconds later with a glass, which he placed on a coaster. "Two bucks."

Willy took a few crumpled bills out of his stained barn coat pocket, separated the money from some old receipts, two rubber bands, and an assortment of small bolts and washers, and paid the man.

Willy waited until the barkeep had turned his back, and then reached into another, inner pocket, extracted a small bottle of amber fluid — actually tea — and poured a generous dollop into the drink. The flask bottle vanished as quickly as it had appeared, but not before the same onlookers had seen the quick and practiced gesture. Comforted by both the supposed alcohol's surreptitious appearance and its owner's seeming need to watch his expenses, the others at the bar allowed their suspicions to be lulled.

He left his subtle communication at that, pretending to focus on his drink and the numbing comfort it promised, while in fact eavesdropping on the conversation around E. T.

This wasn't terribly difficult. Both its volume and its content made for easy listening. In essence, it was the same "guy talk" that Willy had listened to and participated in his entire drinking life, dealing with, in no particular order, engines, guns, dogs, women, a touch of politics, and how to use the word "fuck" as many times, and in as many ways, as possible. It was all as soothing, complex, and subtle as it was outwardly moronic, simple-minded, and gross — a distinctly male medley that was routinely dismissed by most women and academics.

And which made Willy, in a moment's distraction, think of Sammie Martens. As his companion of several years by now, she would not have fit into those judgmental categories — a character trait he valued greatly, not that he'd ever admit it. She was as highly tempered, competitive, and driven as he, and as good at holding her ground. This secondhand conversation would have been a natural for her to consider, had she been here, and one she could have joined at any point.

Not that she was hard or vulgar. In fact, it was her contradictory femininity that most attracted him. It remained his particular secret — as was his inability to tell her — that he found her attractive, endearing, funny, smart, and a terrific cop to boot.

None of which had anything to do with where he was at the moment, except that by the time an outburst of laughter snapped him out of his reverie, he realized that he was on his third bogus drink and had been here for over an hour.

He gazed across at his reason for being here, having subconsciously tracked the entire conversation. He'd noticed that Griffis had participated halfheartedly only, as if his appearance had been stimulated less by pleasure and more by social obligation — a by-product of being a local celebrity. Griffis was listening to one last story with a fixed smile on his face, while slowly pulling his wallet from the back pocket of his green work pants. Willy took this as his cue to simply leave some change as a tip and head out the door for the parking lot, the next step of his plan in motion.

Walking seemingly without care, Willy checked the empty lot for any movement, crossed over to E. T.'s parked truck, quickly bent over and stabbed its front tire with a small knife, and then veered left toward his own vehicle, all in one fluid arc.

There, he started the engine with his headlights off and waited, hoping that his reading of the social mores inside was correct, and that Griffis would be allowed to leave alone by his harder-drinking buddies.

All self-confidence aside, Willy was nevertheless relieved when Griffis did emerge on his own and worked his way slowly — even sadly, Willy thought — to his truck.

He pulled himself up behind the steering wheel, oblivious to the leaking tire, turned on the ignition, and lumbered out of the parking lot with Willy in slow and distant pursuit.

Less than two miles up the road, E. T.'s truck eased over to the side, its brake lights signaling Willy's efficiency.

Willy slowly drew abreast, idling in the middle of the deserted road.

"Great night for that," he observed, looking at the tire.

"No shit," Griffis said, already out of his truck and taking in the damage. "Doesn't make sense."

"Never does. You got a spare?"

Griffis sighed. "Of course not."

"Too cold to change it tonight, anyhow,"

270

Willy commented. "Be easier to deal with it in the morning. Wanna lift?"

E. T. straightened slightly and eyed him more carefully, distracted from his tire, taking in this strange person's gaunt, unshaven face, hollow eyes, and that odd, dangling arm he'd noticed earlier inside. "You were in the bar."

"Yeah. Butch Watters," Willy said, adding, "You're E. T. Griffis."

Griffis straightened slightly. "I know you?"

Willy began applying his homework. "Nah. I drove a rig for Bud Wheeler a while back, in Bradford, right before you put him out of business by buying that gravel pit he used. Best thing that ever happened."

"You didn't get along with Bud?"

Willy laughed. "Nobody got along with Bud. I did worse than most."

"What're you doin' down here?"

Willy pulled out his local trump card. "I'm staying with the Mackies on Five Corners Road. Don and I . . ." he paused tellingly before adding, "were in the service together. I'm sort of between things right now."

He made sure to keep his voice flat, unemotional, matching his appearance, as if uninterested in what he was saying. In fact, he was all but holding his breath, hoping the cover Gunther had set up for him with

271

the Mackies would provide the nudge he needed.

It helped, at least, implying that maybe Don and Sue Mackie *were* the neighborhood stalwarts — and old friends — that Joe had made them out to be. Either that, or E. T. had read between the lines of Willy's inference of a war wound.

In any case, the older man seemed to soften his natural suspicion. "I oughta just call one of my guys out to take care of this."

But Willy could tell the fish was almost inside the boat. He let his pickup slip forward a foot. "Suit yourself. It's your butt to freeze off." He then asked a question his research had already answered. "You got a cell phone?"

E. T. shook his head stubbornly. "Nah. Stupid things. Probably wouldn't work anyhow."

"I can take you back to the bar," Willy offered. "Seems kinda dumb, if you're already half home."

That clearly did it. The older man finally nodded.

"Right," he said. "I guess I could do with a ride. Get my kid on this tomorrow."

Willy nodded without comment, feeding into the traditional New England version of a conversation, where the less you say, the less you have to explain later, not to mention that it's nobody's business anyway.

"Where to?" Willy asked, as Griffis climbed on board.

"Right. Up to the top, then left. I'll show you from there."

After he approvingly watched Willy negotiate the steering wheel one-handed, E. T. stared out the front of the old truck's smeared windshield.

"Sue still have that cold?"

"Pneumonia," Willy said shortly to pass the obvious test. He doubted Griffis cared one way or the other about Sue Mackie's health. "Antibiotics. Guess they're working."

"Not from around here."

No shit, Willy felt like saying. "New York."

That brought a brief stare. "City?"

"Yeah. Been bumming around a lot lately, though — like working with Wheeler."

The truck was grinding uphill, lumbering to overtake the feeble reach of its own headlights.

"New York's a long ways."

Christ, Willy thought. This was going to take a while.

"Figured this would be a better place to die," he said, risking a little melodrama in the hopes of speeding things up.

273

From the corner of his eye, he saw Griffis push his lips out thoughtfully.

"The Mackies know about that?" his passenger asked.

"They know what happened," Willy answered obliquely, nevertheless impressed by E. T.'s practical handling of his statement.

E. T. seemed to accept that and didn't speak until the truck had reached the top of the hill, when he repeated, "Left here."

After a few more minutes, during which Willy could almost hear E. T. arguing with himself, he'd been put in such an awkward spot, Willy took him off the hook with "I had a car crash. Fucked myself up, killed my son. I was drunk."

Both the wording and the tone had been carefully chosen — not so terse as to cut off further conversation, not so confessional that it was best not to ask. Just the facts, but sentimentally evocative enough to get the old man thinking of his own losses.

Willy waited patiently, the heavily shadowed snowbanks to both sides of them slipping past like discarded bundles of laundry.

"That's tough," Griffis finally said heavily. "Know the feeling."

Willy didn't doubt it. Not only had he played to E. T.'s recent loss of Andy, but he knew Griffis as a fellow alcoholic — only a nonrecovering one.

"You, too?" he asked open-endedly.

E. T. bit. "Yeah. My youngest. Hung himself."

Willy thought of Sammie again but didn't correct the other man's grammar. Instead, he faked a theatrical double take. "No shit? A woman, right? It usually is."

But he'd gotten as much as he was going to for the moment.

"Nah," E. T. said under his breath, eyes fixed ahead.

Willy let it be. "I can't get it out of my head, especially with this to remind me." He hefted his useless arm's shoulder. "How do you live with it?" he asked after a pause, trying a different tack, knowing he might be pushing too hard. In truth, it wasn't that important to him. He was doing Joe a favor, it got him out of the office and on his own, and he had nothing to lose if he ended up empty-handed. He could take risks.

But, as if E. T. were eavesdropping and not wanting Willy to betray his boss, the older man met him halfway with "I have another son."

Willy nodded. "Guess that would help."

He hoped it didn't, given Joe's suspicions about why Andy had copped to a crime he'd never committed.

E. T.'s monotone response opened that door wider. "Not even close."

Willy smiled slightly in the darkness. I got you now, he thought.

Willy approached the farmhouse on foot, having parked at the bottom of the long driveway. This was a pure impulse, driven solely by nosiness. He could have called Joe or paged him, or even waited until morning to report on his purely social meeting with E. T. He'd just spent an hour with the old man at his home over a nightcap, further ingratiating himself. But he wasn't interested in seeing Joe — it was the serendipitous proximity of the Gunther farm that had become an irresistible attraction. Willy had heard too much about Mom and Leo and the farm and all the rest not to make at least a covert visit. In a way he couldn't — and certainly wouldn't — have verbalized, it had much of the appeal of catching an eminent presence during an unguarded, private moment.

The night was clear, cold, and brittle as ice, the sky overhead jammed with a shotgun blast of sharp-edged stars. Despite his heavy coat, Willy felt chilled to the bone. The snow under his boots squeaked as he walked.

Lights were still on, spilling over the

white-clotted bushes under the building's windows. He could see dark wood-paneled walls of what was either a cluttered living room or a library, with book-lined shelves everywhere. A gray-haired elderly woman in a wheelchair sat surrounded by document-laden tables, a TV on in the background, its luminescence commingling with the flickerings from a glass-doored woodstove.

"It's more comfortable inside."

Willy whipped around, his feet slipping slightly on the packed snow of the driveway, making him flail out with his good arm for balance.

"Fuck!" he exclaimed.

"Of course," said Joe Gunther, standing in the shadows by the side of the house, "you'll have to clean up your language. My mother's old-school."

Willy recovered himself. "What the hell're you doing out here?"

Gunther chuckled. "You're asking me?"

Willy scowled. "I was around. *You* wanted me to hook up with Griffis."

"So I did," Joe acknowledged affably, gesturing with one hand. "Come on in. I'm freezing just looking at you."

Reluctantly, still embarrassed at being caught so flagrantly, Willy moved toward him. "How'd you know I was out here? You taking a leak or something?"

"I saw your headlights," Joe explained. "Plus, I placed a couple of sensors out there a few days ago." He waved into the darkness. "A little paranoia can be a good thing."

He led the way into the farmhouse's kitchen, around to the side, stamping his feet as he entered the small mudroom. "Better take your boots off. You'll catch hell otherwise. You want a pair of slippers, they're around the corner there."

Willy only grudgingly removed his footwear and skipped the slippers. He hated catering to anyone's precious house rules, even if it meant that his feet would remain cool.

They passed on into the house's true warmth after ridding themselves of their coats, entering an atmosphere redolent of a recent warm meal, a wood fire, and the odor of old books. Joe took him into the room he'd seen earlier and introduced him to his mother.

The old lady gave Willy's hand a firm shake and watched him closely.

"You're an interesting man, Mr. Kunkle. I know that already."

Willy snorted. "That's one word."

"A good word, though," she agreed, adding, "complicated."

He laughed, pointing to Joe. "Is that what he says?"

She smiled. "He says less than you might think. But I'm not too bad a judge of character myself. Would you like a seat by the fire? And maybe something warm to drink? You look like you could use both."

Willy hesitated.

"It won't be held against you if you accept, Mr. Kunkle."

He shook his head, caving in and moving toward the stove. "It's Willy, and I give up. I'll pass on the drink, though. Been doing that all night."

"Willy's been pumping E. T. for information," Joe explained, settling into an armchair.

"Really?" his mother commented. "How did you fare with that? He's a tight-lipped old grouch."

"I laid the groundwork," Willy admitted, picking up from his boss that the conversation was unrestricted. "I told him I lost a son and messed up my arm in a car crash — my fault. Drunk driving."

Joe's mother stared at her son. "You really do that sort of thing, don't you? Lie to people."

Joe laughed. "Yup. Sometimes." He asked Willy, "Did you get anywhere with him?"

"I got friendly," Willy answered, still taking in the surroundings, trying to fit Joe in as a child growing up here. "I figured it'd be better to just break the ice. I'll see him in the bar tomorrow. Pick up where I left off."

"How's that going, the bar thing?" Joe asked pointedly, painfully aware of Willy's alcoholism.

His colleague extracted the flask from his inner pocket and waggled it in the air. "I'm getting sick of this, if that's what you're asking."

Joe didn't laugh. "Maybe this angle's not such a great idea."

Willy's face tightened. "Maybe I can handle it."

"Did he talk about Andy at all?" Joe's mother asked, changing the subject.

Willy gave Joe an extra hard look before answering her politely, "Around the edges. What I got is that Dan is a shitty substitute for the apple of his eye. Sorry."

"That's all right," she answered him. "On that score, E. T. is absolutely correct. Dan has never amounted to anything worthwhile."

Willy eyed her appreciatively and paused a moment before asking her, "Did you know Andy? I mean, well enough to help me open

280

the old man up?"

She nodded. "Oh, yes. A very sweet young boy. Loved by his father, hated and envied by that useless brother, and, until he went to prison, slated to take over all of E. T.'s business."

"You know that for sure?"

She smiled again. "It's a very small town, Willy."

He got her point. "Did Dan go after Andy regularly?"

"As a bully?" she asked, before answering herself. "I think that oversimplifies their relationship. Dan was all of that — still is — but Andy also looked up to him because of it, the way an abused child runs to his abuser for protection."

"Which explains why Andy might've taken the rap for Dan," Joe suggested.

"*You* know that," Willy said, "but would E. T.? He's no shrink. What happened to the mother, anyhow?"

"Two different mothers," Joe's mother said, adding, "The first one — hard as nails — left; the second one — a gentle soul — killed herself, which helps to explain the personality differences in the two boys. And you're right about E. T. not being a psychologist. But he does know men. He has to hire them and fire them all the time. I think he was aware of how his two sons interacted. That's why he tried to protect Andy to a certain extent — sent him to a better school, rode him harder to keep him out of trouble. Dan he let grow up on his own — the wild child of legend."

"But the old man wasn't there when the two boys were together in Brattleboro," Joe said. "And that's all it took."

Willy passed his hand through his hair. "Yeah, except, if that's true, why didn't E. T. raise hell when he heard Andy had covered for Dan? He could've reamed Dan a new . . . Anyhow, he could have set it right."

"Dan was facing the Bitch," Joe reminded him.

His mother laughed at Willy's quick glance in her direction, and added, "Dan is his firstborn. That matters to a man like E. T. I remember hearing at the time how everyone was stunned when Andy was sent to prison. That part wasn't supposed to happen."

Joe was nodding. "Meaning, our theory was probably right. The whole family gambled and lost."

Willy considered that for a moment, his eyes drawn to the flames in the woodstove. "That must be tearing the old man up," he finally said. "He threw his baby boy to the wolves for a loser who's using his business to sell drugs."

There was a silence in the room as the resonances of all this settled in, including one note Joe was surprised that Willy then addressed.

"Mrs. Gunther," Willy said, sitting forward to look her in the eyes, "I wanted to say how sorry I was to hear about Leo. How's he doing?"

She allowed for a sad smile and shrugged under the shawl draping her shoulders. "I don't know. No one does. We can only wait, and hope, and see what happens." She paused and then reflected, "Which is more than E. T. has right now, and for that, I guess, we should all be grateful."

**Mandi144:** U cumming up?

**JMAN:** lol — there's a word I lik

**Mandi144:** me 2. My rules, tho

**JMAN:** rules?

**Mandi144:** no cars, no reel names, not my home

**JMAN:** no cars? Y?

**Mandi144:** fantasy I hav. Saw it in a movie. 2 complet strangers. Luvd it

**JMAN:** wat movie?

**Mandi144:** never nu the name. But he came off a bus. They never even talked.

**JMAN:** we cant talk?

**Mandi144:** lol. Sur we can. But everything else stays.

**JMAN:** kool. Where we meet?

**Mandi144:** motel

**JMAN:** I lik it

# CHAPTER 16

Lester Spinney craned over his steering wheel to better appreciate what he was approaching — a huge, modern, spread-out house crowning a slight rise, overlooking the southern narrowing of Lake Champlain below, and New York's Adirondack Mountains off in the distance. The driveway had already prepared him for something — off Route 7 somewhere south of Shelburne Village, it cut through a sheltering copse of trees and extended a quarter mile before revealing this monster house — but he still hadn't expected the total package of the view. The lake looked almost like a planned part of the landscaping.

He pulled to a stop in the immaculately plowed parking area near the four-car garage — he suspected that the driveway was heated — and slowly climbed out from behind the wheel.

The building's front door opened, and a

woman in her mid-twenties greeted him with a wave. "Hi. Are you Agent Spinney?"

"Yes, ma'am."

She burst out laughing. "That would be my mother. I'm Wendy. Come on in. Dad's in the office."

Spinney grabbed hold of a box from his backseat, containing a laptop and the hard drive with all the Steve's Garage data that Rob Barrows had sent him days earlier, and crossed the asphalt to the girl at the door. He stuck out a couple of fingers from under the box in greeting. "Lester's my name," he said. "Glad to meet you."

She carefully squeezed his fingers and pointed down a long hallway. "Wendy Leppman-Gartner, officially, that is. My pleasure. Go right on down there. Last door on the left. It's open. Would you like some coffee or something?"

He looked over his shoulder as he started off. "Nope. Thanks. All set."

Halfway through his journey, the hallway opened up to a truly enormous vaulted room, with wooden beams overhead and a far wall constructed solely of glass. He suddenly felt there was nothing, aside from the building's own heat, separating him from the wide-open spaces he'd admired on the drive in.

He blinked against the glare, noticing a figure shifting on the couch in the middle distance.

"Hello?" he asked cautiously.

"I'm the wife," came the cheerful reply. "Sandy Gartner. Sandra Stillman Gartner, MD, if you're taking notes, which would be a neat trick, given your load. Just keep on going. John's all set up for you."

Nodding at the shape, which by now had assumed an elegant slimness, Lester marched on, disappearing into the dark hallway beyond.

At the end, as promised, he found another room, lower-ceilinged and slightly darkened by broad wooden blinds that still allowed for the view, along with a man — tall, patrician, and lean like his wife — who rose from an imposing cherrywood desk and crossed the floor to relieve him of his box.

"Agent Spinney?" he echoed his daughter, placing the box on a corner of the table and shaking hands. "I'm John Leppman. Delighted to meet you."

Spinney looked around quickly. The wood motif of the blinds was carried throughout the room, including the ceiling and a parquet floor, making the half-hidden wall of glass an anomaly in what would otherwise have been a good Hollywood stand-in for an ancient, manly British lord's study.

"Wow," he said.

His host laughed. "Yeah — a little over the top. Have a seat. I think I heard Wendy offer you a drink already."

"Yes, sir."

"John, please." Leppman indicated a chair next to his own, both of which faced a bank of oversized computer screens, hard drives, printers, and assorted other paraphernalia. Leppman set about removing Lester's paltry equipment and connecting it to his own, speaking as he did so.

"I gather Tim Giordi steered you my way. Terrific guy."

"Actually, it was Chief Giordi and my boss, Joe Gunther," Lester admitted.

"Right. Gunther." Leppman nodded as he worked. "Famous name. Good to work for?"

"The best."

Leppman laughed. "There are no recorders running, Agent Spinney."

Lester protested, "No, no. Really. And call me Lester, or Les. Doesn't matter."

John Leppman quickly finished up and settled into the seat beside Lester's, making the latter feel as though the room should now take flight toward some galaxy far, far away.

In tune with the metaphor, their captain

rapidly began typing commands onto the keyboard before him, still speaking. "I guess you know by now that I do this a lot for the police," he said, his eyes on one of the screens. "Locals, state, even the odd fed, now and then."

"So I heard," Les commented. "I might have guessed, too, from the way your wife and daughter introduced themselves."

Leppman laughed. "Yeah. Cops are in here all the time. This has become a bit of a passion, ever since I realized you guys didn't have the equipment or the money to compete with the bad guys out there."

Lester simply nodded.

"Not to mention," Leppman added with a self-deprecating snort, "that I've even become a member of the family, if you stretch things a little. I'm the new town constable, and a part-time certified police officer." He cast a sideways look at his companion, adding, "Not that it means much around here, and certainly not to you guys, but it's fun and interesting to do."

"Every bit helps," Lester commented supportively, although constables — or, more precisely, the vague controls overseeing them — made him nervous.

Leppman was back running the computer, his fingertips flying across the keys. "Anyhow," he continued, "it was more of a gesture. This is where I can really help, and certainly Tim's been great about using me whenever he can."

"Internet predators mostly, I heard," Lester said conversationally, watching two of the screens before them come alive.

Leppman tilted his head equivocally. "Mostly, just because of the volume involved — I helped identify eight men in three days about six months ago, and that was only in a twenty-five-mile radius around the PD. But I do other things, too. I did a wire transfer embezzlement case not long ago for a bank that didn't want any bad publicity. And there was a drug deal using e-mails that I just helped Tim and his guys with."

Lester nodded toward the screens. "That's what got us going with this. The sheriff's department is running with it, but the guy had pictures of the stuff and everything."

Leppman shrugged. "It's a shame, really. Chat rooms and the Internet are mostly wonderful outlets — real extensions to how people naturally mingle, while easing the potential social burdens of appearance or social awkwardness. People can be so much more honest there, plus, you can get information, products, services, a few laughs, and even find that special someone. Sad that it's mostly the bad aspects that attract all the headlines.

"Still," he added with an incredulous look, "when people do screw up online, they certainly can do it with style. It's amazing to me — everyone thinks they're all alone when they're on the Net. Totally crazy. I tell people it's like taking your clothes off in a crowded room and thinking you're by yourself just because your eyes are shut . . . Okay, here we are."

Spinney sat straighter in his chair, recognizing the contents of the garage's hard drive. He worked with computers routinely, was young enough to consider them a standard piece of office equipment, and played with them with his two kids at home. They were as natural to him as a typewriter was, or used to be, to Joe Gunther — just as Leppman had been saying.

But this was different — a freeze-frame, forensic snapshot of an entire hard drive's moment in time. It was the computer equivalent of stopping a stage production in mid-motion and then wandering among the motionless, mute actors from all angles, studying their positions relative to one another and the audience, including angles that wouldn't be otherwise available.

Of course, instead of actual people and a

stage, here you had screen-mounted data, only some of it readable. But to Spinney the impression was similar, and he sat transfixed as his host moved the cursor among the serried lines of type.

"This is the main chat room," Leppman was saying. "It's going to be a bit messy. The data is overwritten all the time, kind of like conversations are at a noisy dinner party. What did you say the name was we're interested in?"

Lester paused before answering, thinking of all the various labels they'd attached to the man, including the uniquely descriptive Wet Bald Rocky. "Rockwell," he said.

Leppman typed in a search inquiry with that name and hit "Enter." Instantly it reappeared on the screen, floating clearly among the garbled letters.

"Well, he's here, all right," Leppman murmured, still working the cursor. "Let's see if he's chatting with anyone in particular."

He was. Just below his name, they noticed Mandi144, which Leppman copied down on a pad by his hand. Searching for Rockwell a second time, Mandi was once more right beside him. This trend continued several more times.

"So," Leppman announced, "we've got an

ongoing conversation. That's good — means a relationship is building. You already know about Rockwell, right?"

Spinney was caught by surprise. "What? No, I mean, we think he's a dead man we found in Brattleboro, but that's about it. That's why we're doing this."

Leppman took his eyes off the screen to look at him. "Not Mandi? She's probably the one in trouble here."

Lester's brow furrowed. He felt he was missing something. "In trouble? How?"

Leppman looked incredulous. "Child predation. Rockwell's going after her."

"Why do you say that?" Lester asked. "I mean, I know it's all over the place, so I'm not saying you're wrong. But what did you see?"

Leppman hesitated, blinked a couple of times, and returned to studying the screen before admitting in an abashed tone, "Nothing. I guess you're right. Just jumping to conclusions. Let's dig around some more." He stopped again abruptly to ask, "You do have a way to secure subpoenas as we go, right?"

Spinney nodded. "By phone and fax." He pointed to a fax machine in one corner of the large office, adding, "If that's all right."

Leppman nodded enthusiastically. "No,

no. That's great. Done it before with other agencies. I just wanted to make sure. Don't want any loopholes."

Spinney glanced at him covertly, wondering if this civilian's enthusiasm wasn't maybe getting a little too much stoking by association. He made a note to ask Joe later. It was a common enough sight to see consultants become more aggressive bloodhounds than the actual hunters — and pay a psychological price as a result.

Leppman had returned to the hunt. "We've got snippets of exchange here and there — usual introductory chitchat. Bingo," he finally said, straightening. "What did I tell you?" He tapped the screen with his fingertip. "Right there. She says, '14. U?' See that?"

Spinney was already reading the next line. "And Rocky says, '19.' There's a crock."

Leppman was shaking his head, continuing to scroll the lines before them. "I knew it. There's so much of this out there — guys preying on children." He fixed Lester with a determined look. "That's one of the biggest reasons I do this work."

Lester nodded, figuring the man needed some kind of response.

But Leppman wasn't watching. "These are tricky cases to prosecute — you ever done

one before?"

"Nope," Spinney acknowledged.

"The bad guys — or their lawyers, at least — hide behind all sorts of excuses. And they're getting better and better as they get more knowledgeable about this high-tech world. They can make the claim that what the police find on their clients' computers was put there by a cookie or a virus or Christ knows what else, and then they convince the jury of it. I mean, who hasn't gotten spam in their e-mail? Or all those pop-up ads — where do those come from? Juries absolutely believe that complete strangers can put whatever they want onto your computer, no problem. Blame TV for that — there's no technical wizardry that can't be done if you know how to do it, right? Mostly baloney, of course, but these are paranoid times."

He added a few more notes to his pad. "Okay, I got the date and time stamp for this chat. That'll come in handy when you figure out what Rocky was doing when and where. The biggest catch here, though — since you seem a little vague on everyone's identity — will be the chat room profiles of both Mandi and Rockwell. From there, we should be able to get their IP addresses, which will finally — after you get those subpoenas I mentioned — land us the home addresses through their Internet service provider records. Their monthly bills, in other words."

Lester didn't bother pointing out that he actually understood a great deal of this already.

Leppman had by now switched over to another computer, so that he could access the Internet rather than merely study the static contents of the Steve's Garage clone.

"Huh," he grunted. "Rockwell put a block on his chat room profile. No surprise there. Being a kid, though, Mandi was a little less cagey. She lied about her age — you can't log in, supposedly, unless you're over eighteen — but all the rest looks legit."

He scribbled down her particulars onto his pad. "Okay, so far, so good. She even gave us an address, which is unusual — the standard profile is hobbies, age, gender, general location, and the rest. I guess Mandi's still used to filling out forms correctly. Great for us."

He sat back and rested his hands for a moment, not bothering to turn his head as he spoke. "One last step before we get legal — this is just something I've learned through habit. So far, all this has been pretty much public domain information — something anyone can do with a computer and a connection. I do one more thing along similar lines: I check that address I just got against one of the mapping programs, just to make sure it's not in the middle of the Hudson River, or Lake Champlain, or Christ knows where."

He put his hands back over the keyboard and began typing. Lester watched as the screen did its version of scratching its head — portrayed by a small ticking-clock icon — before finally flashing, "Address not found."

Leppman tried a couple of variations, equally unsuccessfully, and then sat back in his chair again. "Nothing. Well, so much for good little Mandi. I guess she saw me coming after all."

Lester watched his profile, again caught by the man's level of engagement. "No sweat," he said. "I'll get on those subpoenas."

**JMAN:** U there?

**JMAN:** Mandi144. U there?

**Mandi144:** hey

**JMAN:** thot I got the wrong time

**Mandi144:** nop. Probs w/ my mom

**JMAN:** wat?

**Mandi144:** she got fired. At home a lot

**JMAN:** bummer

**Mandi144:** ur telling me. R plans r messed up now

**JMAN:** I cant cum up?

**Mandi144:** Ill tell u when

# CHAPTER 17

"Your mom tells me you're a police officer."

Joe looked up from the coffee machine, where he'd been hoping the spigot over his paper cup wouldn't either miss or overflow. He was so used to everyone knowing what he did for a living — and had been, it felt, for two lifetimes — that he was almost startled at the question.

Karl Weisenbeck, Leo's doctor, was standing next to him with a dollar in his hand.

"Hi, Doc. Yeah. Vermont Bureau of Investigation."

Weisenbeck nodded a couple of times, as if trying to remember the name of a song. "Sounds important."

Joe laughed as he watched the cup filling, successfully so far. "Not if you're in law enforcement. Most cops assume we exist only to steal all the credit and headlines they have coming, not to mention the grant money."

"Do you?"

Joe retrieved his cup and stood back to give Weisenbeck a shot at his own luck. The condition of the floor at the foot of the machine suggested he had a fifty-fifty chance. He enjoyed the man's directness — had from the day they first met.

"Try not to. How's Leo doing? I mean really?"

Now it was Weisenbeck's turn to look up inquiringly. "You think I've been bullshitting you?"

"Not one bit. That's why I'm asking."

The doctor returned to monitoring his progress, even delicately placing his fingers around the cup so he'd be in position to tear it away at the right moment. A veteran.

They both waited until that time when, indeed, he had to extract prematurely and allow the spigot to piddle a little extra coffee into the miniature catch basin, from where it dribbled onto the floor. Weisenbeck shook his head with disgust and began walking with Joe down the hallway toward the ICU.

"He's no worse, which, given what he's facing, is saying a lot. From what we can tell, he's suffered no additional setbacks, which means that time is now playing to our advantage."

"Because of the bone knitting?"

"Right. Once the flail chest is behind him and he can breathe entirely on his own, my suspicion is that we'll see improvement."

"But you did say, 'From what we can tell.' "

Weisenbeck stopped walking to look at Joe straight-on. "Mr. Gunther, as I told your mother earlier, there's a lot we don't know. Sometimes, it can be like driving in winter with the windows fogged up. You trust to instinct, luck, your knowledge of the road, all your other senses, and anything else you can find. In the end, you can usually figure out why you failed — ice on the pavement, a deer jumping out in front of you, a mechanical failure. But only rarely can you do the same with success. Things often work out simply because it wasn't your time for them not to."

Oddly, Joe thought, he found those words comforting despite their absence of medical vocabulary or cant, perhaps because they so eloquently applied to life in general.

Weisenbeck's pager went off. He glanced at it briefly and began making apologies before Joe cut him off with "Believe me, Doc, I know what it's like. Thanks for your time," and headed down the hallway on his own as the doctor disappeared into a nearby

301

stairwell.

In the ICU waiting room, as if in counter-point to the conversation he'd just left, he walked in on Gail Zigman and his mother, sitting side by side near the window over-looking the euphemistically called "floor," their heads together in a deep discussion.

They both looked up as he entered, Gail rising.

"Hey, guys," he said, smiling. "Plotting an overthrow?"

Gail gave him a brief hug as he drew near to kiss his mother, who admitted, "Good Lord, no. We were comparing recipes."

"God, don't tell him," Gail protested. "He always hated my cooking."

"I did not," he exclaimed. "I just could never tell what it was." He glanced at his mom. "Tofu-no-fish? Instead of old-fashioned tuna? I mean, give me a break."

"That's an extreme example," Gail said.

"Tofu instead of tuna?" their elderly spectator spoke up, her interest sharpened. "That sounds wonderful. You spread it on bread?"

Joe left them to exchange details and ap-proached the window, where he watched nurses and technicians in gowns and masks working their way among their swathed, recumbent, immobile charges. It was both futuristic fantasy and lunatic ant farm, where those bedded in the white pods were tended and catered to for reasons far out-reaching their apparent usefulness.

Of course, one of those pods had a very clear use to him personally, and he found himself staring at Leo's supine shape with the intensity of an aspiring mentalist, wishing he could transfer some of his own life force across the sterile space between them.

"What're you thinking?" Gail's voice said quietly from beside him.

He turned to look at her, surprised by her presence. A glance over his shoulder revealed his mother's absence from the room, as well as how deeply in thought he must have fallen.

"Bathroom trip," Gail explained.

He returned to his viewing and answered her question. "I was trying to figure out how to revive him using ESP, or maybe a ray gun."

"It's weird seeing him like that," she said. "A guy so famous for his energy. You learn anything new? I heard you talking with Weisenbeck outside."

"No," he answered simply. He considered sharing some of the thoughts he'd enter-tained as a result, but held back, realizing that he didn't have that kind of bond with her anymore — a continuing revelation, which jarred him still, and which, he knew, was inhibiting his taking any great steps forward with Lyn. He and Gail were friends now — old and deeply intertangled friends, to be sure. But they weren't what they'd once been, and he now found a governor restricting the things that he'd never held from her in the past.

As if to cover his own embarrassment, he added, "It boiled down to no news being good news."

"No news is becoming agony, if you ask me," she said softly. She then checked her watch and added, "I better get going."

They both turned as the door opened and his mother rolled in. Gail crossed to her and made her farewell, giving Joe another brief hug, and was gone before they knew it.

And before she noticed that she'd left her cell phone behind.

Joe grabbed it and jogged for the elevator banks, finding nobody there. He mimicked Weisenbeck earlier and headed for the stairs, taking two steps at a time and hoping the elevator had lots of stops.

When he reached the lobby, he saw her in the distance, swinging through the bank of doors to the driveway outside. He broke into a jog that wouldn't also alarm the small army of people milling around him, and reached the doors in under a minute.

From there, he saw her approached by the well-dressed driver of a fancy waiting car, its exhaust plume thick in the cold air, and greeted with a hug and an intimate, almost lingering kiss.

He stopped dead in his tracks, assessing what to do.

In his training as a cop, public and personal safety were the priorities, followed by tactical considerations — level of threat, availability and nature of countermeasures, and on down the line.

Here there was none of that. The adrenaline rush was similar, but the situation was absurdly benign. He stood rooted where he stood, people jostling him to use the doors before him, and tried to unscramble his synapses.

Fortunately, or perhaps not, Gail ended his dilemma by glancing over her shoulder as she broke away from the embrace and began circling the front of the car.

She, too, froze in place, transparently nonplussed.

Lamely he held up the cell phone he still clutched in his hand, and pushed the door open before him, hoping his expression was within a mile of normal.

The car's owner, one foot already inside his vehicle, was arrested by Gail's abrupt immobility and glanced in Joe's direction, giving the latter more purpose.

This was perfectly reasonable, Joe was thinking as he approached — reasonable and logical. Wasn't he seeing someone else? Hadn't he and Gail both moved on?

He smiled as he reached them. "Can't live long without this, I bet," he told her, sticking out his right hand to the man and adding, "Hi. Joe Gunther. Glad to meet you."

Gail had, by now, returned to that side of the car, a black BMW, her face red and pinched as if from a steady blast of cold air. "This is Francis Martin, Joe. He works with Martin, Clarkson, Bryan."

Joe laughed. "Top of the masthead. Good going."

Martin smiled back, his eyes betraying that he'd figured out what was going on. "Not that tough when you created the company. I'll never have a reputation like yours — or deserve it."

Joe gave his hand a last squeeze and dropped it. "I guess that depends on the reputation and who you're hearing it from."

Martin nodded. "Good one. You'd make a good lawyer. I promise, I've only heard the best." Here, he glanced at Gail, who was standing quietly, her eyes blank, fingering her cell phone.

"You all set?" he asked her. "We'll have to beat feet to make that meeting."

Nicely done, Joe thought, and stepped back. "Have a safe trip," he said, waving to them both, and added to her, "I'll let you know if anything changes, one way or the other."

He stayed standing there, the polite host after the party, until they'd both settled in, slammed their doors, and the dapper Francis Martin had driven halfway down the drive. Gail's pale face was still visible through the back window as Joe finally turned on his heel and went back inside, his heart beating somewhere in between relief and sorrow.

Sammie Martens parked her car on the street, across from the bus depot parking lot on Liberty Street, and paused before getting out, surveying the surrounding bleakness. Springfield, Massachusetts, was huge in comparison to anything in Vermont, or, as most Vermonters saw it, huge and crowded and blighted and depressing. Sammie had personal knowledge of the social troubles this area visited upon her state. She'd gone undercover in nearby Holyoke for a while in a vain attempt to stifle some of the drug flow heading north.

Of course, she knew that her prejudice was unfair. Springfield was an oversize urban center, no more or less saddled with its ills than most places of its kind. And no bus terminal that she'd known was located in a town's upscale section. This one was wedged against two interstate overpasses, surrounded by industrial-style low buildings and adjacent to the train terminal, which looked as though it dated back to when robber barons called the shots.

Barely visible in the gray, flat daylight, a strung-up sign of extinguished lightbulbs was attached to the low, arching stone overpass that carried the railroad tracks between the depot and the rest of the city, to the south. The sign spelled out, "City of Bright Lights."

Sam popped open her door and got out into the kind of harsh cold that only miles of concrete can exude, the wind whipping between the nearby buildings and shredding the warm cocoon around her. She stood next to the car, getting her bearings and noticing the contrast between the bland, towering, modern Mass Mutual building in the distance, and the ornate, Italianate campanile beside city hall behind it — the only sign of grace within sight. Her contact had told her, on the phone, to park where she had and that everything else would become obvious.

It did. She saw, over the tops of a row of salt-streaked, dirty parked cars, a clearly marked police van, the glimmer of some yellow tape, and several cold human shapes standing around, most nursing coffee cups. She crossed the street and walked down the length of cars to join them.

As she drew near, a tall, white-haired, red-faced man in a down jacket that made him look like a tire company mascot broke away from the small group and approached her.

"Agent Martens?" he asked. "Steve Wilson, Springfield PD."

She nodded in greeting, not bothering to shake, with everyone wearing gloves. "How'd you know?"

A wide smile broke his craggy face. She imagined he was old-school — hard at work, hard at play, and no stranger to the bottle. Some stereotypes existed for a reason. "You walk like a cop."

That made her smile. A cop was all she'd ever wanted to be. She pointed to a small, dark sedan parked almost nose to nose with the police van and surrounded by the yellow tape. "Don't tell me — that's the car, right?"

He laughed. "I wish I could tell you we'd wrapped the wrong one on purpose, but that's it, all right. Good detective work."

Several of Wilson's companions chuckled in the background, eavesdropping and, she knew, checking her out. Not that she minded especially. Guys she could handle. Women cops were tougher to figure out.

She stepped up to the car's hood and looked at the vehicle straight on — a dark blue Ford Escort, several years old, but in pretty good shape. A middle-class car, economical and dependable. Its inspection sticker was up to date and issued from Connecticut.

"You run the registration yet?" she asked.

Wilson nodded. "Frederick Nashman. A couple of old moving violations, nothing big. That's assuming the car wasn't stolen to get it here."

She looked at him.

"It's not reported stolen. I'm just saying . . ."

"Got ya." Sam went back to studying the car, slowly walking around it, her hands in her coat pockets. "Anybody notice it out here before we raised the alarm?"

Wilson was walking with her. "Nah.

Would've happened eventually, but they can be parked out here a long time."

She finished her tour and straightened to give him an eye-to-eye, as best their relative heights allowed. "This when you tell me you've gone through it all already and have everything bagged and tagged in the back of the van?"

His eyes and eyebrows expressed theatrical shock, but his laugh gave him away. "It did cross our minds, what with the weather, but given the respect we have for . . . What do you call yourselves again?"

She gave him a friendly sneer. "Cute. You got the paperwork at least?"

He nodded, adding, "And we popped the lock, just to make sure we wouldn't be screwed after you got here. Thing opened like a soda can. No one's been inside yet, though."

Sam nodded. "That was nice — I do appreciate it."

"No sweat," he said, liking her more and more as this went on. He made a gesture to the people behind them before saying, "And now that you are here, we got a little extra comfort to throw you."

She looked over at the van as the others swung open its rear doors and pulled out a long, bulky, brightly colored tarp with bundled aluminum tubing, a generator, and an oversize space heater. She recognized the package immediately and smiled at her host. "A heated tent. Sweet."

Steve Wilson bowed. "We try."

Some 250 miles to the south, following a seven-hour drive from Vermont, a stiff and tired Lester Spinney crossed a sidewalk in Ardmore, Pennsylvania, near Philadelphia, and entered the Lower Merion Police Department, where he'd been told to check in on arrival.

"Help you?" the man behind the bulletproof glass asked.

Les pulled out his badge and held it against the window. "I'm here to see Detective Cavallaro. Lester Spinney from Vermont."

He studied the man's face, expecting the usual Vermont-directed one-liners, but got nothing for his effort. The dispatcher merely glanced at the ID, picked up a phone, and said over the tinny loudspeaker between them, "Have a seat."

Five minutes later, a tall woman with short-cropped hair stepped into the lobby, smiling. "Agent Spinney? Detective Cavallaro. Call me Glenda. You have a good trip?"

He shook her hand. "Lester — Les is okay,

too. And the trip was fine. More people than I've seen in a while, though."

She looked at him quizzically. "Where? On the road?"

"The road, the streets, the towns, even the sidewalk outside. We only have about half a million in Vermont, and a third of them are clustered around one town."

She visibly had no appreciation for what he was saying. "Huh," she said. "Interesting. I was born and brought up around here. Never saw it as crowded. New York — *that's* bad. Most of what you drove through is tied into there, one way or the other."

Spinney chose to drop it. No one outside Vermont could be expected to understand a setting where starlit skies, complete silence, and empty downtown streets at four in the morning were the norm. Except maybe far out west. He'd heard that even a Vermonter could get lonely in Wyoming.

"You want to find a motel and start on this tomorrow morning?" Cavallaro was asking him.

Lester checked his watch. It was five o'clock. "Seems a little early," he murmured.

"Not a problem," she said immediately, with enough enthusiasm that he took her word for it. "Let me get my coat and bag and we'll head out."

It was barely a minute before she re-appeared.

"I can't believe they didn't put you on a plane instead of making you drive down," she said, slipping into her coat as they crossed the lobby.

"We don't have much of a budget," he admitted.

"Really?" She looked at him. "The Vermont Bureau of Investigation? Sounds rich enough."

"Yeah — well, we're kind of new. Still muscling our way into the pack."

She turned right out of the door and headed for a parking lot to the side of the building. "Where did you work before?"

"State police."

"No kidding? Didn't like them?"

"Loved them. But I thought I was running out of options. Numbers again."

She pulled keys from her pocket and aimed toward what was clearly an unmarked cruiser — the kind of thing street kids love to decorate with "Narc," written on the dusty side panels.

"How so?" she asked.

"They hover around three hundred and fifty people in uniform, depending on the year and the budget," he told her. "Upward mobility gets tight. When the Bureau came up, it looked more interesting, less bureaucratic, and now I'm working with the field force commander. Plus, I keep all my benefits and retirement."

She was already laughing. "Three fifty? We've got almost half that in this department alone."

She unlocked the doors and they both got in, their bodies jarred by the frozen hardness of the seats. Apparently, the car hadn't been out all day.

She started it up as he changed the subject. "You said on the phone that the IP address I gave you for Mr. Rockwell was an Internet café. You ever have any problems with them before?"

Glenda Cavallaro shook her head. "Nope. And I checked every database we have. Nothing. Just for kicks, I also looked up N. Rockwell. There're more than a few with that name, but nothing for any cyber crime or sex stuff. That's what you're looking for, right? Child predator shit?"

"We think so," Spinney answered cautiously, looking out the side window as they pulled into traffic and headed west along Lancaster Avenue.

He watched the buildings slide by, mostly brick clad and older, few above a couple of stories tall. Soon, on the left, the view opened up, and a large, deep expanse of cold-bitten lawn appeared, with a frozen pool in the middle and a row of imposing buildings skirting its borders.

"Haverford College," Cavallaro explained. "Pretty good place."

He'd noticed it earlier, having come this way to reach the police department from the interstate. He'd also gone by both Villanova University and the village of Bryn Mawr, home to that college, where he'd also noticed dealerships for Ferrari, Hummer, and Maserati. Despite the main drag's almost pedestrian, weathered brick appearance, there was obviously serious money lurking just beyond sight, here and there.

Cavallaro snapped him from his reverie. "The café is up ahead." She pulled into a shopping area parking lot and killed the engine, pointing through the windshield. "Over there."

They got out and crossed the asphalt to the place she'd indicated, its windows fogged by moist heat and the presence of a sizable crowd. Spinney suddenly realized that coming at this time of the early evening was probably not a good idea. His companion, however, didn't seem fazed.

She walked up to the counter and asked

to see the manager, showing just a glimpse of her shield. As they waited, Les took in their surroundings — a sprinkling of small tables, each adorned with a computer, catered to by a counter stuffed with coffee choices and sweet comestibles. Adrenaline times three, he thought, watching the largely young crowd, the majority of them men, quietly hunched over their keyboards. The room was filled with the tinny clatter of fingertips stuttering across plastic keys.

"May I help you?" a smooth voice said from behind him. "I'm the manager, Bruce Fellini."

Cavallaro was already staring at the short, goateed man in a black turtleneck who'd appeared from the back room. She displayed her shield again, along with a folded piece of paper. "I'm Detective Cavallaro of the Lower Merion PD. This is Agent Spinney of the VBI, and this" — she waved the document — "is a subpoena for the contents of one of your computers. We have reason to believe that one of your customers was using your place to sexually pursue underage girls."

She placed the subpoena in front of him. Fellini looked down at it, otherwise not moving.

"How's this work?" he finally asked. "I've

never been involved in something like this before."

Both cops looked at him carefully, their instincts immediately sharpened by the line.

Spinney removed another piece of paper from his pocket before slipping out of his coat. It was hot to stifling for him in here, although he noticed that Cavallaro hadn't even unbuttoned hers yet. Cultural differences, once more.

He laid the sheet beside the subpoena and placed his finger on the line that John Leppman had highlighted in yellow, back in Vermont. "This is the computer's address, along with the time and date it was being used."

Fellini studied the line of type briefly. "Officers, I'd be happy to help. I'll show you the computer and do whatever else you'd like me to, but I gotta warn you: You're not going to find anything. Our computers get used all the time, by dozens of people a day, and that's day after day. You might get a time-date stamp somewhere from the guy you're after — I'm not saying that." He tapped the sheet of paper with his finger. "But you got that already. Otherwise, that computer's going to be blank, or covered with gibberish. We set the temp files to be overwritten immediately, and I also

318

happen to know that the settings on that particular instant-messaging program are defaulted to wipe the record clean whenever the user exits the program. It's what we do to keep clutter to a minimum."

"So you don't want us to tear into the computer?" Cavallaro asked.

Bruce Fellini held up both his hands in surrender. "Hey, I'll even let you take the whole thing out of here, for as long as you want, if you give me some paperwork. We got insurance for things like this. I was just warning you, is all."

Spinney had lost interest in the conversation a few sentences ago and was back to surveying the room. Now he returned to the manager and asked him, "Your security camera working?"

Fellini stared at him for a blank second before his brain kicked in. "Oh, yeah. Sure."

Lester pulled out the photograph of Rockwell that they'd circulated to the newspaper, and displayed it. "This is the guy we think used your computer. He look familiar?"

The small man shrugged. "Vaguely, I guess."

"How far back do you keep the security tapes?" Lester asked next.

This time Fellini smiled, pointing to the date on Spinney's printout. "Long enough."

# CHAPTER 18

"Butch — hand me another beer."

Willy reached over the side of his bedraggled armchair, flipped open the lid of the cooler parked on the floor, and fished around in the cold ice slurry for a can, which he then handed the older man.

E. T. took it from him, peeled back the tab with a snap, and brought it to his lips in one smooth, well-practiced gesture. He didn't put it down until it was half empty. On the wooden floor by his feet, scattered among other discarded trash, were the rattling remains of most of a twelve-pack.

They'd settled on the unfinished but enclosed back porch of E. T.'s shambles of a house, dressed in coats, accompanied by two glowing parabolic space heaters and an old sleeping dog of confused lineage.

They were surrounded by frosted glass on three sides and perched on the edge of an enormous gravel pit that fell away from the rear of the building like a meteor crater, revealing a snow-covered assortment of piled stones, sand, and rock, and a haphazardly parked collection of ten-wheelers, a stone crusher, and two enormous backhoes. Willy understood that this was E. T.'s working-class version of a landed lord taking some time to enjoy a small drink while surveying his hard-won worldly assets. Had the setting been conventionally staged, and the old man's son here instead of an undercover cop pretending to be a newfound friend, the next line would have been a variation on "In a few years, my boy, all this will be yours."

But E. T. Griffis was not a man of conventional trappings. True to his roots, and regardless of his accumulated wealth, he was happiest — or perhaps least unhappy — when in proximity to the world that had given him birth: trucks, cheap beer, and the fruits of hard labor. New and shiny things, not to mention the commercial world that hawked them from all sides, were not for him, including a new roof on his house, or a truck built in the current decade, or any clothing from somewhere other than Goodwill. Money had become a way to keep score or, perhaps, to exact revenge on ancient devils Willy knew nothing about, but it was not to be used on glitzy frivolities — like insulation or central heating. Or cell phones.

Willy had heard that E. T.'s first and only legal wife had walked out on him so long ago, few people recalled what she looked like. Now that he'd become the man's newest drinking buddy — following a week of nightly encounters at the bar — and been allowed into the sanctum sanctorum of his home, he didn't doubt it.

Which wasn't to say that he didn't like the guy. For all his renowned faults as a father and husband, E. T. was the proverbial salt of the earth — honest, practical, hardworking, and, at long last, much to Willy's present benefit, becoming sentimentally philosophical.

"So, anyhow," he was saying. "Dan's mother wasn't Andy's, and Andy's mother and me weren't ever legal. Not that it mattered. She had the first one beat all to hell, and that was everybody's opinion, including Dan's."

"What happened to her?" Willy asked, sipping from his hip bottle of amber fluid. This was the third time they'd ended up here to share an afternoon drink — presumably in preparation for the standard evening encounters — but the first that he'd gotten

E. T. to open up personally. And, as was so common with otherwise taciturn people, it seemed to Willy that he would never shut up.

"She died," he said simply, taking another deep swallow.

"Must've been hard on the boys."

"Hard on Andy. He was like her. Dan didn't give a shit. He's like the first one."

Joe's mother had described that death as a suicide. Willy now wondered if even the method had been similar for mother and son. He wasn't about to ask E. T., but he made a note to check into it.

Given the broad nature of Joe's assignment to him, Willy was in the comfortable position of considering everything E. T. said to be of potential value. After all, from Andy's fate in prison to Dan's side business in drugs, to the car crash that had hospitalized Joe's family, even to the true story about why Andy had pleaded guilty in the first place, Willy and his colleagues had nothing but unanswered questions.

"How long ago was that?" he asked.

"Ten years."

"That when Dan started acting up?"

E. T. paused then, staring out at how the ebbing light was casting his pit into shadow, almost like a premonition.

"Nah, Dan was always a bad kid," he said darkly. "Annie's death only took off the last set of brakes. What was yours named?" he asked suddenly.

Willy hesitated, at first wondering what he meant, before remembering his own cover story. He then couldn't resist answering, "Joe."

"Huh," his companion grunted.

Willy then realized the fringe benefit of his private joke.

"That mean something?"

"Just a coincidence. I got a guy named Joe causing me problems."

Willy pushed his advantage, trusting E. T.'s inebriation to have dulled his perceptiveness. "Gunther? The Mackies were telling me there was bad blood there. He's a cop, right? VSP or something?"

"Yeah — something. Not state police. The new one. Bureau of something. Anyhow, a pain in the ass."

"I hate cops," Willy said. "He after you for the business? Is he like the Better Business Bureau?"

E. T. looked at him with widened eyes. "Better Business Bureau? Jesus Fuck, Butch. You don't get out much, do you? The Better Business Bureau is a bunch of limp dicks. They don't have cops. I don't know what this prick is after. He's just chewin' on me, is all — fucking dog with a bone."

Willy took another pull on his bottle of tea, wincing at its bitter taste. E. T.'s response didn't imply that Joe was much more than a generalized pest. But if Willy kept probing, even Griffis was likely to notice. He decided not to respond, but to do some of his own silent gazing out the window, not that the sunset was allowing for much of a view anymore.

"He's the one who got Andy in trouble," Griffis finally said in a low voice, having obviously been mulling over the subject for the past couple of minutes.

"Andy got in trouble?" Willy asked. "I thought he was your good kid."

"He is," E. T. answered angrily, throwing his empty can into a corner. "Was," he added a moment later. "Give me another beer."

Willy complied without comment.

"Gunther arrested him on a bullshit charge a few years back. Got him sent to prison. That's why he killed himself."

"I thought you said it was a woman," Willy protested.

"You said that," E. T. countered, knocking off another half can.

"What kind of charge gets you to jail first

time out?" Willy asked. "I thought Vermont was super soft there — never putting anybody behind bars."

"You thought wrong," Griffis replied.

Willy was starting to worry how much he should pursue this line of inquiry. He'd gotten a fair amount so far. But that was part of the game — how much to pay out versus how much to reel in.

He went for one more try and then figured he'd give it a rest. "I did time once," he said. "Wasn't too bad. Three hots and a cot, like they say. Mostly boring. Your kid must've been the sensitive type."

That hit a chord. E. T. swung on him in a rage, spilling beer on his pants. "What the fuck you know about it? Three hots and a cot? Like it was some fucking summer camp?" Griffis lurched to his feet and half fell toward Willy, trying to take a swing at him, the forgotten can still in his hand. "He was fucking raped, you asshole."

Willy easily swiped away the punch with his good hand, which threw E. T. off balance and sent him stumbling straight into Willy's lap, breaking the arm of his chair. They collapsed into a pile on the floor.

"Get off me, you son of a bitch!" E. T. yelled, thrashing around.

Willy kept his composure, speaking clearly

326

but quietly into the other man's ear, "You're on top of me, E. T. Take a breath. I didn't mean any harm. I didn't know." He repeated slowly, "I did not know."

Griffis settled down, still lying across Willy like a dropped bear, staring at the ceiling with a wondering expression. "Shit," he finally muttered. "I know that."

Willy planted his hand against E. T.'s back and pushed him to an upright position, rising behind him. He decided to go for broke then and there, figuring the opportunity would never come up again.

"Who did it, E. T.?" he asked softly. "Who really killed your son?"

There was no response at first. Griffis just sat there, his legs splayed, his hands in his lap, staring at the floor. For a split second, Willy wondered if he might not have passed out, or whether he was even breathing.

But E. T. proved him wrong with two words. "Wayne Nugent," he said.

The name Sam hadn't been able to uncover. Griffis couldn't see the smile on Willy's face. Well, that was at least one puzzle solved.

In Ardmore, Pennsylvania, and outside Waterbury, Connecticut, Lester and Sammie, respectively, in the company of their host police agencies, conducted separate searches of the homes of the two men they'd once referred to as Wet Bald Rocky and Dry Hairy Fred.

Lester had gotten lucky with the videotape in the Ardmore Internet café. On film, the same man in the postmortem mug shots that Spinney was carrying around was seen sitting at the right computer and at the same time and date that John Leppman had dug up. Bruce Fellini, the café manager, still didn't know the man by name, but he did recognize the teenager at the neighboring console. That boy, a regular, was then located and told Lester that the person he was after was Norman Metz. With Detective Cavallaro's help, the last step to finding Metz's address — a single room in a house he shared with others in a run-down neighborhood — had been easy.

For Sam, the journey had been farther but easier still. The car abandoned at the Springfield bus depot had been eloquence itself, containing all the myriad details of its owner's vital records and habits, from his address to his birthdate, to his taste in music and candy. It had also confirmed the name that Detective Wilson had found through its registration — Frederick Nashman — whose identity was confirmed photographically by comparing Sam's mug shot with Connecticut DMV computer records.

Unlike where Lester was searching in Ardmore, however, Nashman's home outside Waterbury was a sedate, middle-class two-story house. Unfortunately for Sam, it also came equipped with a wife and teenage child.

Joe sat on what Lyn and he now viewed as his traditional perch, established when they'd first met in Gloucester — at the end of the bar, with his shoulder against the side wall and his hand around a Coke. He watched her traveling along the line of noisy, appreciative drinkers, chatting, laughing, making small talk and change as she served drinks, waved away compliments, and kept an air traffic controller's eye roaming across the room. He remembered what she'd told him then, after he'd plied her with a milkshake and a lobster roll. She'd said that the bar — the actual physical object — was like a barrier that allowed her access to the public while protecting her from it, thereby becoming the perfect platform for a shy person who longed for company. It had been a comment both intriguing and startling, since he'd always believed — as he figured most people did — that anyone in this business had to be a glutton for bad jokes, other people's miseries, and attention in general.

It was Friday night and the place was packed — a harbinger, he hoped, of her business prescience. He knew that many were here out of curiosity, of course. She'd even warned him about that. Not to mention the offer of opening night discount beer.

Bars weren't really his preference. He spent most days out in the public eye. Rest and relaxation for him came in isolation, most happily in the woodworking shop that he'd attached to his house on Green Street. He'd supplied almost everyone he knew with lazy Susans, birdhouses, and magazine racks as a result, and himself with some substantial furniture.

But he recognized the value of bars, and their historical place, as among the earliest of democratic gathering places. Vermont's own independence, it could be argued, found birth in Bennington's Catamount Tavern, where the likes of Ethan Allen — an archetypal barroom bully — took time off from being a lout to act like a leader.

Joe's gaze swept across the crowd. There were Allens aplenty here tonight, if appearances were telling, from the brooders to the boisterous. But, in Lyn's favor, they remained a minority, vastly outnumbered by those simply seeking a good time and companionship.

If she was able to maintain the present mood and clientele, her prospects looked good.

"How's it going, boss?" Sam asked, having appeared at his shoulder.

Joe waved at the activity before them. "See for yourself. A runaway success. You come home with the bacon?"

But she wouldn't be so easily derailed. "Dispatch said I'd find you here, with what they called your 'person of interest.'"

He smiled, shaking his head. "That sounds like Maxine. God, what a small town."

"So, where is she?"

Joe finally turned in his seat to look at her. "You that much out of the loop?"

Sam punched him gently in the shoulder. "Come on, boss."

Joe faced forward again and gestured to Lyn, who'd been subtly keeping tabs on him.

She came down the length of the bar with a smile.

"Lyn Silva," he said as she drew near, "this is Sam Martens, my right hand. You don't call her Samantha, and she won't call you Evelyn."

The two women exchanged greetings, laughing at the introduction and eyeing each other carefully.

"I have to go," Joe told Lyn. "Duty calls. Congratulations again on making the deadline."

Lyn leaned over the bar and kissed him on the cheek, which he felt was as much for Sam as for him. There were a couple of moans and whistles from nearby customers.

"Thanks for coming, Joe. If you're still up at two, come back."

"I will," he said, sliding off his stool and heading toward the door with Sam.

"Dishy," she said, grabbing the knob and letting in a blast of cold air.

*"Dishy?"* he asked, incredulous.

# CHAPTER 19

Lester Spinney was already at the office, writing his report about the Pennsylvania trip on his computer. It was late, after nine.

He looked over his shoulder as Joe and Sam entered, and raised his eyebrows at Sam. "So, what does she look like?"

"Enough," Joe told him. "Her name is Lyn Silva. She just opened up the new bar on Elliot, and we're just friends." He circled his desk and dropped his coat across the back of his chair, sitting down heavily before adding, "Christ. I can't believe I just said that."

"It's okay, boss," Lester said. "Rumor has it that's a nice way to start a relationship. Good going."

"Thanks," Joe said, hoping to end the conversation. "What did you both find out?"

Fitting her character, Sam began first, pacing the small office as she spoke off the cuff. "Red Fred, Ready Freddy, or R. Frederick, as he registered at the motel, turns out to have been Frederick Nashman, of greater Waterbury, Connecticut. Middle-class, married with a kid, worked at an insurance office. He had no record to speak of, was unremarkable at work, according to his boss, and, from what I could get out of the wife, was about the same at home. He bowled, played cards with the boys every Saturday night at the Elks, took the family out to the movies about twice a month, and — again per the wife — spent a lot of time online, alone, in his office. He told her he had an eBay business going on the side to benefit the Legion, which wasn't true when I checked it out. What I found after we got past the locks on his desk and filing cabinet . . ."

She stopped and looked pointedly at Gunther, adding, "Legally — don't worry. The locals were great. I got names and numbers for your Christmas card list. Anyhow, what I found was a huge collection of child porn — pictures, articles, X-rated stories, DVDs, videotapes. Some of it printed or downloaded off the Web, some of it ordered through various sites. It was all neat and tidy and organized like a stamp collector's dream world, with categories and subcategories in carefully labeled files and boxes. It was textbook obsessive-compulsive."

"The wife was clueless?" Joe reiterated.

"Totally. I even tried the girl-talk approach, to see what he might've been like in bed. Nothing. Unless she was either bullshitting me or as dumb as an ox — which I didn't get — he performed perfectly normally, if maybe not like a sexual athlete."

"The kid a boy or girl?"

"Boy. I only met him in passing, since I didn't have that much time, but he seemed as normal as his mom."

"So did his dad, from the outside," Joe mused.

"True," Sam agreed. "It's early yet. We'll get a better crack at both of them soon enough."

"How come they didn't report him missing?" Lester asked.

"They didn't think he was," Sam told them. "He said he'd be in Vegas at a week-long convention, and that maybe he'd extend his stay to enjoy the sights afterward."

"It's been a hell of a lot longer than a week," Joe commented.

"I said the same thing," Sam agreed, adding, "I guess it was that kind of marriage. In her defense, I don't think the wife missed him any. When I told her he was dead, she took it pretty well — more like he was a relative they hadn't seen in a while. Sad, but not destroyed."

"Married how long?"

"Sixteen years."

Gunther cupped his chin in his hand thoughtfully. "He ever do this before? Go off to quote-unquote Vegas?"

"Nope — overnights only."

"Meaning what?"

"Business trips. I checked with his boss. Nashman didn't have the kind of job that called for any trips."

Joe straightened. "Huh."

"What?" Lester asked him.

"Just a thought," Joe told them both. "Earlier we played with the idea that both he and Rockwell came here following a recipe — come by bus, get two keys at the desk, stick one on the door, etcetera. How 'bout a part of that being that they were supposed to tell everyone they'd be gone for a week or more?"

Spinney was already nodding enthusiastically. "That's what happened with my guy. Told his roommates the exact same thing."

"Makes sense," Sammie agreed. "It would guarantee the trail being pretty cold before anyone like us started backtracking."

"Except," Joe then countered, playing devil's advocate, "why would they agree to that? It would sure make me suspicious."

"You aren't horny out of your mind," Sam answered. "We don't know what they were promised."

"Okay," Joe said to Lester. "How 'bout you?"

Spinney read from notes, sitting at his desk, while Sam settled down on the edge of hers to listen.

"Rockwell, or Wet Bald Rocky, was actually Norman Metz. Totally different outward appearance. Or maybe just further down the slippery slope than Red Fred. He was divorced, unemployed, living in a dump, and nobody's best pal among the other tenants I interviewed. They all thought he was weird and antisocial, what little they saw of him. He kept all hours, didn't go out much, and, like Fred, seemed to spend all his spare time on the Net."

"How did they know that?" Joe asked.

"When it was hot, he'd leave his door open a bit, to allow for circulation. The only thing people saw or heard was him tapping on the computer. Bit of an assumption, I suppose, but borne out by what I found once we got access."

"Which was what?" Sam asked.

"Like you did," he said, "but a lot messier. Metz had porno all over the place, including on the walls of the bathroom — that was gross; I didn't want to know what he did in there."

"You interview the ex?" Joe asked.

"Yup. She didn't live far away. She knew all about it, or him. That's why they broke up. He had a good job — prospects, as she called them — but got hooked on the Internet and went off the deep end. That's her take, by the way. I'm not playing shrink here. Anyhow, lost her, lost his job. All this wasn't long ago, which explains why his clothes were good but worn when we found him, and probably why he checked into the cheaper motel."

Once more Joe thought back to Hillstrom's comment about Rocky's — now Metz's — middle-class toenails. She'd been right — again.

Joe leaned back in his chair and steepled his fingers against his chin, thinking over what they'd reported. "You check into Metz's background?"

Lester nodded, scanning his notes. "Not lily white like Nashman. He was busted in a prostitution raid, had a couple of minor drug possession charges. There was at least one propositioning-a-minor case that was dropped. There's probably more, since he didn't come from Ardmore originally — moved there only about ten years ago from further west. I've got a request in for a total records check."

Joe was shaking his head slightly. "If Metz was going down the tubes and his place was such a mess, with porno all over the walls, why did he use the Internet café? He had an online computer at home. What're we missing here?"

After a moment's contemplative silence on all parts, Sam suggested, "Maybe he was asked to."

Joe stared at the far wall as he spoke slowly. "I like that. All right, let's recap a bit. So far, in a nutshell, we have two possibly minor league perverts with an interest in Internet porn involving underage kids." He paused before asking, "Boys or girls mostly?"

"Girls," they both said.

"Okay — another overlap," Joe commented, holding up a fist and raising one finger at a time. "Child predators interested in girls; under instructions on how and why to come here; living relatively nearby to us." He let a second lapse before adding, "And dead under suspicious circumstances."

"In Brattleboro," Sam added.

"And as for Metz using the café," Joe continued, "maybe Sam's right. Nashman was secretive. That probably came through in his communications. Metz could've been told to use a neutral computer so nothing could be traced back to him."

Lester raised his hand as if answering a question in class. "I can confirm that Nashman was careful. After I got the subpoenas to go after Freddy's IP address, John Leppman told me that Freddy used what they call a shadow address, meaning that if we hadn't found Nashman's car and backtracked it to Waterbury, we'd still be clueless about him and Freddy being one and the same."

"Looks like we're after a homicidal avenger — a father?" Sam mused.

"Possibly," Joe agreed. "At least someone with a specific grudge fitting both victims. Both of you got their computers, right? The hard drives?"

They nodded in unison.

"Process them like you did the garage computer, then. Use Leppman if he's amenable, or the state police, if they have anybody, or anyone else who's credible and trained in this. Do it by the book, keep the prosecutor on board, and let's see if we can figure out who or what is the common denominator between Nashman and Metz. We do that, maybe we find out whoever got them traveling here in the first place."

He got up from his desk to look out onto the darkened streets of Brattleboro, or what little he could see of them. "Also, let's throw out a net for angry parental types across the state who've voiced any outrage against Internet predators. Not letters-to-the-editor types," he added, "although we may get there. But violence-prone ones — people who've been arrested or detained for acting out. Mothers, fathers, aunts, uncles — the works."

He reached up and wiped away where his breath had fogged the windowpane. "Somebody is seriously pissed off out there, and I have a sneaking suspicion they may not be through."

It was long past two in the morning by the time Joe drove by Silva's, knowing it was well after hours. Still, his spirits sank when he saw the lights out and the place closed for the night. Unsure he should risk aggravating his disappointment, he nevertheless swung by Lyn's apartment on his way home, his growing anticipation making him feel embarrassingly juvenile.

There was at least one light on in her

window, in the living room, and, as he got out of his car, he could see the rosy flickerings of a dying fire reflected off the ceiling.

Quietly, he climbed the stairs to her apartment, his doubts growing as he went. He liked this woman very much — always had, in fact — and having seen Gail with a new companion, he now knew absolutely that both of them had moved on. Nevertheless, he was torn. With Leo still unconscious, his mother hanging from an emotional thread, and several major investigations crowding his brain, Joe knew for a fact that he was poorly placed to begin a new relationship.

And yet, he kept climbing the stairs, trusting to instinct, Lyn's freely admitted enthusiasm, and the pure dumb luck that had brought them together.

He reached the landing and stopped, the pounding of his heart contrasting with the utter silence all around him. He stared at her door, wondering, still, if he should knock.

Putting an end to his doubts, the door opened. Lyn stood on the threshold, wearing a long, sleeveless nightdress, buttons running down to the hem, her hair loose around her shoulders.

She smiled at him and reached out with one hand. "I was hoping you'd make it."

He took her hand and followed her through the room with all the boxes. She didn't lead him to the living room, though, but chose another door to the side, crossed a hallway, and entered a warm, sweet-smelling bedroom, lighted by a single candle beside a large, old-fashioned four-poster bed.

She turned in the middle of the floor and placed her hands on his shoulders. Without a word, she slid his coat off his arms, letting it fall to the ground.

He removed his jacket and shirt, and the rest of his clothing, with her help, until they stood as they had upon entering, she still in her nightdress, he now totally naked.

Only then did he rest his hands on her waist, his fingers warming to the feel of her skin beneath the thin cotton. He drew her near to him, her arms slipping around his shoulders, and they kissed as never before — slowly and deeply. Joe moved his hands up across her shoulder blades and down along her sides, over her hips, feeling his excitement building.

He stepped slightly away and began unbuttoning her nightgown, not hurriedly, enjoying how the candlelight caught her eyes, and the smooth contours of the skin he was revealing.

When he'd reached her navel, he returned to her shoulders, slipped the nightdress's straps off, and let the garment gather in a circle around her waist.

"My God," he murmured, drawing her near again, feeling her shiver slightly as her breasts pressed against his bare chest. They kissed again, and with one final sweep, he slid his hands under the swath of cotton at her hips, dropped it to the floor, and lifted her up, feeling her legs lock around his waist.

He carried her the short distance to the bed, and they both half tumbled into its embrace, laughing.

# CHAPTER 20

Willy stood perfectly still in the darkness, adjusting to the cold. He was beyond the glare of a nearby streetlight, in the shadow of a rickety, wooden triple-decker dating back a hundred years, in one of the poorer sections of the village of Bellows Falls.

There wasn't much activity. It was late, the traffic all but petered out. The weather was keeping most pedestrians off the sidewalks, and although there were windows still glowing with light, Willy was pretty sanguine he'd be left alone.

Not positive, though. Bellows Falls was quirky enough to hold back a surprise. A pretty village, with ancient mills, once fueled by the power of its namesake cascade, it was wedged between the Connecticut River and a prominence named Oak Hill, whose sheer bulk appeared to shove and compress the village onto a narrow shelf paralleling the water's edge.

Unfortunately, Bellows Falls had a reputation at odds with its appearance. Where once those mills had kept both mansions and worker housing bustling and trim, now their stagnant silence had relegated too many buildings to the status of neglected, parceled-up tenements.

The spirit of the place struggled on, the efforts of its boosters telling and ongoing, but the sheer weight of its financial challenges was like an iceberg's bulk — just under the surface and massive in proportion.

Sadly, as a result, Bellows Falls was a prime place to conduct police business. Which was why Willy was here now.

He checked his watch slowly, sensitive to making any sudden movements. He'd been here two hours. Ever since being told by old man Griffis that Wayne Nugent had raped Andy in prison, Willy had been in quiet pursuit of the man. E. T. hadn't stopped at just the name. With prompting — and occasional breaks for more beer and some sobbing — he'd also delivered other pertinent details, all of which had helped Willy get a line on Nugent and begin tracking him down.

Not that it had been a huge challenge. Nugent was one of humanity's too common

346

opportunists — neither clever nor calculating, but certainly unhesitating to grasp every offer that came within reach. He randomly raped or robbed or simply self-indulged with drugs and liquor. He stayed with people, sleeping with them, robbing them blind, or both, leaving behind a wake of disgruntled sources all too happy to unload into Willy's accommodating ear.

His latest harbor was a woman in Bellows Falls who lived on the second floor at the top of a narrow exterior staircase, across from where Willy had been waiting ever since he'd spotted Wayne downing shots at one of the watering holes on Rockingham Street.

It wouldn't be much longer. It was after two a.m., when the bars closed. Nugent was guaranteed to push the limit and then stagger out toward his latest version of home.

It was then that Willy intended to intercept him, between one oasis and the next, and to begin a conversation he anticipated would result in Nugent's arrest. Lord only knew how many times Willy had made just such things happen in the past — and Wayne Nugent was just the kind of guy he loved to go after. The fact that the man's involvement with Dan Griffis's misbehavior or Leo's car crash was peripheral mattered less to Willy than his own discovery that a bad man had gotten away with driving a fellow human being to suicide. In Willy's mind, this was merely a logical extension of Joe's initial assignment to pump E. T. Griffis for everything he could get.

Nugent first emerged as little more than a dark motion against a somber background, although Willy, a combat-trained sniper, had little trouble spotting what most would have missed entirely. He pulled back farther into his own shadows and watched as his target drew nearer, studying his hands, his gait, his manner of dress, and estimating from his body language how he might react to a sudden crisis. He also studied the man's clothing to see if any allowances had been made for quick access to a weapon.

Satisfied, he waited for Nugent to walk past, trailing a cloud of cheap beer and cigarette smoke, and soundlessly fell in behind him.

As Nugent reached the bottom of the exterior staircase and placed his hand on the wooden railing, Willy clearly but quietly ordered him, "Police, Wayne. Do not move."

Nugent's reaction was hair-triggered and totally unexpected. He didn't freeze, startle, twist around, or shout in surprise. Instead, as instantly as if he'd been launched from a cannon, and using the riser under his foot as a push-off, he simply propelled himself backward, guided solely by Willy's voice.

Caught completely by surprise, Willy tried fending off the sheer bulk of the body hurtling at him, sidestepping and throwing up his good arm for protection. He staggered backward, hit the hood of a parked car with the small of his back, and catapulted over as Nugent, deflected by the impact, came up against the car's side instead, thereby managing to stay on his feet. As Willy rolled off the hood and fell hard to the ground, Nugent took off at a sprint.

"God damned son of a bitch," Willy swore as he staggered to his feet and gave chase, amazed by the other man's reflexes. Already, Nugent was halfway down the block, despite his inebriated state.

Willy had given no thought whatsoever to asking the local police department for assistance with this, purely on principle. And even now, as his quarry began vanishing into the darkness, he didn't rue his decision. He was hoping, however, that Nugent's adrenaline would run out sooner rather than later.

As it turned out, that didn't matter. When Nugent reached the next major cross street, a car pulled up out of nowhere and — in defiance of typical behavior — came to a complete stop at the sign. With the same reactive fluidity that he'd used against Willy, Nugent ran straight up to the driver's door, yanked it open, pulled out the astonished young man at the wheel, and all but threw him across the sidewalk. In the time it took Willy to cover five yards, the car's rear wheels were burning and squealing as the vehicle peeled away, its open door slamming shut from the momentum.

"Shit!" Willy yelled, shifting directions to aim for his own car, parked within sight. No longer simply irritated at his man for being half rabbit, he was already visualizing ranks of irritated senior officers looming in his proximate future.

He unlocked his car at a run using the remote, half fell in behind the wheel, and jammed the key into the ignition. His one hand controlling the car, he used the same technique as Nugent to slam his door, and swerved around the baffled, dispossessed driver, now staggering in the middle of the street.

From the air, Bellows Falls fit roughly between two major streets that matched up at either end like parentheses placed too close together, and which therefore formed an oval-shaped loop. The one cutting through downtown proper was named Rockingham — where Nugent had spent half the night drinking. The other was Atkinson, where, with Willy in hot pursuit, he was now driving north at exuberant speed. As Willy could have predicted given his present turn of luck, the Bellows Falls Police Department was located just beyond the northern juncture of this loop. And, naturally, it was just as Nugent was approaching this spot, hoping to burst through it and beyond to the interstate entry ramp some five miles off, that a patrol officer, no doubt bored with his own paperwork, left the office in his cruiser and began heading south.

He didn't need a radar to interpret what was approaching. Nor did he have to think twice before hitting his blue lights.

Willy saw the light bar burst to life ahead of Nugent's stolen car. This time, however, his reaction was almost muted. "Christ," he snorted quietly, by now philosophical. "What next?" He quickly moved to turn on his own hidden grille strobes.

Nugent's response was finally predictable. He cut his wheel right, went sliding broadside toward the oncoming cruiser, and, just shy of collision, shot into the parking lot of a gas station at the juncture of Atkinson and Rockingham, intent on heading down the latter in the opposite direction.

The cruiser skidded to a stop, unable to turn without hitting Willy, and swung around instead in his wake, his siren now joining the light show that was jaggedly bouncing off the nearby buildings.

Willy hit the radio transmit button he had mounted to his steering wheel to favor his disability.

"BFPD, this is VBI two-four, directly in front of you. Do you copy?"

The response was a delayed and breathless "Ten-Four. This is M-eight-five-one. What's going on?"

By now, all three cars were tearing down Rockingham, the nearby red-brick walls whipping past at white-knuckle speed. Willy could only hope that no one else would be taking in the sights on a wintry night.

"In pursuit of a stolen vehicle. Better alert everybody on both sides of the river."

A woman's calm voice then broke in. "This is Bellows Falls Dispatch. Do you have a description of the vehicle?"

With a small sigh at the inevitable reprimands to come, Willy rattled off the make, model, and registration of the car ahead, mentioned that it was stolen, and identified Wayne Nugent, knowing that his criminal record would pop up on the dispatcher's screen.

Nugent, in the meantime, was fast approaching a choice: to turn left at the bottom of the village's small square and cross the bridge into neighboring New Hampshire, or continue south to the village limits and select Route 5 into Westminster and the interstate's southern ramp, or west toward Saxton's River and the back roads beyond.

He skipped the bridge, eliminating New Hampshire for the moment, and led the way up and out of town, abandoning, among other things, its quaint and demure twenty-five-mile-an-hour speed limit — something Willy thought he'd include on the list of offenses he was mentally tallying up, for fun if nothing else.

"Eight-five-one — Dispatch," he heard over the radio from the car behind him, "we're proceeding south on Westminster toward Red Light Hill."

"Ten-four," was the laconic reply.

Westminster Street was merely Rockingham renamed, wider and flatter than it was in the village. Nugent took advantage of this to extend the gap between himself and his pursuers, apparently not knowing, as they did, what lay ahead. At the aforementioned

Red Light Hill — actually a four-way intersection — his two easiest choices were either a hard left or a steep hill straight up, unless he opted for an even tougher right turn back onto Atkinson all over again. In all cases, the one common denominator was a need to slow down.

Willy didn't know if Nugent was too new to the area or too drunk and scared to care, but as they approached the junction, he began to realize that the lead car wasn't going to survive.

He eased off the accelerator and keyed his mike, "This is VBI two-four. I think we're looking at a ten-fifty in the making. I recommend we drop back."

The cruiser driver didn't answer, but he made no effort to pass Willy in the straightaway.

Now far ahead of them, the stolen car chose the left-hand turn, not surprisingly shooting for the distant interstate he'd been aiming at when the patrolman had changed his plans. Willy saw little puffs of smoke in the car's red lights as the rear end swerved and the tires burned with a sudden braking, and then the whole package yielded to simple physics. Nugent broke into an uncontrolled skid, his car slithered both sideways and to the right until it caught the edge of a concrete median, and then it flipped, vaulting spectacularly into the night air. It hung there for a split second, as if arrested by a movie projector glitch, before coming down into a gas station driveway, careening into both of the station's outermost pumps.

There was a flash, a flicker, a long and bated pause, and then, almost mercifully, a fireball explosion that made Willy drop onto the passenger seat for cover. A thunderous *whump* filled the air and compressed his lungs, even inside the closed car, followed by a showering of small, hard objects all around, including one that smashed his windshield.

With the patrolman's yelling on the radio as a backdrop, Willy got out of his car and surveyed the scene before him — a beautiful, constant fountain of flame, with the car and the mangled pumps at its heart.

"Guess there won't be a trial," he said to himself.

# CHAPTER 21

Joe heard about Wayne Nugent while he was lying in bed beside Lyn, shortly after his cell phone started vibrating from deep within his pile of clothes on the floor. He'd tried sliding his arm out from under her head in order to retrieve the phone and slip out into the hallway, but she'd heard it, too, and urged him to get back into bed with it in order to stay warm. It was an attractive offer, and not only because of her presence. She'd been right — the rest of the apartment had become uncomfortably cool.

"Gunther," he answered, pulling the covers back up over them both.

"Hey, boss," Sammie said. "Sorry to bother, but I thought you better get this hot off the presses. Willy was just in a ten-eighty in Bellows Falls with the guy he says raped Andy Griffis. Swears he was just going to talk to him, that he came on soft and gentle, but that he got knocked on his ass for his efforts. Wayne Nugent's the dirtbag's name — did I mention that? Sorry. Anyhow, Nugent took off down the street, jacked a car at a stop sign, blasted off like a rocket, and then proceeded to lose control and blow himself up at that gas station on the south side of the village. He's dead."

Joe didn't respond. He was too busy both processing and stifling a collection of mental outbursts.

"Oh," Sammie continued, either oblivious or, more likely, nervous for her partner, "Willy's fine. Bellows Falls PD was there with him — at the end — so it looks pretty up-and-up."

"Willy's solid on Nugent being the right guy?"

"Absolutely, boss." Sam's emphasis betrayed her own initial misgivings. "E. T. gave it up first, a few days ago, and Willy really checked it out. I mean, nobody *saw* Nugent do it, of course — except Andy — but he was at the right place at the right time, has a history of doing that shit, to men and women both, and, finally, even bragged about it to some of his buddies. Willy got it all down — sworn statements, the works. That's why he made the approach. He was going to bust him."

Joe checked the glowing clock on the night

357

table. It was four a.m. "When did this happen?"

"About ninety minutes ago. It's been kind of a mess to sort out." Sam suddenly stopped before adding in a guiltier tone, "I tried calling your home phone earlier. When you didn't answer, I didn't want to disturb . . . Well, you know, you've got a bunch of things going on. I didn't want to . . ."

Jesus, he thought, this'll make the rounds. "That's fine, Sam. Don't worry about it. You still in BF?"

"Yeah. We got VSP doing the investigation. We're all hanging out at the PD."

"Was anyone else hurt?" he asked.

"Nope — just Nugent. The gas station is half toast, but the owner says he's insured. Nothing else caught fire, and the fire department had a blast putting it out — big-time war story material."

Joe shook his head slightly — the circles he traveled in. "Okay, Sam. I'll be heading up soon."

He snapped the phone shut and rested his head against the pillow, staring at the ceiling.

"That didn't sound good," Lyn said quietly.

"Could you hear both sides?" he asked.
She nodded.

"Well, it could've been worse — if it turns out the way Sam just said. People bolt all the time when we get too close, and get into deeper trouble because of it. Let's just hope there's no surprise hiding in the bushes."

"Like what?"

He immediately thought of Willy. "You know how it is," he answered vaguely. "Just something you don't expect."

He sighed and slipped his arm back where it had been, enjoying the way she slipped her thigh up over his leg and placed her warm hand on his stomach.

"Mostly, I just hate to go," he admitted. "Not the way I figured tonight would wrap up."

She kissed his neck. "Exactly how much time do you think you do have?" she asked, biting his earlobe lightly.

He laughed. "A few more minutes than I thought I had?"

She slid her hand down farther. "Good."

He only got to drop by in Bellows Falls, long enough to show a command presence to both the state police investigators and his own people. During the half-hour drive up the interstate from Brattleboro, he'd received a second phone call, this one from his mother, who told him that the hospital had called.

His heart had dropped at the news. Given his profession and the surprises it often bore, he'd been dreading this call while expecting it, too.

"It's good, Joey," she'd told him, however, falling back to a nickname she rarely used. "He's coming out of it, just like the doctor said he might."

"I'm already heading your way, Mom," he'd told her. "I'll be there in under an hour."

Karl Weisenbeck looked as fresh at 5:15 in the morning as he always did — affable, neat, and completely focused on his patient's mother.

He was also overflowing with enthusiasm. "In a nutshell, Mrs. G.," he said, crouching down to her level. "We hurt your son and he said 'ouch.' Best news in the world."

He laughed at her concern. "Remember what I told you?" he asked, supplying the answer. "That we were looking for the improved oxygenation to do the rest of the work for us? Well, that's what's happening — the paradoxical breathing has stopped, he was taken off positive pressure several hours ago, and he's not only holding his own, but his O-two saturation has reached normal levels and his consciousness has surfaced to where he responded when we applied a painful stimulus." He reached out and patted her hand. "That's what I meant. I've been told I probably shouldn't try to be funny in situations like these, but it's just such great news."

She squeezed his hand in return, her eyes bright with gratitude. "No, no, Doctor. It's quite all right. We'll take humor any day. Would it be all right to see him?"

Weisenbeck stood up. "Of course. Now, he's not going to start up a conversation, you know. He is still asleep. But you can check out his improved breathing for yourself, and see how much better he looks without all that plumbing stuck down his throat. You might even get a response if you squeeze his hand." He laughed and added, "especially if you use a little rough stuff."

A nurse came in to get her ready for her visit, and Joe and Weisenbeck stood side by side before the viewing window overlooking the rows of beds.

"Straight?" was all Joe asked.

Weisenbeck smiled without looking at him. "Straight. I'm not saying something can't still go wrong — it definitely can. But the odds are hugely in his favor now. If his progress is any indicator, all he has left to do is wake up, get his strength back, and go home. All of which, I won't deny, will take time, but still . . ."

Joe patted his shoulder. "Thanks, and not just for the doctor stuff."

Weisenbeck glanced quickly at his watch, looking pleased, and then moved toward the door. "Happy to help, Mr. Gunther. Call me anytime, for any reason."

Joe waited until he saw his mother being wheeled into the ICU before going outside to his usual cell phone corner in the hallway. He dialed Gail's number, got her answering machine, and said, "It's Joe. Good news from the hospital. Leo's not fully awake but he's starting to come out of it. The doc's pretty optimistic. Just thought you'd like to know."

He then called Sammie. "How're things going?" he asked.

"I should ask the same thing," she answered.

"Good," he said. "He's starting to improve."

She laughed. "I should probably say the same thing. The chief down here is being a little starchy about Willy not checking in before all hell broke loose, and the VSP is curious if we always run solo after suspects in major cases, but no one's really faulting what happened. We got lucky with a bunch of realists, for once. I'm betting he gets a clean bill on this one."

"And there's no doubt about Nugent being the guy? 'Cause I plan to tell Andy's father that we got him."

"I double-checked, boss — promise. He did it. By the way, we got a hit on that long shot you asked Les and me to check out — the irate parental type who might go after people like Nashman and Metz? Lester found someone named Oliver Mueller. Lives in Bratt, heads up a bereaved-parents support group, writes letters to the editor all the time, rants at selectmen meetings, hassles the police chief for more action against child molesters. He's been arrested for disorderly a few times, including once for resisting and assaulting a cop. His daughter's death two years ago is about all he lives for anymore."

"I don't remember that. What was her name?"

"Didn't happen here. He's a New Jersey transplant. Kid died, and everything went with her — the marriage, the job, the house, you name it."

"What makes him homicidal?" Joe asked, unsure that his own reaction to a child's murder wouldn't push him at least a little off center.

"Last year, there was an incident in Brattleboro. The cops thought a guy in the neighborhood might be going after kids. Mueller caught wind of it, bushwhacked the guy, and threatened to kill him. I won't bore you with the details — I'll be writing them all down anyhow — but, long story short, lawyers made it all go away. Point is, five months later, the guy wound up dead in Massachusetts, and Mueller had a bulletproof alibi. But the cop I talked to down there is convinced Mueller did it, or at least hired it out."

"Based on what?" Joe asked.

"Pure gut," Sam conceded. "When Lester was asking around, Mueller was the first name that the Bratt PD's Cathy Eakins thought of — said we'd be dumb not to check him out, although she wasn't as gung-ho as the Massachusetts cop."

"Still, better go for it," Joe recommended.

"You gonna stay up there awhile?" she asked.

"Yeah," he told her. "I got a couple of loose ends I have to take care of. Let me know how you fare with Mueller."

"Roger that."

There was a café in Thetford, serving only

breakfast and lunch, that was cheap, familial, offered good basic food, and had been long known in the neighborhood as E. T. Griffis's home away from home. Joe timed his arrival there for about half an hour after E. T.'s usual appearance, when he hoped the man would be just nearing the end of his meal.

He was sitting in a corner booth, beside the window and facing the door — the perfect place for the best view — in front of the remains of some spaghetti and meatballs.

He and Joe spotted each other as soon as Joe entered, and exchanged the barest of nods. Joe walked down the length of the restaurant to stand before him.

"E. T. How've you been?" They didn't shake hands.

The old man picked up a piece of bread and sopped up some sauce with it. "Fair."

"Sit down for a second?"

He didn't look up, concentrating on his task. "Free country."

Joe slid in opposite him. A waitress appeared, and Joe asked for coffee. E. T. made no comment.

"I was sorry to hear about Andy," Joe said.

E. T. paused in mid-motion for several seconds, then resumed eating, as if alone.

"I looked into what happened to him in prison," Joe continued. "I know about Wayne Nugent."

E. T. stopped chewing. Joe remained silent. The waitress came with the coffee and silently placed it on the table, looking at the two men quizzically.

"Good for you," E. T. finally said, still stubbornly refusing to make eye contact.

Joe sipped from his coffee before saying, "The reason I'm here is because you'll be hearing about Nugent in the news today. He died while one of my men was trying to arrest him for what he did to Andy."

That did it. E. T. looked up and stared at Joe, his lips parted in surprise.

"He was escaping at high speed in a stolen car. Lost control."

E. T.'s hand moved to his chest, seemingly on its own, and Joe wondered if he might not be having a heart attack. He certainly looked ripe for one.

"You okay?" he asked. "You need anything?"

The old man glanced around the table, saw his water glass, and grabbed hold of it for several deep swallows.

Again Joe waited, nursing his coffee. Griffis finally put down the glass, hung his head, and sat there with his hands in his lap.

"Fuck off," he said at last in a quiet, slightly tremulous voice. "Leave me alone."

Joe stayed where he was, the blood pounding at his temples. "In a minute. I have one last thing to say to you. I also found out why Andy pleaded guilty to what I busted him for in the first place."

E. T.'s head snapped up and he slapped both hands onto the edge of the table, as if prepared to tear it off its moorings and throw it.

Joe, just as fast, leaned forward so his face was inches from the other man's. Behind him, he heard several voices questioning what was going on.

"You made a choice, E. T.," Joe said, barely above a whisper. "Then you stuck me with the blame. I did my job — twice now, counting Nugent. Don't tell me to fuck off, asshole, because all I've done is clean up your messes. Talk to Dan about this, like you should've in the first place, when you had the chance to save the right son."

He slid out of the booth, dropped two dollars on the table for the coffee, and left E. T. staring at the empty seat across from him.

■ ■ ■ ■

Joe was halfway to Chelsea, approaching it from Thetford this time, when his pager went off. It was Beverly Hillstrom's number. He pulled out his cell phone and watched its screen periodically as he drove, waiting for the reception indicator on the tiny screen to reach the level where he could have a decent conversation. It took him ten minutes before he could pull over, predictably at the top of a hill.

"Hi, Beverly. It's Joe."

"I tried calling you," she said, "but the message said you were out of the area."

"I'm in Vermont," he laughed. "So in their terms, I guess they're right."

"I heard back from toxicology about Mr. Nashman. That is the current name you're using, isn't it? The ex-Ready Freddy? I received an update from your office."

"Yup, that's it. The Freddy part turned out to be his first name. Anything interesting?"

"Oh, you bet," she said in a rare burst of exhilaration. "His system had a lethal dose of fentanyl."

He hesitated. "I've heard of it. An opiate? But I don't know why it's ringing a bell."

"Excellent. That's exactly right. A synthetic opioid, fifty to eighty times more potent than morphine, patented in France in the late fifties or early sixties. I had to look it up — fascinating. It's used in childbirth, to control cancer pain — anytime a truly heavy gun is required. The biological effect is identical to heroin but much, much more potent, and it's metabolized at a much faster pace.

"But the reason it probably sounds familiar," she continued, "is because, in 2002, either it or something just like it was used by Russian security forces as part of an effort to take back a theater that Chechen rebels had seized, complete with some eight or nine hundred people."

"They put gas through the ventilation system," Joe blurted out, his memory revived.

"And killed over a hundred people in the process," Hillstrom agreed. "All of the rebels died, but so did fifty hostages or so. I may be a little off with those numbers, but you get the idea."

Joe made a face. "What I'm getting, I don't like."

"Oh, yes," she reacted, "I see what you mean. You're thinking of the terrorist angle. Well, that may be, although I think that's a stretch. For one thing, I doubt that Nash-man's motel room was filled with fentanyl gas — sounds a little too James Bond, don't you think?"

Joe thought back to all the careful planning that had gone into the killing of these two men. James Bond didn't seem like such a stretch.

But he played along. "How else does it get administered?"

"Any number of ways, including a lollipop. When we and the Mossad and a few others were considering it as a chemical weapon years ago, all sorts of delivery systems cropped up. I read that we used it in darts during the Vietnam War, since, in the right dose, it can knock you out in a snap."

He heard her fingers click over the phone.

"If it doesn't kill you first," he muttered.

Her mood was not to be dampened. "Right," she said brightly. "That was the problem, and why we supposedly dropped its use for that purpose — the margin between effective and lethal was too narrow. But it does still work as a painkiller."

"In more ways than one," he added.

She chuckled. "True. But your question is directed at how this particular dose was delivered to Mr. Nashman."

"Do you know?"

"I think I do. Did you find any food in his motel room — specifically cookies?"

Joe thought back. "No."

"Well, there were recent remnants of a cookie in his stomach, which I also sent along for analysis. They found traces of DMSO — dimethyl sulfoxide — along with the fentanyl, mixed in."

"What's that tell you?"

"DMSO is a super carrier of other compounds through the skin and other membranes. By itself, it's used as a topical analgesic and as a liniment for horses. It's good for joint pain. But I think it was its first application that came into play this time. Whoever killed Mr. Nashman wanted to make sure the fentanyl really did its job and was taken deep into the body systems. Putting both it and the DMSO into a cookie guaranteed that the fentanyl would hit home like a bullet."

Joe gazed out onto the snow-covered hills around him for a moment, mulling the scenario over in his mind. It was so far removed from the run-of-the-mill, whack-'em-over-the-head murder that he was having a tough time accepting it.

But he wasn't moved to challenge Hillstrom's findings. One thing she never did was stray too far into supposition. She always had the science to back her up.

He did see one loophole, however. "Doesn't it sound like overkill to you, using both?"

She hesitated. "I know what you're saying, Joe. I thought the same thing. You're asking me to theorize, though, and I don't feel comfortable doing that."

"Humor me. I won't quote you."

He could hear her frustrated sigh in his ear. "It struck me like the belt-and-suspenders metaphor."

"He wasn't sure of just the fentanyl, so he threw in the DS . . ."

"DMSO."

"Right . . . For good measure."

"You asked what I thought," she agreed halfheartedly. "But I have no evidence to back that up."

He laughed at her predictable discomfort. "I know, I know. That's my job."

"Correct, Agent Gunther."

"Doctor, as usual, one hell of a job. I have no clue what to do with this, but it's got to be a smoking gun somehow. I just need to find which hand it fits."

"Have fun, Joe. Glad I could help."

"Thanks, Beverly. As always."

■ ■ ■ ■

This time, since Joe had called ahead, finding Rob Barrows at his Chelsea office wasn't simply dumb luck. The deputy met him in the diminutive front lobby and led him back to the tucked-away basement corner they had used the time before.

Barrows cleared a guest chair of a pile of papers and offered Joe a cup of coffee — not quite to café standards but appreciated nevertheless. The younger man was in high spirits.

"I'm guessing you've been busy," he said as they both settled down. "I heard half of Bellows Falls blew up last night."

Joe laughed. "Hardly. The gas station owner's going to get a couple of brand-new pumps, though."

"But the bad guy," Rob persisted. "Wayne Nugent — he ties into what we've been doing, right? I ran him through Spillman, soon as I heard, and made a bet right off with one of the other guys that I was right."

Joe nodded — this was, after all, in large part why he'd made the trip. He owed Barrows that much. "Yeah. He was the one who did Andy in prison. One of my people dug it out and was trying to arrest him when he took off."

Barrows shook his head. "Wow. That must've been something to see."

Joe couldn't argue the point, but he doubted that public opinion was going to be quite so appreciative statewide, especially in Bellows Falls, where sensitivities about police actions ran high.

"I also wanted you to know that I told E. T. about Nugent's connection to his son — just so you aren't blindsided later."

"I appreciate that," Rob responded. "Especially since we're about that close to nailing his firstborn." He held up his right hand with thumb and index finger a quarter inch apart.

"Really?"

"I got lucky with the hard drive we confiscated," Rob explained. "Since you were focusing on the Internet porn material, I just went after the drug deal between Car-Guy and SmokinJoe."

"And you got something?"

"Oh, yeah." He suddenly slapped his forehead. "Geez, what a dope. I'm really sorry. I forgot to ask how your brother was doing."

Joe blinked at the interruption before murmuring, "Fine, thanks. Better. Doc is pretty confident."

"Very cool," Rob said, changing topics. "You know, I did hear back from the crime lab about those tools we seized. They got a positive match between a pair of Vise-grips and the nut we found in the snow. But there were no prints on the handle — too smeared. The only way I can think we can move forward there is to get somebody to squeal. That's actually kinda why I put all my energy into the drug deal — figured if we could get somebody uncomfortable enough, we might get the information about the sabotage as a freebie."

"And it looks like you're almost there?" Joe asked, to bring him back on track. Not that he hadn't been interested in hearing the lab results.

"I knew from the start CarGuy was probably Dan Griffis," Barrows answered. "I mean, we both did, but I didn't have any proof. It could have been Barrie McNeil, just pretending to be too dumb to operate a light switch. But, in any case, I thought it might be cleaner to chase after CarGuy's correspondent first, SmokinJoe. That way, nobody could claim I got where I did through prejudice. Anyhow, it worked like a charm. SmokinJoe had about as much survival smarts as a deer on a highway. John Winston is his name — called Joe for short;

the Winston is self-explanatory, but he actually does smoke, like a chimney. Stinks of the stuff."

Rob reached behind him and handed Gunther a file folder containing various printouts, including a color faxed mug shot of a narrow-faced man with bruised-looking eyes.

"I poked around a little to start," Rob went on. "Checked him out, talked to a few people, dug into his habits and background, put him under surveillance. And then I pulled him in for a little one-on-one. It was almost a letdown — soon as I opened the door, he couldn't wait to charge through. Gave me a full confession — dates, contacts, even had some samples at home. Not to mention his own computer, which has more on it than I know what to do with."

"And Dan Griffis is implicated?" Joe asked.

Rob's eyes widened. "Like Don Corleone, implicated, you bet. He's all over the place — dirty as hell. I laid it all out for the SA, who brought in the drug task force. We wired Winston up and had him make a couple of buys off of Dan — just to put a cherry on top. Now we're coordinating everyone's calendar on when we should drop the hammer on him."

"When's that going to happen?"

"Very soon. I was actually going to call you about that. I figured you'd want to be in on the action."

"Tempting," Joe conceded. "But a potential conflict of interest. Too many tight corners in all this. I don't want anything coming back on me in court."

Barrows smiled. "Got it. You threw me this steak — just wanted to offer to share a little."

# CHAPTER 22

The meeting this time took place downstairs, in Ron Klesczewski's bailiwick, the police department's detective squad. Joe always felt odd returning to his old haunts of over twenty years, finding them both familiar and fundamentally altered. Klesczewski, at least, was among the former, looking older outside his white crime scene suit, but as comfortably in place as Joe imagined he felt anywhere. No one who met Ron out of context ever guessed what he did for a living, but he was a good cop, reliable and intuitive, and perhaps, Joe believed, precisely because it had never come naturally.

Joe, Ron, Sam, and a detective named Cathy Eakins were sitting around the battered conference table in the small catchall room adjacent to the actual squad room.

"Okay," Ron was saying, "so — Oliver Mueller. What did you want to know?

Cathy's our resident expert, by the way, so now that I've brought it up, don't ask me anything."

"Same for me," Joe echoed. "Sam just told me that he'd come up on our radar and that you guys had dealt with him more than anyone else in the area."

"We have a lot of good intel growing on him," Cathy Eakins acknowledged, patting a thick folder before her. "And it's all pretty recent. He's only been up here a couple of years."

"That's what I heard," Joe said. "Sam told me his daughter was killed in Jersey by an Internet stalker?"

Eakins flipped open the folder. "Yeah. Very sad, but not particularly original. Teenage girl on her home computer, hooks up with some creep who sweet-talks her. They meet at a motel outside Summit, New Jersey, and he murders her. He was caught within two days — basically, the local cops told the girl's computer, 'Take us to the creep,' and it did."

"What was the creep like?" Sam asked.

Eakins shrugged — a no-nonsense type. "A middle-class worker bee — a bean counter in the business office of a large bank, stuck in a cubicle for fifteen years with his packed-at-home sandwiches, his dead-end life, and his out-of-control fantasies."

"And Mueller wigged out afterwards," Joe suggested.

"Yeah," Eakins replied. "He might've anyhow, but the killer only got twenty to life, instead of the death penalty, which they still have down there. That pretty much pushed Mueller over the edge."

"She was his only kid?"

Eakins's eyes widened. "No — that part was weird. She was the middle of three. Not even the only daughter. But he still walked away from all of them, including the wife. He's up here solo."

"Still? No girlfriend?"

"All by his lonesome."

Klesczewski laughed softly. "He has us, instead."

"Okay," Joe broke in. "The reason we're interested is because we want to rule him out for our two killings — Nashman and Metz. From what we can figure, both of them were lured here by a phony teenage girl, told exactly what to do and how — all the way from what transportation to use, to how many key cards to take from the front desk — and then murdered, almost immediately upon arrival. Does Mueller strike you as someone who could do that?"

Eakins pushed her lips out thoughtfully

before answering, "I don't want to be a wise-ass, but what did the people working right next to his cubicle think of the predator I just described? Mueller's a pain in the butt. He walks into closed meetings, trespasses onto people's lawns, protests without permits, gets into fights, and even decked one of our own. And, yes, he did threaten some poor bastard who was accused of stalking kids and later proved innocent. All that makes him angry, short-tempered, and violent. Does it also make him a calculating killer? Maybe. Or maybe it takes off the steam and just makes him another of Brattleboro's run-of-the-mill wackos."

"I heard the supposed stalker ended up dead in Mass a few months later," Sam said.

Eakins let out an exasperated sigh. "You been talking to that cop — Mr. Conspiracy Theory. Yeah, I checked into that. It's bogus. I mean, he's entitled to his opinion, but I gave it a good, long look. There was nothing there. I think Mueller's a total pain in the ass — don't get me wrong. But he didn't do that one. Probably the victim got into the same kind of jam in Mass he did up here, and didn't get off so lucky. Maybe the cop's just covering his own inability to solve the case. I don't know. But Mueller's alibi was solid and he's a loner, like I said — not too likely to hire a hit man."

"Let me ask it another way, then," Sam suggested. "If I pulled him in and asked him to help us out with the investigation — as a good citizen — do you think he'd shut down, or maybe give me something I could use later to jam him up?"

Eakins was unequivocal. "The second. You won't be able to shut him up. Even if you accused him head-on, he'd still talk his head off. If there's one impression Oliver Mueller has made on me, it's that he has only one cause to live for and nothing to lose."

It was slow going on the interstate, the snowstorm being one of those thick, blanketing, cotton-wool events. Joe drove north as if poking through whipped cream, the only hint of something dark in a universe of white being the faint trace of the paved road ahead. To the uninitiated, it was a white-knuckle, hunch-over-the-steering-wheel, squint-your-eyes affair. For that matter, even most native Vermonters were notoriously cautious in such weather. But Joe loved it. The music on the radio was good and the traffic virtually nonexistent, his snow tires were new that year, and he'd just gotten the news that Leo had at last woken up.

It still took him two hours to drive roughly sixty miles, and the light was just starting to ebb as he crawled around the hospital parking lot, looking for an opening. For that bit of timing, he was grateful. Driving in the dark in the same circumstances was hair-raising even to him.

He stopped inside the hospital's vaulted entranceway to stamp the snow from his boots and brush himself off.

"Hey, Joe."

He looked up, startled to hear the familiar voice. "Hey, yourself. What're you doing here already? You hate driving in this junk."

Gail gave him an awkward smile. "I came down just before it hit. I heard he was doing better and hoped I'd get lucky."

"So, you were here when he woke up?" he asked, giving her a quick one-armed hug as they fell into walking side by side.

"Yes. What a relief. Your mom started crying."

They quickly reached the building's central, mall-like first-floor corridor, which towered several stories overhead to a skylight a city block long. The Dartmouth-Hitchcock Medical Center was class A, from the ground up — at least, that was the way Joe was feeling about it right now.

"Were you just walking by and happened

to see me?" he asked her. "Nobody knew when I'd make it."

"I've been waiting awhile," she confessed. "I figured it would take you a couple of hours after you got the call. I wanted to see you before we went up."

"Oh?" he asked. "What's up?"

She seemed to take a small breath before speaking. "I just felt badly about how you met Francis . . . Martin. You know, the man who picked me up here last time."

"Yeah," he said lightly. "The Bimmer."

She seemed slightly flustered by his response. "Oh, the car. Right. He's thinking of getting rid of that. Not very practical."

Joe reached out and touched her elbow. "I was surprised, Gail, that's all. I think it's great. I'm happy you found someone a little less hazardous to be around."

"It's not just that, you know."

He thought back to the mood that had carried him here, and decided to do what he could to maintain it, even if slightly at her expense. "Gail, it doesn't matter. It's just semantics now. I've found someone else, too."

She stopped in her tracks, her smile at odds with the look in her eyes. "That's great."

He touched her elbow a second time, this

time to get her going again. "Yeah," he said, looking down the vast hall. "She runs a bar in town. Is Leo still in ICU?"

Gail took the out. "No. They moved him. I'll show you." She moved ahead and led the way to the elevators.

Upstairs, they found Leo and Joe's mother and the ever-present Dr. Weisenbeck all in a regular-looking patient room, with Leo lying in bed without a single tube hooked up to him. He was as pale as the sheet underneath him, about twenty pounds lighter, and, ironically, looking as if he needed a good night's sleep, but he gave Joe a broad smile as they entered, which, to Joe, made all the rest of it irrelevant.

He crossed over to the bed, ignored his brother's thin out-stretched hand, and planted a big kiss on his cheek instead. "Welcome back, you crazy bastard."

Leo laughed softly and patted Joe's shoulder. His voice, when he spoke, was hoarse. "You, too. Weird to have the tables turned for once, huh?"

The reference bore weight. Joe had been in such a bed any number of times during his career, and while Gail was correct that it hadn't been the sole reason she left him, it certainly played a big role.

Joe looked him over. "Not even an IV?"

Weisenbeck spoke up from the back of the room. "He's not off meds completely, but we thought he'd enjoy at least the sensation of being free. And while he probably won't admit it, he has a terrible sore throat, so try not to make him talk too much. The breathing tubes take awhile to recover from."

Weisenbeck checked his watch, which, by now, they'd all come to know as more of a nervous gesture than a real consultation. He walked to the doorway, adding, "I'll leave you be. Congratulations to everyone."

He left to a chorus of thank-yous as the small group clustered more closely around the bed, most of them unconsciously touching some part of its occupant, as if still unbelieving that he had appeared back among them.

A hundred miles away, Matt Aho was buried in his office in the depths of the Burlington Police Department, far from any windows and oblivious to any snowstorm. He made a tidy pile of some printouts and a couple of logbooks and trudged down the hallway toward the chief's office, feeling like a penitent heading to church.

He knocked on the open door and stuck his head in. Tim Giordi was sitting at his desk, scrutinizing his computer screen.

"Chief?"

Giordi looked over his reading glasses at his supply officer. "Yeah, Matt. Come in."

Aho waggled the pile he had clutched in his hand as he approached. "I've been researching the missing Taser cartridge situation."

Giordi raised his eyebrows. "And?"

"I think I have at least part of it figured out."

"Oh?"

He laid out some of his documentation, upside down, so Giordi could read it. "When this first came up, I consulted only the dispersal log, which showed that Officer Palmiter had been assigned three cartridges. He, of course, said he only got two and didn't think anything about it. That left me trying to figure out not only how it might've gone missing, but from where. The biggest flaw I've found so far is that after I've barcoded what's headed out to the airport, the stuff's actually carried over there in bulk. It gets signed out by the individual officers who requested it, but the airport log and mine aren't connected electronically. I think I might've discovered this sooner or later the old-fashioned way, but that's why that one cartridge fell through the gaps."

Giordi, knowing his subordinate's meticulous style — one of the reasons he'd been given this job — nodded patiently.

Aho continued. "So I went over the outgoing transfer manifests and the airport receiving logs, totaled everything that I'd signed out against everything that everyone I interviewed claimed to have received, and I found that the missing cartridge never made it out of my office — at least not officially."

"Meaning somebody walked in, when you weren't there, and swiped it?" Giordi asked, thinking privately that was what he'd assumed from the beginning, even though he was sympathetic to Aho's resistance to the idea.

As if reading his mind, Aho flushed slightly. "It seems that way, yes."

"Yeah," Giordi mused. "That's not too surprising. Your office is off of a high-traffic corridor. What's your suggestion for a more secure setup?"

Aho brightened considerably at that. "I've already put in a requisition for a security Dutch door kind of arrangement, with a grilled upper half. It shouldn't be much more inconvenient than the present system, and it'll make things much tighter. But that's not actually where I was headed."

"I see." Giordi smiled. "And where was that, exactly?"

Aho didn't react to the question's wry tone. "Well, having narrowed down the *where* part of the puzzle, I now had to find out the *when*."

"Right," his boss coaxed.

Aho pointed to an entry on one of his logs. "As you know . . . Actually, maybe you don't . . . but I try to do things like receiving, unpacking, and cataloging at regular times, so that I have a routine I can follow. It helps keep me on track. As a result, I have a pretty good idea at what time of the day I probably set the cartridges out to be shipped to the airport division, putting them on the corner of my desk, as usual . . . well, as usual in the old days."

"Right," Giordi repeated.

"Not to make a big deal out of it," Aho continued without irony, "I pretty much identified a half-hour time slot when somebody could have taken that cartridge — right here, between eleven thirty and noon."

"Okay."

Aho straightened triumphantly. "Well, the rest was easy. We know what shifts were in the building then, and we have the visitors' log for people from the outside." He laid a final sheet before his chief. "So, there you have it — a complete listing, as best I can figure it, of everyone who had access."

Giordi glanced at the list — a significant number of people — and sat back in his chair. "Nice job, Matt. Above and beyond the call. I'll make sure to check this out and share it with Agent Gunther and his people, and I'll also make sure that your new door gets priority treatment."

Aho smiled nervously, gathered up his exhibits, and headed out the door. Giordi waited until he'd left before getting out his bottle of aspirin.

An hour later, Lester Spinney crossed the VBI office in Brattleboro and retrieved the fax that had just arrived.

"Who from?" Sam asked from her desk.

"Burlington PD," he answered vaguely, reading its cover sheet and contents. "It's a list of all the people who were in their building when that Taser cartridge went missing."

"Huh," she reacted. "I thought that was a lost cause."

Lester stopped in the middle of the floor, bringing the sheet closer to his eyes. "I'll be damned."

"What?"

"One of the visitors was John Leppman. Small world."

# Chapter 23

Deputy Sheriff Ted Mumford drove his cruiser gingerly down the narrow lane. It was banked with walls of fresh snow, no doubt disguising parallel ditches that would strand him for sure, and it hadn't been plowed in hours or sanded at all. On top of that, it was late, he was tired, this was the middle of nowhere, and he was responding to his least favorite type of call — a noise complaint.

With the worst snowstorm of the season at last behind him, ten hours of accidents, traffic control, domestic disputes, a lost child, no time off, and God knows how many cups of coffee, Mumford was in no mood to deal with some barking dog or loud stereo. He'd done an uncountable number of these in his years as a deputy, and only a few times had the complainant actually deigned to call the source of the problem and simply ask them to stop it. "I won't call that son of a bitch" was the usual reply. "That's what you cops are for."

Ahead, Mumford made out the glimmering of two houses among the thick tangle of trees — one doubtless belonging to the complainant, the other to the subject. Now that he was near, he could imagine the scenario all too easily: the sole two neighbors inside a square mile of wilderness, hating each other and using every excuse to exchange mutual misery.

He rolled down his window as he drew abreast of the first driveway, or at least the car-size furrow of snow leading to the house, and listened. He would have to give the complainant that much, if nothing else — there was a dog barking down the road, loudly and nonstop, with the same dull rhythm as someone repeatedly thumping the side of your head with a finger.

On the other hand, if Ted were a dog chained outside in this weather, he might have done some barking of his own. Maybe he'd be able to slap an animal cruelty charge on top of the disturbance citation.

Often he would stop at the complainant's on such a call, both to placate and to work up a little departmental PR, but he was too tired and pissed off to bother this time. Instead, he kept crawling down the road, his snow-encrusted headlights doing their feeble best to lead him along, until he reached the second house's blanketed dooryard. Or what he could find of it — there were already three white-shrouded vehicles filling the space. Informing dispatch of his arrival before getting out of the car, Mumford figured he'd have to back all the way to the first driveway in order to turn around later. Great.

The dog, of course, had climbed to a new plateau, having discovered something real to complain about. Also, to be safe, Ted had shined his powerful flashlight right at it to make sure it couldn't suddenly break free and come at him from across the yard. That had done nothing to calm things down.

Holstering the light and relying on the glow from the house's windows to show him the way, Mumford shuffled through the thick and slippery snow, careful of any obstacles possibly lurking beneath it.

He reached the bottom of the front porch steps, and was two treads up when the door above and ahead of him abruptly flew open, revealing a man in a checked shirt, holding a beer in one hand and a joint between his lips. A handgun was shoved into his belt. Although only ten feet separated them, the man missed seeing Mumford entirely, swung on his heel, faced the length of the porch, and bellowed, "Rollo, you stupid mutt. Shut the fuck up."

Mumford stared through the gaping open door into the ram-shackle log house — and directly at two more men who were sitting at a table, placing carefully measured amounts of white powder into small transparent glassine envelopes that they were holding up to the light.

One of them was Dan Griffis.

That's when the man on the porch saw Ted Mumford.

"Who the fuck're you?" he blurted, reaching for his gun and drawing the attention of the other two.

Mumford instantly inventoried the trouble he was in. His own gun was hard to reach, half hidden by his winter jacket, he was wearing nonregulation woolen gloves for their warmth, and he'd just found out how poor his footing was.

As a result, on pure instinct, and seeing the other man's gun starting to level in his direction, Mumford charged up the steps like a linebacker.

Checked Shirt was caught by surprise. Mumford tackled him around the middle, lifted him off his feet, and propelled him backward, flying into the cabin beyond.

They both landed on the floor in a heap, with both of Mumford's gloved hands anchored around his opponent's gun.

As plans went, of course, it was short-term at best. Dan Griffis leaped to his feet at the violent intrusion, grabbed the back of his chair and swung it over his head in the same movement, and brought it crashing down onto the back of the deputy's head.

Mumford let out a groan and stopped struggling. Checked Shirt wrestled free, scrambled to his feet, readjusted the gun in his hand, and took aim. Griffis smacked him across the mouth with the back of his hand, sending him staggering.

"Hey, genius," Dan yelled at him, "why don't you blow your own brains out instead? And ours, too, for that matter. You wanna kill a *cop?* Get the fuck out there and find out who's with him. For all we know, he's got the DEA with him."

He then quickly knelt by Mumford's slowly stirring body, pulled the man's handcuffs from his belt case, and secured his wrists behind his back, commenting as he did so, "Always wanted to do that. Hope they're too goddamned tight."

Checked Shirt, for his part, angrily replaced his gun in his belt and sat in a chair in the far corner of the room, growling, "Up yours. I already been out there. There ain't no raid."

The third man in the room, sitting dumbfounded at the table, a glassine envelope still in his hand, finally spoke. "Jesus, Dan. What the fuck was that all about?"

Griffis looked up at him. "What was it *about?* What the fuck do I know, Charlie? How many times have you had a cop fly through the door and fall on your floor?"

Charlie seemed to consider the question seriously.

"We need to get out of here," Griffis said. "Mike," he ordered the man in the corner, "get your ass out of that chair and go outside. Humor me, okay?"

Without a word, Mike rose and stepped outside, closing the door behind him.

Griffis rolled the deputy over onto his back, removed his gun from its holster, and pointed it into Mumford's face. Mumford blinked a few times, slowly regaining his wits. A large knot was already growing on his forehead where the blow from the chair had driven his face into the floor.

"What's your name, cop?" Griffis asked.

"You know me," Mumford told him.

Dan straightened and looked at him more closely, trying to put him in context. "Mumford!" he finally exclaimed. "You sorry son of a bitch. I should've let Mike kill you. What the fuck were you doing out there? You're no drug cop."

"I wasn't here for drugs. Your stupid dog was barking."

The gun was lowered, already half forgotten. Griffis rubbed the back of his neck with his other hand. "You are shitting me. You came for a dog complaint? What? From the neighbors?"

Mumford merely gave him a wilting look.

Dan stared back at him, muttered, "Up yours," and got to his feet, adding, "Fucking Mike and his fucking mutt. I told him to shut it up. But, oh, no — he's a good guard dog." He began pacing. "Goddamned guard dog just about put us in jail."

"Are we going to jail?" Charlie asked.

Dan kept going in circles. "You can if you want, but I'm never getting out. No fucking way I'm sticking around for that."

Mike reentered the cabin. "Nothing," he reported. "He was alone, just like I said."

Griffis confronted him. "He was alone, *Michael,* because the neighbors called in a barking-dog complaint. I thought you should know that. Asshole."

Mike laid his hand on his gun butt but otherwise remained silent.

"What should we do?" Charlie asked, at

last putting the small envelope down.

Griffis addressed them both. "I don't care. Me, I gotta get out of here, and I mean, way out. We need to put Deputy Mumford here back in his cruiser and squirrel it away somewhere where they won't find it for a while, but after that, it's every man for himself. You guys want to stick around, you can do that, too. They'll probably just slap you on the wrist. But I'm gone."

"You gonna go to Canada?" Charlie asked.

Griffis looked down at Mumford and shook his head. "Yeah, Charlie. To Canada, and I'll give you the address, too, just so the deputy here will remember it and have the Mounties drop by."

He tilted his head back and glanced at the ceiling meditatively. "Why am I surprised I ended up here?"

Joe was back at his favorite office contemplation spot, perched on his windowsill, overlooking the now snow-clotted parking lot. "John Leppman?"

They were all four there, including Willy, since the Dan Griffis situation had blown up and Dan was on the lam. Deputy Mumford's colleagues had taken about five hours to locate him, cuffed and stuffed into his own backseat, hidden inside an abandoned barn — time enough for Griffis to return home, clean out his effects, and vanish.

"Guess you never thought to check out the good guys," Willy gratuitously volunteered.

Joe took it in stride. "Never crossed my mind. He's worked with all sorts of agencies for years, got thumbs-up all around, is even part-time certified."

Sammie was less charitable, glaring at her companion. "Like *you* blew the whistle on him."

"He wasn't my assignment."

"Les," Joe asked, cutting in. "What do we know about him now?"

Lester, having worked the closest with Leppman, was understandably the most embarrassed. He kept his eyes on his paperwork as he reported. "Right now it's just background stuff, but it's bad enough. The whole family moved up here from Virginia about five years ago. Very successful — she, the doc; he, the big-name psychologist. They set down roots fast and wide, made lots of contacts. He started working with the police on computer crimes. Nobody gave it a second thought. But the reason they'd moved was that they used to have two daughters. I should've known that — I even saw family photos in his office showing two girls. Wendy is the older one. Her sister was named Gwen, Gwennie to them, and she was abducted, raped, and murdered by an Internet predator a little over a year before they pulled up roots. The killer was caught almost immediately, tried, convicted, and thrown in the hole, but the family couldn't stand living there, so it was off to Vermont to start over."

"Why wasn't any of that ever picked up?" Joe asked.

Spinney looked up for the first time. "It's not that rare, anymore, boss. And it was a fast case. I found local headlines, but not much else. These people were just victims. If you don't ask, and they don't tell . . ." He left the sentence unfinished.

"Okay," Joe conceded. "That goes under sad but true. What else?"

Lester's tone became more rueful still. "Turns out the choice of a Taser wasn't so random. When Gwennie was abducted and raped, a Taser, or at least a stun gun, was used by the rapist."

"Jesus," Sammie said softly.

"The connection to a stun gun doesn't stop there," Lester continued. "This may be a stretch, but soon after Leppman started helping out the Burlington PD, he was on a ride-along with a patrol unit when they responded to a burglary. It was a sporting goods store, but heavy into personal protection. Among the things missing was a Taser — the store owner's private property, taken from his office. Later, when they caught who did it, the Taser never reappeared."

"Did everything else?" Joe asked.

Les held up a hand. "Like I said, this is a stretch. No, a bunch of it was gone forever, sold for drugs."

"But our boy was at the scene," Willy commented.

"And according to the case narrative I read," Lester said, "the Taser was the only thing missing from the office. Everything else had been out front."

"Was Leppman ever suspected?" Sam asked.

"No," Lester told her. "They had no reason to."

"What's the Burlington PD doing about him now?" Joe wanted to know.

That brought Les up short. He hesitated before answering. "I don't think anything. They just sent me the list of people who were in the building when the Taser went missing. They didn't even comment on Leppman. He's in the building so much, he doesn't stand out."

"If he already had the Taser," Willy asked,

"why did he need a cartridge?"

To Joe, the question didn't have much weight. Every cop has to take at least one practice shot with a stun gun before it's officially issued. He was therefore surprised that Spinney had an answer.

"When it was stolen, the Taser didn't have a cartridge. That's one of the reasons it caught my eye. And since, as we know, every cartridge of that brand has a traceable serial number, he didn't want to just go out and buy one — not considering the use he had in mind."

"All right," Joe said, getting up from the windowsill and walking over to the coffeemaker. "So much for the Taser. What about the chemicals that Hillstrom's tox screen dug up — the fentanyl and the DS . . . DM . . ."

"DMSO — dimethyl sulfoxide," Spinney finished for him. "Both it and fentanyl are used by vets, especially large-animal vets. The Leppmans have horses, and Leppman himself is the one who rides the most. I made a discreet call to their stable, pretending I was shopping around, and got chatty with some woman up there. I couldn't get a lot of details, but I dropped Leppman's name, and she told me he was like a groupie, hanging around, asking questions and learning how everything's done. I specifically asked about vet visits, and she said the same thing applied — he loved grilling the vet and learning the ropes. So he had access and probably had or got knowledge."

"Why hit both guys in Brattleboro?" Sam threw out.

"And why move one of the bodies and dump him out of town?" Willy added.

A silence filled the room momentarily.

"Because Brattleboro's not near Burlington and Shelburne?" Joe suggested without much conviction.

After another pause, Willy shrugged. "I can live with that," he conceded. "Why the river?"

"If the logic works for one, why not both?" Joe countered. "For all we know, the original plan wasn't to have either one of them found in a motel room. Could be Brattleboro was chosen because of its distance, and the river so that not even Bratt would be pinned down — it would also make it look like an accidental drowning."

"Meaning something went wrong?"

"Could be. We certainly know both crime scenes were almost antiseptically cleaned up," Joe said. "What was Leppman's office like?" he asked Lester.

Spinney leaned back in his chair, by now

feeling much less self-conscious as someone who'd dropped the ball. "I almost hate to say this, since I really do like the guy, but it was spotless."

"I've got a question," Willy asked generally. "Whatever happened to Oliver Mueller? I been out of the loop for some of this, but weren't we all hot and bothered about him at some point?"

Sam answered that one. "I put him on the back burner. He *was* looking good for a while — same kind of profile as Leppman, maybe better, with a history of violence — but he had alibis for both killings, and witnesses, too. I haven't written the report yet, but I'll spell it out there."

Joe took a long swallow of his coffee before finally announcing, "All right. We need to see about a search warrant for Leppman's computer before we put him in a room for a talk. And before all that, let's track his past movements — where he was when Nashman and Metz were killed being the big ones. Bring in extra help if you need it. Put everything about him under the scope. When that conversation takes place, I want all questions already answered and that warrant ready to be used. He needs to know that the only reason he's there is to confirm what we already know. Everybody good with that?"

Predictably, Sammie answered for them all. "Good, boss."

# CHAPTER 24

Joe raised his glass and addressed everyone more or less gathered around the table, which really meant Leo, who was propped up in a rented rolling hospital bed nearby.

"To old returnees and newcomers alike," he toasted, nodding toward Lyn and her daughter, Coryn. "May you forever be welcome at our table, and may you forever stay out of all ditches. But if you've got to do what you've got to do, then speedy recovery and consult my brother and mother on matters of technique."

To the general laughter following, he added, "I cannot tell you how happy I am with this outcome. You two scared the bejesus out of me."

They were all back home at last, Leo having been released earlier in the day, with home nursing and physical therapy visits scheduled for the next few weeks. By pure coincidence, Lyn had said that Coryn was visiting from Boston, so Joe had brought them north for the day's major event, much to Coryn's satisfaction — she had wanted to check him out in any case, and now had been handed serendipitous access to the entire diminutive clan.

Joe couldn't be sure, of course, since he'd only just met the girl, but she seemed to be liking what she saw. Certainly, that was true for him. He found her genuine and honest and funny — a natural offshoot of her mother, all the way down to the same almost lissome frame.

Unfortunately, they weren't going to have her for long, since she had to be back at work the next morning and was driving south in an hour, leaving Lyn behind to spend the night. This was, therefore, a celebratory dinner for more reasons than just Leo's return to the fold.

The meal was easy, relaxing, and filled with laughter. Joe kept glancing at his mother and seeing in her expression the pure joy of a return to normalcy. The proximity of her own mortality, which, he knew, had loomed large in her mind with Leo's disability, seemed to have slipped back once more. She looked more relaxed and self-confident than he'd seen her in weeks.

By the end, when all except Leo were gathered by the door to send Coryn off with hugs and best wishes, Joe was back to feeling that his out-of-kilter world might be resettling on a more even keel. Lyn and he seemed on the right track, with her daughter's blessing; the double homicide investigation in Brattleboro was gaining credible steam; the source of Leo's accident had been addressed with Dan Griffis's flight from the area — even if for unrelated reasons; and Leo was on the mend.

Life had been worse, and not that long ago.

Later, in his old bedroom at the front of the house, with the walls glowing in candlelight and the two of them buried deep under old family quilts, he and Lyn made love quietly, with an ease and a familiarity that each found at once surprising and confirming.

But this peacefulness proved short-lived. In the middle of the night, Joe heard the phone ringing in the living room — an unheard-of occurrence in most rural settings, and a nearly guaranteed harbinger of ill tidings.

He slipped out of bed fast and focused, getting to the phone by its third ring.

"Gunther?" said a familiar male voice.

"Yes."

"It's E. T. Griffis. My son Dan is headed your way right now. I told him you got Nugent and that you know why Andy went to jail. Do what you have to do. I'm done with him."

The phone went dead.

"What's happening, Joey?"

He turned and saw his mother in the hallway door. Lyn had also appeared across the room.

"Trouble," he said, dialing the phone to no avail. "That was E. T. Dan Griffis is coming here to take a bite of me, or maybe all of us. Shit."

Joe gave up on the phone just as the warning system he'd set up — which Willy had triggered earlier — started pinging near the front door, where he'd put the receiver.

He looked at both women. "He's cut the phone line and is coming up the driveway now. Chances are, he doesn't know we're up, so no lights. Lyn, call 911 on a cell, use my name, and say that a home invasion's about to start. Mom, go back to your room, close the door, grab Dad's shotgun, park yourself in a corner, and blast whoever comes through without announcing themselves. Can you do that?"

"What about Leo?" she typically asked.

"I'll take care of him. Will you do what I asked? I want to know where you'll be."

"I will," she said, and swung around in her chair and rolled out of sight.

Lyn was already dialing her phone.

He motioned to the staircase lining the living room wall. "You go upstairs. Can you shoot a gun?"

"Yes."

He ran back to their bedroom, quickly grabbed his pistol, and thrust it at her, pushing her toward the stairs. "Go, go, go."

"What'll you use?"

"I'm set," he told her. "Dad had more than one gun."

She ran for the stairs, now speaking quietly into the phone. Joe crossed to his father's old office, now mostly used for storage, climbed onto the cluttered desk, and pulled a World War Two–era M1 carbine off the wall. On top of the bookshelf beside it, he found a fifteen-round magazine, fully loaded, which, he knew, Leo kept there for varmints or just for plinking when he was in the mood. He slapped the magazine into place, chambered a round, and returned to the dark living room.

Time was running short. It had been awhile since the warning sensor went off.

Joe, moving fast and by instinct, knowing

411

to avoid furniture he couldn't even see, ran in his bare feet to the guest bedroom they'd set up for Leo, off the kitchen.

He'd barely entered the room when he heard his brother whisper, "What's happening?"

"Home invasion," Joe said quietly, laying the rifle on the bed and rolling the whole unit toward the bathroom. "Dan Griffis is coming to get me. E. T. called to warn us. Stay put and stay quiet, Leo. You want the gun?"

"What'll you have?"

"I don't know. I gave mine to Lyn. Mom has the twelve-gauge. Maybe I'll grab a knife."

"Don't be a jerk. Keep the M1," Leo said, "I probably couldn't lift the goddamn thing anyhow."

Joe didn't argue. He finished rolling the bed through the — luckily — unusually wide bathroom door, stepped outside, almost completely closed the door, and then reached inside to pull the bed against it, making entry as awkward as possible.

"Go get 'em, Joey," he heard his brother say.

He knew he was out of time. He left the guest bedroom quietly, slipped into the hall, bypassed the kitchen, and froze, listening intently and thinking of all the things he should have done but hadn't had time for, including putting on anything besides his blue jeans.

The first sound came from the building's south wall — a single sharp snap, as from a twig breaking. Joe jogged through the house, flattened against the south wall from the inside, and glanced through one of the windows in time to see the bulkhead door to the basement swing open, dumping its load of snow. A dark shadow disappeared into the cellar's void.

"Okay, you bastard," he muttered, and much more stealthily made his way to the door leading down to the basement, off the hallway between the living room and the kitchen, painfully aware that any misstep or creaking floorboard would resonate below him.

In the hallway, he positioned himself so that he was partially protected by the width of a waist-high bookcase, across the top of which he steadied the carbine, pointing toward the door.

Then he waited.

There had been times in combat like this, with an attack anticipated, when all bodies had been called to the perimeter. As now, every minute had stretched to absurdity, and every slight noise had cracked like a shot. By the time the cellar door began swinging back on its hinges, barely visible in the moonlight from the distant windows, Joe's face was damp with sweat.

He waited until the shadow emerging from below was fully in the hall before he said quietly, "Do not move. I have a rifle on you."

The man opposite him froze.

"Lie facedown on the floor before you," Joe ordered. "Arms and legs outstretched. Hands open."

The shadow did as it was told. Joe reached across the hallway, inside the nearby kitchen door, and switched on a light. Ahead of him, looking up with pure venom in his squinting eyes, was a man Joe had never before seen. He was wearing a checked shirt.

Just as his heart sank with the realization that he'd been had, Joe heard Dan's voice behind him, farther down the hall: "Nice try, Gunther. Real tricky. Leave the gun alone and put your hands up."

Joe followed instructions, aware of the man in the checked shirt getting up as Joe glanced over his own shoulder at Dan.

He'd barely registered that Dan was standing right across from his mother's bedroom door when one panel of the latter blew up with a shattering explosion that sent Griffis smashing against the far wall with a scream, his right knee torn apart.

Purely on instinct, Joe didn't even look back at the man who had emerged from the cellar. He simply dived through the nearby kitchen door, rolled into a forward somersault, and then pushed himself off and to the side of a cabinet front as a bullet smacked into the place he'd just been occupying.

But he was now exposed in the light, sprawled on the floor, and knew he was out of luck.

The man in the checked shirt stepped into the room, the gun dangling by his side, his face malevolent. In the hallway, Griffis was screaming, "Kill the prick, Mike. Blow his fucking head off."

Through the kitchen's other door, leading to the dining room, one arm and half of Lyn's face appeared, her eye sighting down the length of Joe's pistol.

"Don't do it, asshole. Drop the gun or you die."

Before Mike could respond, Lyn fired, the sound enormous in such close quarters. The gun in Mike's hand flew away from him with a spurt of red blood, and he spun and crouched simultaneously, doubling over his wounded hand. Joe leaped to his feet, ran back to the hallway, and snatched up his carbine. He brought it to bear just as Dan Griffis, lying on the floor and bleeding, reached for the pistol that he'd dropped moments before.

*"Don't move!"* Joe yelled.

Simultaneously, the barrel of a shotgun appeared through the hole in his mother's door, followed by her almost sweet advice. "Dan, I think you should stop this."

Griffis glanced up at the barrel and over to Joe, and slumped back against the wall, effectively putting his gun beyond reach.

"Shit," he moaned softly.

In the meantime, Lyn had entered the kitchen and was aiming at Mike in a combat stance, as if on the range, looking incongruous only because of her nightgown.

"Is that it?" Joe asked Dan. "Just the two of you?"

Griffis sighed, both hands now wrapped around his shattered knee. "Yeah. The other guy wimped out."

Lyn glanced at Joe quickly, breaking her focus on Mike for only a fraction. "This something I should start getting used to?"

He considered that for a moment. It had some painful relevance, given how things had worked out with Gail.

"Maybe," he answered as truthfully as he could.

She tilted her head and smiled — the daughter and sister of men lost at sea. "Okay," she said simply.

In the distance, they heard sirens approaching.

# Chapter 25

Willy Kunkle looked over the top of his magazine as Joe walked into the office the following morning.

"Heard your mom and your girlfriend saved your butt last night."

Joe laughed. "Yeah — I heard yours does the same for you all the time."

"Bullshit. She say that?"

Joe crossed the room and dropped his newspaper on his desk. "It's her constant burden — lugging you through life with minimal damage. Where is she, by the way — and Les, for that matter?"

"Doing one of your errands," Willy told him. "It's all about Leppman nowadays. Rumor also has it E. T. gave you a phone call before his Son Wonder showed up with the artillery."

Joe nodded as he poured himself some coffee. It never occurred to him to ask how Willy knew all he did so shortly after it happened. The man had his methods, after all, and his pride.

Moreover, it was an interesting point — one that had made a crucial difference in the night's outcome.

"Yeah, he did. From the sound of his voice, I think it almost killed him, but it was clear he'd had enough. I talked to Dan after the state police got there, while EMS was wrapping him up."

"What'd he say?"

"He'd come back to E. T.'s house to get an extra gun before heading out for good — didn't expect to see the old man. They had a blowout. E. T. told him we knew Andy had taken the fall for Dan. I guess Dan answered that he'd put things right by knocking me off. And that did the trick — E. T. finally saw him for what he is."

Willy tossed the magazine aside and stared into middle space. His tone surprised Joe with its gentleness. "Poor old bastard."

"You got to like him, didn't you?"

"You kidding? A ruthless, manipulative, unscrupulous alcoholic who drives what family members don't commit suicide to acts of homicidal excess? Of *course* I like him."

Joe was laughing. "Well, since you put it that way . . ."

But Willy was only half kidding. "Hey, the sins of the fathers . . . Maybe all of them were screwed before they drew their first breaths. God knows what E. T.'s old man was like." His tone changed slightly as he asked, "Did you ever find out if Dan rigged Leo's car?"

Joe had settled behind his desk and interrupted taking a sip of coffee to answer, "Yeah, threw it right at my mother. Said he was sorry things hadn't worked out as planned. She was great — shot right back that she was happy they had. He got her point. Later, he told me he regretted he hadn't just planted a bomb. Guy's such a winner."

The door opened, and both Les and Sam walked in, chatting.

"Hey, boss," the latter said, shucking off her coat and hanging it in the corner. "Everybody okay at home? I heard your mom's quite the shot."

"Both of them are," Joe conceded. "I asked Lyn afterward if she planned to shoot the gun out of the other guy's hand. Her comeback was, 'That's where I aimed.' "

"Ouch," Lester said. "Watch out for that one, boss."

"Turns out she used to target shoot with her father and brothers when they were

420

kids," Joe explained. "Throw bottles into the ocean and blow them up. Not PC, but I guess a lot of fun."

Sam was already typing at her computer, checking her morning e-mails. "Useful, too, as it turns out. I can't believe the bastard attacked your house. It's like a big-city war story from the flatlands."

"Speaking of flatlanders," Joe segued, "you and Les get anything on Leppman?"

Sam looked up from the screen. "Yeah. We just drove down from Burlington this morning."

"Didn't trust our own people?" he asked.

She pursed her lips, considering how to answer that. In fact, the VBI had five offices strategically located across the state, staffed with squads like their own. That was what he'd meant when he encouraged her to bring in extra help if needed.

He interrupted her with a raised hand. "Don't worry about it, Sam. I know what it's like to share. Tell me what you got so far, instead."

She gave him a slightly embarrassed, rueful look. "Yeah, I'm a little possessive." She then pointed at Lester. "He's just as bad, though. Didn't once suggest farming this out."

"It was worth it," Spinney said defensively.

"Nobody knows the case like we do." Not having all the years the other three had shared working for the Brattleboro PD, he was a little less sure of the limitations to this sort of banter.

Sam returned to the question. "It was good news, bad news, to be honest: the good part being that we got a solid picture of his activities and whereabouts; the bad being that, as a result, we couldn't put him in Bratt on the dates of either killing."

Joe scowled slightly. "No doubts?"

"Not much," she admitted. "We got the right judge, which got us access to Leppman's phone records and credit card receipts. We talked to neighbors, a package delivery driver who handed him something on one of the days, a few other people we found out about. All this was on the q.t. — not that he won't find out eventually — but every time, we came up empty for both dates."

"And it wasn't just the timing," Lester added. "We asked about his demeanor, too. I mean, I know he's a shrink, but they all said he's been fine — upbeat and cheery, just like he was when I was with him. No signs of stress at all."

"What about the phone records?" Joe asked. "Anything stick out there?"

Sam shook her head. "Nope. And sure as hell nothing to Pennsylvania or Waterbury or anything as easy as that. It was like taking apart Mr. Average Joe Citizen."

"You interview the vet?"

"Yup," Spinney answered. "Followed up on that phone call I made back when. What the stable lady told me was right — Leppman does like to hang out and ask questions — but the vet said he never thought anything about it, that Leppman never asked him any leading questions about overdosing or lethal chemicals, or even anything about fentanyl or DMSO."

"They use those, by the way," Sammie interjected. "But nothing's gone missing from their stock."

"What about the wife and daughter?" Joe asked. "Pardon my prejudice, but when I hear horses, I hear more their gender than Leppman's. Did they hang around the vet at all, or visit the stables?"

"No on the first," Sam told him, "but yes on the second. They both ride, but neither of them seems to have Leppman's curiosity about everything. In fact, a stable girl we talked to said none of them really liked the women that much — thought they were kind of snotty."

Joe let out a sigh. "All right, so, right now,

all three are a wash."

" 'Fraid so."

"What else?"

"We met with Matt Aho and really went through his list of possibles," Les volunteered, trying to sound helpful.

"You get anything?" Willy asked.

Sam answered from her desk. "Could be." She sat back to explain. "We not only ran Aho through the wringer, trying to get him to remember anything he could, but we also chased after most of the people he'd highlighted, just in case one of them might've seen something."

"What we found," Spinney picked up, "maybe falls into the category of pure dumb luck. The day Leppman came to visit, he had an escort from their patrol division — not for security, since they considered him an insider, but to introduce him to a couple of people he didn't know."

"Richard Lloyd's his name," Sam resumed. "But he wasn't there when we were, so I left a message that we'd like to have a chat." She tapped her computer screen. "I just got an e-mail from him that he's in the office right now if we want to talk to him."

She looked questioningly at Joe.

"Go for it," he urged, his frustration mounting.

She reached for the phone, dialed the number, and hit the speaker button. In less than a minute, they all heard a young man's voice fill the room.

"Hello, this is Officer Lloyd."

"This is Special Agent Sam Martens of the Vermont Bureau of Investigation, Officer Lloyd," she said in her official voice. "You're on speaker phone, just so you know, and you and I are not alone."

"Okay" was the hesitant reply.

"A few weeks ago, you escorted a man named John Leppman while he was visiting your PD, is that correct?"

"Sure," said Lloyd, some of the tension easing in his voice. "He had to meet with a bunch of people, like the chief, somebody from accounting, and a couple of the detectives. I guess it was the deputy chief who didn't want him to get lost in the building."

"And how did that go?" Sam asked leadingly.

"Good. Fine. He met who he was supposed to meet, and then he left."

"You were with him the whole time?"

"Yeah. Never left his side."

"What kinds of things did he do there?"

"I didn't get it all. It was computer stuff. He helps out catching people through the Internet, so some of it was case related, some of it was schmoozing — like with the chief — and the accounting part was so he could get paid back for something. I don't really know what that was."

"How would you describe his demeanor during the visit?"

"He was cool. A nice guy. Relaxed, friendly. I didn't pick up on anything wrong."

"He never tried to ditch you, however subtly, like with a sudden trip to the bathroom?"

Lloyd thought back for a moment before answering. "No. He was only there for a little over an hour. Guess he never got the urge."

"And you didn't, either?"

"Nope. Just his daughter."

There was a sudden silence in the room.

"Hello?"

"Yeah, hi," Joe said, speaking for the first time. "This is Agent Gunther. Leppman had his daughter with him?"

"Yeah."

"And she did go to the bathroom?"

"Right — once."

"She asked to do that shortly after you passed the supply room, is that correct?"

Now, the pause was on Lloyd's part, as he assimilated the question and its possible meanings. "Yeah — I think it was. How did you know that?"

"It connects to something we're looking into. What was she like? Wendy, right?"

"Yeah — Wendy. Gee, I don't know. Nice enough lady — a little older than me . . . kind of wired. She laughed a lot, talked too much. I remember her father asking if she was all right."

"What did she say?"

"Just that she was in a really good mood. She seemed more nervous to me."

"And after she got back from the bathroom?" Sammie asked.

"Kind of the same."

"She carrying a bag or purse?"

"Purse."

"And she kept that with her at all times?" Joe asked.

"Yeah."

"Officer Lloyd," Joe continued. "This is important. Think back and tell us if her body language concerning the purse was any different after her trip to the bathroom."

There was a thoughtful hesitation before the young cop said, "She wore it slung across her body when she came back. And it was slid forward, so that it rested less to her side and more across her stomach."

"Great," Joe told him. "You're really good

at this. One last question: Did anything at all happen when the three of you passed the supply room?"

"Not really."

"What's that mean?"

"Well," Lloyd answered, "neither one of them did anything, but I noticed that the door was open and Aho was gone."

"Nothing was said?"

"I might've said, 'Huh — wonder where Matt is?' or something like that. It surprised me, 'cause Matt's a real stickler about keeping that area secure."

"The Leppmans didn't say anything?"

"He asked me what the room was, and I told him, but that was it."

"Could you see anything through the open door?" Sam asked him.

They could almost hear him shrug over the phone. "Usual junk — ticket books, pads, a few Taser cartridges, bundles of those plastic envelopes they use for parking tickets, maybe some pens." He thought some more. "I don't know. There might've been a couple of those Cordura equipment pouches, like for cuffs or OC spray, for our duty belts. Guys are always asking for things like that."

Joe glanced around the room to see if anyone had any more questions. "Okay,

Officer Lloyd. Appreciate your time. This has been a big help."

"Sure. My pleasure."

The line went dead and Sam hit the Disconnect button on the phone console.

"No question Wendy swiped the cartridge," she said before asking rhetorically, "but was Dad in on it?"

Joe was staring at the floor, buried in thought. "We better find out," he responded, adding, "and I'm not so sure I'm going to like the answer. Something's making me think maybe Leppman's used his daughter for more than just that Taser cartridge."

"What d'you mean?" Willy wanted to know.

"Something Hillstrom discovered," Joe answered him. "Remember? She said the chemicals that killed Nashman were mixed in with a cookie he'd just eaten."

"Yeah?"

"Well, how does that fit? The guy checks in, takes his two key cards, goes to the room, sticks one of the keys to the outside of the door in an envelope, and waits for his date. Where's the cookie come in?"

"With the date," Lester said simply.

"I'm not gonna open my door to you, big fellah," Willy told him, seeing Joe's point. "Not if you're carrying a goddamn cake with candles."

Sam and Lester looked at him.

"He's a *guy*," Willy said with eyes wide. "I'm expecting a girl, for Christ's sake."

"My point exactly," Joe said with a smile. "But there's more. He *is* expecting a girl — a young girl. And what he sees walking through the door — which is why there had to be a key outside, or he might not have let her in — is a woman in her twenties."

"Bummer number one," Willy chimed in, playing Joe's second fiddle.

"Correct," Joe resumed. "So, she's got some seductive one-liner or something to stall him, and a cookie as a peace offering. He eats because that's what you do for a pretty girl when she's caught you off balance."

"And then you die," Willy concluded. "Bummer number two."

"Which," Sam suggested, dragging out the word for emphasis, "now means you have a one-hundred-and-ninety-pound body on your hands."

"So what?" Willy asked. "Nashman wasn't moved."

Sam laughed. "*Exactly.* Metz was. Why? Same basic m.o., same motive, same people."

"Because with Metz, you had more than

one person in on it," Joe suggested.

"Yeah," she agreed. "So, who was stuck alone with Nashman?"

He looked up at them. "I think it's time for that chat with the Leppmans."

# CHAPTER 26

The initial sound was slight to almost unnoticeable, making Joe look up from his paperwork for no reason he could fathom. Its source, once revealed, however, held no mystery whatsoever. A woman was standing like a wraith at the office door Joe had left open for circulation. Her features were indistinct, the only lighting coming from Joe's desk lamp, but her intent seemed clear. She had a gun in her hand.

Joe had seen only one photograph of this woman — from a brochure that Sam had collected while visiting her medical practice — and it was hardly reflective of the person standing before him now. But it seemed reasonable when he asked, "Dr. Gartner?"

"Don't move." John Leppman's wife's voice was a taut monotone.

"I'm not. What do you want?"

"That you leave us alone."

"Am I bothering you?" Joe's brain was

working overtime, trying to bridge the gaps between what she knew, what he knew, and what she thought he might know. Incongruously, he also made a mental note to address the building's lax security — the door downstairs had no metal detector, and a lock so flimsy, Joe himself had popped it open one night when he forgot his keys.

At the time, that had been a good thing.

"Spare me. You people have been digging into every corner of our lives."

"Are you surprised?" Joe switched to considering his own survival. No one rational walked into a cop's office with a gun — not that someone hadn't done precisely that in his home just twenty-four hours earlier. But what was this one hoping to gain? Joe doubted that it was her own self-preservation. Sandy Gartner was here for her sole surviving daughter.

"Nothing wrong was done by anyone."

"Those two men deserved to die," Joe suggested.

"They were hoping to rape teenage girls — children."

"So, you wanted to be helpful."

After a moment's pause, Gartner said, "Yes."

Joe was torn between the conversation and its context. The gun was no prop, and its eventual use depended on the depth of Gartner's self-delusion. On the other hand, if he played this right, her very words could close the case, here and now.

He decided to try inching her back toward reality, while fantasizing that if the movies were right, a sudden leap by him — as he whipped out his own gun in midair — would result in a full confession and his not lying dead on the floor.

"And you did that by using the stolen Taser on the first man, and the chemical cookie on the second. You know, according to our lab, the DMSO probably wasn't needed. The fentanyl would've worked on its own."

Sandy Gartner took a few paces toward him, revealing more of her face to the light. Joe could tell from the confusion in her eyes that his comment had hit home. The problem was that he was now approaching the very edge of his knowledge and had already taken a huge, albeit calculated, risk. He and his squad had assumed that those two drugs had materialized via the horse vet route, despite the vet clinic's having told them that none had gone missing. But as Joe had uttered Gartner's name out loud, it occurred to him for the first time that the easiest, least complicated source of both chemicals could have been a doctor's office.

But what about Wendy? Joe had convinced himself that she'd delivered the cookie to the second victim and stolen the Taser cartridge used on the first, both with her father's involvement.

The woman with the gun suggested otherwise.

"Did you know their names?" Joe asked her, hoping her answer would start to clarify who had done what.

Her eyebrows rose slightly. "They don't have names."

"These two did. One of them even had a wife and child."

Gartner held out the gun and sighted along it. Joe watched her eye floating just above the black hole of the barrel as she aimed at his face. Her hand was trembling slightly.

"They were monsters," she said. "I saw them."

Maybe now's the time to jump, he thought. I might get lucky.

A soft male voice floated into the room. "Sandy? Sweetheart? Put the gun down."

She startled. Joe winced, surprised that, in fact, she didn't fire and he didn't jump.

But the gun didn't go off. Nor was it lowered.

A second shadow entered and stood quietly by the door.

Gartner shifted her weight. The gun wavered.

"Go away, John," she said. "This doesn't concern you."

"Of course it does," he said gently.

Joe slipped his oar into the water, hoping to normalize the mood. "Mr. Leppman? Your wife and I were starting to sort all this out. My name's Joe Gunther."

Leppman picked up his cue. "Glad to meet you, Mr. Gunther. Sorry about the intrusion."

"That's okay. I was planning to talk with you both anyhow." He made the smallest of gestures with his hand. "Would you like to sit down?"

That was too much. Sandy Gartner poked the gun at him. "Don't move. I told you."

Joe remained silent. Leppman took two silent steps farther into the room. "Sandy? I wouldn't mind sitting down. I'm very tired. I bet you are, too. There're two chairs — one right beside you."

She glanced to her side, which Joe took as a good sign. Apparently, so did her husband, since he finished approaching, grabbed the other chair, and sat down. In a typical mental aside, so often rued later, Joe hoped this shrink knew his business and wasn't acting without a single thought toward Joe's survival.

Gartner hesitated, seeing her husband unbutton his coat and get comfortable. She glanced at Joe, who did his best to appear the genial host, and finally folded at the knees, perching on the chair's edge. The gun stayed pointed at Joe.

"What are you doing here?" she asked Leppman.

"I followed you," he said simply. "I overheard the phone call you got from the stable, telling you the police had been asking questions, I heard you say the same had happened at your office, and I saw you take the gun."

"Where's Wendy?"

"She's at home," he reassured her. "She doesn't know anything. She's fine, Sandy. Like I want you to be."

Gartner looked down at the gun and watched it slowly lower to her lap as if it belonged to someone else.

"What did you want to have happen here?" her husband asked her.

With her left hand, she reached up and touched her forehead fleetingly. "I wanted some peace and quiet. I thought maybe we could talk this out."

Joe saw what he hoped was his opportunity. "I'm listening," he said.

"I am, too," her husband echoed, which struck Joe with its implied ignorance.

"You had your police consulting," she said to him, her eyes fixed on the floor. "You had a way to channel losing Gwennie."

Joe saw her husband's brow furrow. He imagined what was going on inside the man's brain. The psychologist battling with the spouse and fellow mourner — one wishing to counsel and soothe, the other urging to argue and fight for turf.

Joe was having some of the same problem. Intrigued as he was with the direction this was taking, his right arm, as slowly as a minute hand, was also moving to where he could casually drop it into his lap — and closer to his holstered gun.

"You could get your revenge," she was saying. "Putting all those men in jail. I had nothing. I had to put on a brave face for Wendy, keep running my office, listen to all my patients complaining, even encourage you as you bragged about how you nailed this guy or the other. I wanted to find some relief, too. But no one was listening."

The husband in Leppman slipped out for a moment. "You never told me."

"You never asked. You never looked. John,

we left our home on your recommendation, to 'leave it all behind us,' you said. We were supposed to get a fresh start in Vermont. Well, I tried that, but you didn't. You started right up with all this Internet police work. That wasn't leaving it all behind. You were the only one of us who never even tried."

She suddenly straightened in her chair. "My God, John, you planted the seeds of all this. Remember that night you went riding around with your cop friends? You came home with a Taser — like it was a talisman you'd found on the edge of Gwennie's grave, instead of something you'd stolen. What were you thinking? That damn thing took on a life of its own. You moved on — forgot all about it. But I kept thinking about it, wondering how a Taser had so cleverly worked its way into our home."

Leppman's brow furrowed. "My God," he said. "I didn't know. I stole it from impulse, because of what it represented. I never thought . . ." He rubbed his eyes. "Maybe, subliminally . . ." He lapsed into silence.

Joe watched them both — highly schooled, well spoken, respectfully mannered — their emotions muffled under the careful professional language of their analytical training. Still, what they were saying didn't differ from what he'd heard between the down-

and-out of his experience. People made assumptions, took one another for granted, behaved selfishly, maybe even acted to correct the wrongs the other refused to address.

He wondered if, given the mood, that last point might not be broached, the half-forgotten gun notwithstanding.

"Dr. Gartner," he began, "what made you focus on these two? Were they like the man who went after Gwennie?"

"I thought so," she agreed. "They were so quick to assume . . ."

She paused. He waited a couple of seconds and then tried a slightly different approach. "What made you go online in the first place?"

That seemed to help. Her face became more animated, the latent researcher brought to life. "I wanted to find out what the appeal was. I wanted to understand what Gwennie was looking for. It was amazing. I only read the exchanges at first, people going back and forth. Some of it was like eavesdropping on any conversation — even most of it, I guess. But there was this undertone. Maybe I was looking for it, too, reading into the comments. But I began to see where a lot of the chats were leading. I could see how seductive so many of the men were, and how willing the girls were to follow them — the total anonymity breeding a lack of inhibition."

She stopped again, still staring at the floor, but neither man interrupted. They could instinctively tell she was gathering her memories, putting them in order to get them out at long last.

"I began to get angry," she continued. "All the sadness, the loss. Everything we'd gone through was brought together in my head. It was like a laser beam gathering light. I began to fantasize putting an end to it all. It made me feel better."

Joe glanced at John Leppman, trying to read his mind. His face was slack with remorse and guilt — his closest and most valued patient had been overlooked or, perhaps worse, dismissed.

"I don't know why I chose those two," Sandy said. "Something clicked with the first one's name. Gwennie loved the Rocky movies, and I always loved Norman Rockwell. Maybe that was it. And he was so horrible, too. When I started chatting as Mandi, he came on like a boy in high school, all awful one-liners and disgusting innuendos. He thought he was such a Don Juan."

Her cheeks had colored as she spoke, and her voice grew in strength. The growing rage she was describing hardly needed better illustration.

"I began fantasizing about him — what I would do if I ever got him into a room alone." She laughed once, very quietly, almost a sob. "I came up with plan after plan, each time making it more real. The Taser had to be a part of it — the same thing that pig had used on Gwennie. That seemed only fair."

"You got Wendy to steal the cartridge without her dad knowing?" Joe asked.

She looked up at him, a sad smile on her face. "Poor Wendy. I didn't ask her to do that . . ." She stopped in mid-thought, reconsidering. "Not directly, but I suppose I did. I'd been telling her of my fantasies."

Her husband groaned next to her, barely audibly. Her head jerked in his direction, and Joe thought she'd break from her monologue to give him a tongue-lashing. But she stopped at the last second and merely stared at him for a moment.

She returned to Joe, ignoring Leppman. "She was feeling as I was. Dangling. She needed an outlet, too. She wanted to help, and when she was with *him* on that tour of the police department and she suddenly saw the cartridge we needed, she took it."

By now Leppman had slumped into his chair, his hands in his lap, his eyes unfocused, all energy seemingly drained from his body.

"She also helped you drop his body into the river," Joe suggested.

She shook her head but answered affirmatively, "That was wrong. I shouldn't have involved her so much. But I believed she wanted to. She told me the two of us had to do everything together, every step of the way. I went along because I wanted the company. And she was so enthusiastic." She said this with emphasis, her eyes bright.

Joe stoked the mood of the moment. "You were like sisters," he suggested.

She nodded. "After we dropped him into the water, we hugged and laughed. It was the best I'd felt in years."

Joe knew he should probably get as much detail as possible — the gap between using the Taser in the motel and subsequently drowning Metz miles away suggested a horrifying picture of many repeated electrical impulses in order to keep the man subdued. But he wasn't sure how much longer this moment would last. It had come about spontaneously, and could just as quickly vaporize. These kinds of confessions were tricky enough in the best-planned environments, let alone something like this.

He forged ahead to get as much as he

443

could. "But by the second time, things had changed."

Her face fell. "Yes," she conceded. "That's when I realized how wrong I'd been. Such a fool. I should have thought of that. We planned it together, worked out all the details. But when it came down to actually doing it, Wendy balked."

Joe was watching her every gesture, every shadow that crossed her face. She was discussing this as if she'd chosen the wrong dress for her daughter's coming-out party — an important glitch in an otherwise well planned event. The fact that they were discussing a double homicide had slipped into irrelevance.

Not that Joe was outwardly behaving much more rationally. Since Sandy Gartner had brought herself to this level of reality, Joe wasn't about to disabuse her.

He glanced quickly at Leppman, who seemed almost catatonic by now. "So, you had to act on your own," Joe suggested helpfully. "Is that why you left him in the motel room instead of taking him some-where else, like you did the first guy?"

Gartner nodded. "Yes. It all happened at the last minute. Wendy came with me, but then she wouldn't get out of the car. She was supposed to open the man's door, carrying the cookies. She's so much prettier than I am — and younger, of course, which was the whole point. Fortunately, that part didn't matter. He was so hot and bothered, I could have talked him into anything."

"What did you say to him?" Joe asked. "He was expecting a fourteen-year-old."

She looked straight at him and smiled sadly, her head slightly tilted to one side, as if mystified by every aspect of her own tale. "I offered him one — I showed him Gwennie's picture and told him she was waiting for him." She paused and leaned forward in her chair, her body language seeking confirmation. "And she was, wasn't she?"

He was hard-pressed to argue, while at the same time wondering how many people might have seen her ploy as victimizing Gwennie all over again. It wasn't lost on him that at the very same moment, Wendy had sat in the car, traumatized and guilty, feeling that she had let mother and sister down, alike. "I guess so — as things turned out."

John Leppman, however, was having no more of it. Mirroring the apparent family tradition of impulsive rashness, he suddenly stirred from his torpor, pushed himself up from his chair, and launched onto his wife, flailing with both fists and knocking them both onto the floor in a struggling heap.

Gunther pushed backward in surprise, smacking against the wall behind him, and scrambled to his feet, trying to circle his desk to intervene.

Almost predictably, the gun went off as he was halfway there. There was a startled cry from Leppman, and he rolled off his wife, clutching his left upper arm, just as Joe arrived over them both.

Sandy Gartner, her eyes wide, focused suddenly on Joe and brought her gun to bear on him next. He struck out with his right foot and caught her straight on the wrist, sending the pistol skittering across the floor.

With a yelp of pain, she curled into a ball, striking a curious counterpoint to her husband, who was doing much the same thing a few feet away.

His adrenaline pumping and his own gun out by now, Joe stared at them both for a few moments, wondering what might happen next, even glancing at the door once to see if their one remaining daughter might not be standing there with a shotgun.

But all was finally at rest.

"Jesus" was all he could summon up in the end, reaching for the phone. "What a bunch."

**JMAN:** hey — Mandi144 u out ther?
**LoneleeG:** don't no Mandi, but im here
**JMAN:** kool. ASL
**LoneleeG:** 15/f/Burlington
**JMAN:** Vermont? Wurks 4 me

# CHAPTER 27

Joe switched off the table saw and examined the edge of the board he'd just pushed through the blade.

"No blood?" a voice asked from behind him. "I would've thought by now you'd be missing a thumb at least."

Joe put the board down and dusted his abdomen free of sawdust. "Hey, Willy. Slumming in the neighborhood?"

Kunkle shrugged, looking around the small barn that his boss had converted into a woodworking shop attached to his house. "Something like that."

"You stand a cup of coffee?" Joe asked. "I made it an hour ago, and I'm having some anyhow."

"Sure," Willy answered, pointing at the table saw with his chin. "What're you making?"

Joe laughed, removing the thick apron he wore. "If I'm lucky, an end table for Lyn's daughter, Coryn. Her apartment is supposedly like a sixties college museum of stacked bricks and orange crates."

They left the shop for the living room next door and the kitchen beyond. Joe lived in what might have been a gatehouse had it not been stuck onto the back of a Victorian monstrosity fronting the street. In any case, it was also inexplicably and oddly proportioned, so that anyone taller than five and a half feet looked shoehorned into the place.

"You two still tight?" Willy asked.

"With Lyn?" Joe responded, taking out a mug. "So far, so good. I take it you're asking because Sam just threw you out."

"Fuck you," Willy said without emphasis. He watched Joe pour out the coffee in silence. Only after he accepted the mug did he add, "We just had a fight. I left. She wanted to talk — as usual."

Joe poured his own mug and sat on a stool near the counter. "You do talk sometimes, though, right?"

Willy took a sip and answered, "Yeah, Mom. We talk. I wasn't in the mood this time."

"It's tough," Joe commented vaguely, knowing his audience. "The price we have to pay for companionship. Still worth it to you?"

Willy stared a moment into the depths of the mug. "I guess."

A thumbs-up, given the man, Joe thought.

"How's your brother doin'?" Willy asked, changing the subject.

"Close to good as new. Using a cane only, driving on his own. He's even back at work half days."

"That was a weird deal."

"You mean Dan Griffis going after him?" Joe asked. "Yeah. I never thanked you properly for doing what you did, by the way, getting close to E. T. In the long run, that probably saved all our bacon the night Dan came hunting for me and mine."

Willy nodded. "No sweat. Got me to hang out in a bar again. I always liked bars, even if what they had in them didn't like me."

Or liked him too much, Joe thought.

"E. T. was a good enough guy, though," Willy continued unexpectedly. "A fucked-up dad, maybe, but okay in the end. Did you ever get together with him after?"

Joe shook his head. "The night he called, I could tell it was about all he had left in him. The local scuttlebutt has it he hasn't left his house since — not to see Dan in jail, not to run the business, not even to have a drink. From what I hear, the lawyers are gathering to figure out all his businesses."

Willy laughed. "Any lawyers left over after the Leppman-Gartner clan got through hiring?"

"Good point," Joe agreed.

Willy put his coffee down and gazed at his host. Joe had rarely seen him in such a contemplative mood. "This family shit is so weird."

Joe smiled at him. "How so?"

"I don't know. Getting ticked off at Sam tonight and driving around, I got to thinking. Seems like all we do is piss and moan about breaking up or sticking together, and when we're not doing that, it's family, family, family. I mean, what do you get out of that whole deal with Gartner using the death of one daughter to screw up the other? Or E. T., for that matter? He puts Andy in jail to spare Dan and then has to drop the dime on Dan because the bastard's about to kill a cop and his entire family. How messed up is that? How wrong can you get it?"

Joe absorbed all this, knowing that an answer wasn't requested. But it did make him think of Lyn and her family, half destroyed by the sea; of his own mother and brother, almost lost through capricious

451

malice; and of how fragile and tenuous even the best of bonds could become, through no fault of one's own.

None of which considered the other, more willful human dynamics that Willy was talking about: divorce and abandonment, revenge and paranoia, murder and mayhem.

"How bad is it with you and Sam?" he asked.

Willy made a dismissive face. "Just a pissing match. No big deal."

Joe nodded and gazed out the darkened window for a while in silence. "I guess we just do the best we can," he finally said, "and keep our fingers crossed."

Willy took a final sip, put his mug down, and slipped off his stool. "Okay, Obi-Wan. I'll go home now. Thanks for the java, if not the bullshit."

Joe nodded. "Take care, Willy. I'll see you tomorrow."

The employees of Thorndike Press hope you have enjoyed this Large Print book. All our Thorndike and Wheeler Large Print titles are designed for easy reading, and all our books are made to last. Other Thorndike Press Large Print books are available at your library, through selected bookstores, or directly from us.

For information about titles, please call:
    (800) 223-1244

or visit our Web site at:
    http://gale.cengage.com/thorndike

To share your comments, please write:
    Publisher
    Thorndike Press
    295 Kennedy Memorial Drive
    Waterville, ME 04901